vox 'n' roll

....

fiction for the 21st century

vox 'n' roll

....

fiction for the 21st century

edited by
Richard Thomas

Library of Congress Catalog Card Number: 00-100220

A complete catalogue record for this book can
be obtained from the British Library on request

The right of the individual contributors to be
acknowledged as authors of their work has
been asserted by them in accordance with
the Copyright, Patents and Designs Act 1988

First published in 2000
by Serpent's Tail,
4 Blackstock Mews, London N4 2BT

website: www.serpentstail.com

Set in Plantin by Intype London Ltd.
Printed in Great Britain by Mackays of Chatham plc

10 9 8 7 6 5 4 3 2 1

contents

....

introduction

....

If you live outside London you might have picked this book up and thought 'Vox 'n' Roll Presents', what is 'Vox 'n' Roll?' To the uninitiated, Vox 'n' Roll is the name given to the literary readings held at Filthy MacNasty's Bar & Whiskey Café in Islington, North London. Filthy MacNasty's was opened by Sligo-born Gerry O'Boyle in August 1993, located between King's Cross and the Angel, on the fringes of Clerkenwell. With a huge selection of different whiskies and award-winning food, it quickly became one of the best bars to be in and be seen in in London as musicians, actors and authors made it their local.

In 1995 Gerry O'Boyle changed the direction of Filthy's into an 'Irish-led' art house and joined up with music promoter Richard Thomas, who had previously worked with literary musicians such as Nick Cave, Henry Rollins, Richard Hell and Lydia Lunch, to set up the concept of Vox 'n' Roll. A very simple and effective idea: take a writer and ask them to read three ten-minute sections of their work interspersed with ten-minute bursts of recorded music chosen by the author. The music may be what inspired them, come from the era of the writing or simply whatever turns them on.

The aim of Vox 'n' Roll was to create pleasant and informal surroundings for authors to read their work and to stress the links between literature and music.

Several of today's writers like Ian Rankin, Nicholas Blincoe, Charlie Higson, Kinky Friedman and Jeff Noon started off as musicians and musicians such as Patti Smith and Leonard Cohen had poems published before they turned to music. In the last decade, authors as diverse as Salman Rushdie, Nick Hornby and James Kelman have written novels heavily featuring contemporary music.

The first Vox 'n' Roll show took place in February 1996 with Booker Prize-nominated author, Patrick McCabe, and the shows became a success. There are currently eight to ten Vox 'n' Roll shows a month in Filthy MacNasty's. Apart from the authors in this book, writers who have appeared at Filthy's include James Ellroy, Nick Hornby, Frank McCourt, Helen Fielding, John Cale, Richard Hell, Lawrence Block, A L Kennedy, Hanif Kureishi, Meera Syal, T C Boyle, Kathy Acker, Ian Rankin, Eddie Bunker and Charlie Higson.

The press quickly caught up with Vox 'n' Roll and it has been described as 'the grooviest literary salon in London' by the *Independent* and 'the best literary evenings in London' by the *Guardian*. The *Evening Standard* voiced the opinion that 'when Vox 'n' Roll is in full swing, you will see something that has no equivalent in London', while *GQ* rated the Patrick McCabe/Sinead O'Connor show as one of the literary highlights of 1998.

The stories in this book are not meant to represent a 'greatest hits' collection of the biggest authors who have performed at Vox 'n' Roll, but rather a selection of writers to show the diverse range of writing that you will find at Vox 'n' Roll shows. We hope you enjoy this book and look forward to seeing you at Vox 'n' Roll.

acknowledgements

Vox 'n' Roll would like to thank:
Pete Ayrton at Serpent's Tail for commissioning this book and all the authors who kindly agreed to write for it. In addition, a huge thank you to all the authors, publishers, agents and journalists who have supported Vox 'n' Roll and especially the audiences who keep turning up for the shows.

Richard Thomas would like to thank:
For their help and support at Vox 'n' Roll, Acushla Bastible, Bleddyn Butcher, Susan Ferguson, Phil Griffiths, Mike Hart, Tim Jones, Mike Oldfield, Nick West, John Williams and for her long distance support Julie Taraska. I would also like to dedicate this book to the memories of Rob Gretton (1953–99) and Claude Bessy (1945–99), from both of whom I learnt a lot.

Gerry O'Boyle would like to thank:
Pat McCabe, Abner Stein, James Brown, Geoff Mulligan, Ann and Mary Scanlon, Aine O'Connor RIP, Murphy Williams, Cathy Wilson, all the staff of Filthy MacNasty's Bar and Whiskey Café, our clientele and friends, Edel Quinn for divine intervention and Wilke Rodrigoz for the shirts.

sparkle hayter

how i met your father

How did my cat Bastard get his name? That's a funny story. I had recently moved into the Chelsea Hotel after divorcing my second husband and bumming around Europe for a year, where a series of romantic misadventures soured me on love almost completely. I'd given Mr True Love another year to show up and if he didn't, I was going to give up on true love and become a whore-queen, a powerful, sexual woman who bestows her favors on a variety of desperate young men willing to perform heroic quests to please her.

That year was almost up when Crazy Anna befriended me, more or less. The fact that she was known as 'Crazy Anna' should have tipped me off that she was someone to avoid. To be known as the crazy one in an unusual place like the Chelsea Hotel, the legendary bohemian landmark and historic artist residence on West 23rd Street in Manhattan, was some accomplishment. There was a reason residents called it 'the mothership'.

Under other circumstances, maybe I wouldn't have gotten to know Crazy Anna at all, but I was particularly friendless back then, having just moved back to New York, and my other neighbors at the Chelsea Hotel didn't seem very neighborly. I had Anna on one side of me, a guy I knew as Cousin It on the other. Across the hall was a bald, mucho-tattooed body-builder whose apartment was completely painted black. He stood in his doorway lifting hand-weights and staring into the hallway at nothing in particular. The rest of the third-floor denizens consisted of secretive artists, musicians, magicians and writers who scurried in and out of their apartments, all in a frenzy, facing deadlines for manuscripts, shows, etc. You'd see them on the elevators, the lobby, the deli, locked into their own heads, staring past you, clearly not wanting to be bothered with small talk. One of them, an actor preparing for a role, wore a 'Do Not Disturb' sign, from the Waldorf-Astoria, around his neck as he wandered around the Chelsea Hotel, brooding and muttering to himself in character. The place was not lacking in humanity and humor, it's just that people were very busy and/or in creative isolation on my floor when I moved in, and suspicious in general of newcomers, something I would understand better later.

But at the time, I was very lonely.

The first time I saw Crazy Anna, she was cursing, 'Fuck you! Fuck you! Fuck you!' at a plump, pale, half-dressed man, who was pleading with her in some foreign language, largely drowned out by Anna's 'Fuck You's. The only word he said that I could make out was something Seussian, like 'loobloo'. There were clothes scattered all over our hallway. The man's trousers were unzipped, his underwear was showing, his torso was bare. Anna, tall and thin with the body of Wallis Warfield

Simpson and the blonde hair of Ivana Trump, was wearing an aqua-colored dressing gown with scarlet feather trim. She seemed drunk, and she was so loud she drew even more hermetic neighbors into the hallway to see what was going on. 'What is it?' I heard a woman say. 'Just Crazy Anna and some man,' said another woman.

'Don't give that bullshit,' Anna shouted at the man. She had just the trace of an accent. 'You don't love Anna, so don't say you do.'

With that, she stomped off, cursing some more. The man began picking up the rest of his clothes from the hallway floor. Being a good Samaritan on my better days, I began to help him.

'She's crazy, she's crazy,' the man said.

One of his shoes was missing, but then Anna's door opened, and the shoe came flying down the hall, just missing the pale and plump man's head.

As my last marriage had foundered on calm, chronic indifference, and had ended with a mutual shrug, I couldn't help but be impressed by this level of passion, and be a little frightened by her raw energy.

When I next saw the pale, plump man, he was carrying an orange cat and a bouquet of cheap flowers, the kind you can buy at a greengrocer for a few bucks, and heading towards Anna's apartment.

Almost every time I saw Crazy Anna she was in a different over-the-top outfit, shimmery silver prom dress with matching shoes, a blue sequin gown with matching gloves and hat. Her hair was long, curly, artificially blonde and kind of trashy, as was her heavy, flamboyant makeup. But somehow she was able to elevate this 'Ivana

Trump for K-Mart' aesthetic and make it seem like a bold, individual statement.

Though I saw Crazy Anna almost every day, we didn't speak until the day she had a heated discussion with another man, a good-looking brown-haired man, in the stairwell. He said, 'You have no idea what you're talking about. That's Chopin. Now, leave me alone.'

'It was not Chopin, it was Mendelssohn!' she insisted, furiously.

'Have it your own way then. It was not Chopin.'

'Don't agree with me just to shut me up!' she raged.

'I can't disagree nor agree with you without you getting angry. Why don't you just leave me alone?'

The brown-haired man shook his head at Anna, gave me a dirty look for watching the exchange, and walked upstairs. Anna looked at me and said, in her throaty voice, 'He's just angry because I won't sleep with him. He's a drug dealer, and he's in love with me. Do you have a cigarette?'

'In my room,' I said, and invited her in for coffee.

After breaking the filter off the cigarette, she lit it and sat down at my kitchen table. She was wearing a bright yellow dress with big red appliquéd flowers.

'You have any whiskey?' she asked.

I didn't, but she had some in her room. She left and returned a few minutes later with a half bottle of Canadian rye. She poured it straight into her coffee, and then into mine, though I hadn't asked for any, and told me some of her life story.

The child of a Rio businessman and his secretary, Anna was born on the wrong side of the blanket, she said. She spoke of herself in the third person, 'Anna was born on the wrong side of the blanket.' She had a materially comfortable childhood with her mother, until her father died when she was seven, with no provision for his mistress and illegitimate daughter in his will. Her mother lost her job when her lover's widow took over the business, fell into even harder times, and died when Anna was twelve, leaving Anna to run wild in Rio until she was arrested for theft and put into a convent-school-prison for bad girls. According to Anna, it was a terrible place where penance meant kneeling on dried corn or bramble to pray 'for hours'. When she was thirteen, the nuns caught her masturbating, and put her in a straitjacket at night 'to keep Anna from hurting herself, ha ha ha'. The only good thing about the convent was that it was where she developed her singing voice. At sixteen, she escaped from the convent, she said, bummed around Rio until she was nineteen, when she hooked up with an American businessman, 'a bastard', who brought her to California. As soon as she got to California, she ditched the businessman and ran off with a biker, whom she married, and ultimately ditched to make her way to New York. At the moment, she was singing at some club. She now lived with her cat, a gift from her boss, who was a 'big cheapskate', in one of the European-style rooms, which meant she shared a bathroom with several other tenants on the third floor. She knew a lot about them from their bathroom habits, along with other information she happily shared about them. Cousin It, for example, drank absinthe, 'real absinthe', and believed that the United States government had destroyed his music career, and the body-builder who stared into the hallway was some kind of Zen master Anna had recently offended.

'He doesn't talk much, but when he does, he says things, they sound smart, but if you think about them, they're very stupid,' she said. 'He told Anna, "The ultimate goal is to pass through this life and have absolutely no effect at all." No effect? Excuse me, but what is the fucking point, then? So full of shit. He claims he sees all, because his invisible third eye has been opened.'

She sipped at her spiked coffee and then said, 'An invisible third hand would be more fun and more useful.'

A couple of nights later, I ran into her at the bar of El Quijote, the Spanish seafood restaurant in the Chelsea, an odd place in its own right, a shrine to both the Cervantes character and the tasty crustacean, with decor that mixed 1962 lounge with Moorish brothel. Anna was dressed in a tight, sequin dress embroidered in a peacock feather motif.

'Hello!' she called out, waving me over. She was sitting with the plump man I'd seen her screaming at the first time I'd noticed her, only now he wasn't angry and wasn't red-faced. He was quite pale.

'This is Anna's boss,' she said of Pale and Plump.

The man half-smiled, half-leered, giving off a powerful smell of raw meat, and it occurred to me that if Anna thought all men were bastards then it was, in part at least, because she had bad taste in men.

'We go now, Anna,' Pale and Plump said.

'Ah, to work,' Anna said to me, and exited with Pale and Plump, getting into a chauffeured limousine.

Early the next morning, she was at my door. She was wearing a white winter coat with white feather and rhinestone trim and a matching hat. Under one arm was her orange cat. On the floor beside her was a litter box.

'Anna has to go away for the weekend,' she said. 'Will you please look after the cat?'

'I don't know. I . . .'

'Please. It's an emergency. Just until Monday. The cat hates to be left alone.'

What the hell, it was just for the weekend. I love cats, and I felt for Anna. I took the cat and the litter box. She opened her purse and gave me two cans of cat food and a few crumpled bills to buy more.

'His name is Bastard, after the man who gave him to Anna,' she said, and hurried off.

Monday came. No Anna. Tuesday, no Anna. Wednesday came, still no Anna, and a strange black woman calling herself Sequoia moved into Anna's room.

I went down to the Chelsea front desk and asked them what the hell had happened to Anna. The Chelsea staff claimed they knew nothing. This, I would learn later, was part of the Chelsea's protective ethos, that the staff was close-mouthed about its sensitive tenants.

'You do remember Anna?' I persisted, and the short, inscrutable Sikh behind the desk said, 'We have several hundred long-term residents and hundreds of tourists here. I can't remember everyone.'

'Is there a forwarding address?'

'No. Nothing.'

Sequoia claimed she didn't know Crazy Anna or anything about her. At the local precinct the cops asked if I was a relative and when I said no, took my statement with seeming indifference. How bizarre. You'd think these people would be as worried as I was about what had happened to crazy Anna.

My third-floor neighbors weren't helpful. Cousin It, who evidently had no left brain left, couldn't even remember who Anna was, and the Zen master body-builder said nothing, just lifted weights and stared past me.

A whole woman disappears without a trace, and nobody knows a damned thing about it.

The hub of social activity in the Chelsea is the lobby and I started hanging out there, keeping an eye out for people I'd seen Crazy Anna talking to in the past. The Chelsea Hotel lobby was eclectically decorated, with artwork covering every available space. The walls were full of paintings, and there was sculpture scattered around the seating area. A papier mâché woman in a swing hung from the middle of the ceiling. The black iron fireplace was guarded by two snarling black griffins. Above the mantle was a carved wood tableau depicting different artists at work. And on the mantle were two strange silver filigree vases that looked like ancient Phoenician cremation urns, flanking a bust of Harry S Truman. Behind the lobby desk, where the mail was held in hundreds of tiny cubbyholes, there was more art, on the walls, even on the ceiling. Not an inch of wall space was wasted.

It was like being inside a brain.

The nice-looking brown-haired man I'd seen, and heard, arguing with Anna about Chopin, was sitting on an ornately-carved church pew near the window. After Anna told me he was a drug dealer, I'd avoided him, but now all bets were off. I sat down across from him and introduced myself. He did not respond with his name, or anything more than a slight nod.

He was reading something called *The Journal of Recreational Mathematics*. I joked that it was a much more fun magazine since Tina Brown took it over. He did not respond, just looked at me, and then looked back at the magazine, turning away slightly.

So much for icebreakers. 'You know Anna, on three?' I said.

'Yeah, I know who she is. Haven't seen her around lately.'

'She hasn't been around. I'm trying to find out where she has gone.'

'I wouldn't know,' he said.

'How well did you know her?' I asked.

'We had a conversation one day about music that turned into a recurring argument whenever I was unable to avoid running into her,' he said, getting up and walking away.

As I tried to find out more about her, I got to know more of my neighbors, and every one of them had a different spin on Crazy Anna. I discovered that not everyone in the Chelsea was a nut, that there were a lot of more ... maybe not 'normal', by most definitions of normal, but more normal*ish* people who didn't drink absinthe, or lift weights and stare into the hallway for hours, or grunt, or believe that the CIA and George Bush had destroyed their music careers.

'Brazilian? I thought Anna was Russian,' said Charles, a French painter who had had a brief conversation with Anna once. 'And I don't think she was a singer. I think she was a hooker.'

'She told me her ex-husband was in the Hell's Angels, but he lost a leg, so he decided to make his wife famous,' said the bartender at El Quijote. 'But she ditched him and came to New York. Maybe the one-legged Hell's Angel came back for her.'

Anna had told someone else she was from Argentina, that she had had a baby when she was younger and the baby had been taken away from her. Everybody who had met Anna had met a different Anna, it seemed. Nobody knew where she'd gone, though, and nobody knew who Pale and Plump was, or what club Anna had worked in out in Brooklyn.

No good leads, no ideas, and I was stuck with a cat I didn't want and an unsolved mystery, a very worrisome one – what had happened to poor Crazy Anna? What if Anna was dead in a gutter, or being held as a sex slave by some perv, or wandering disoriented somewhere?

It was making me depressed and crazy, which colored everything. The whole world took on a very dark tone for a while. I hated the Chelsea Hotel and began looking for a new place to live.

One day, coming home from work, I was in the hallway on three and I heard someone say, 'Anna's gone. You won't be seeing her here again.'

I looked up. It was the All-Seeing, Three-eyed Zen master, Mr No Effect, lifting hand weights in his doorway, looking into the hallway. He was stony-faced.

'Do you know where Anna went?' I asked.

'No,' he said.

'Do you know why?'

He said nothing.

'Do you think she's safe?'

'Yes,' he said.

I wasn't so sure he wasn't completely whacko – the guy rarely spoke, had a body-building fetish and thought he had an invisible third eye, so what were the odds he was completely toons? But nobody else had had anything reassuring to say about Anna, and so I chose to believe him, to believe she was safe somewhere, and continued looking for another place to live.

Three weeks later, I was in the lobby waiting for the elevator, carrying a bag full of cat food and Czechoslovakian beer, and I ran into Mr Recreational Math/ Drug Dealer, the one who had argued about Chopin with Anna in the stairwell the day I formally met Anna. He was standing by the newspaper rack, reading the *Daily News*. When he saw me, he said, with surprise, 'You heard about Anna?'

'What about Anna?'

He handed me the *Daily News*, turned to page five, and a headline that read, 'Mystery Mob Moll is No Lady'.

Below that, it said, 'Key Witness against Brighton Beach Mob Boss Stuns Courtroom!'

A photograph of the reputed Russian mafia boss identified him as Ilya Odyotikov. It was Pale and Plump.

Below that was a modelling photo of a tall, thin woman in a gold lamé evening gown, her face obscured, with the caption, 'She's a Man!'

A Russian transvestite prostitute, code named 'Tootskie', had been secretly taping conversations with one of his lovers, the suspected Russian mob boss Ilya, who worked out of a Brighton Beach nightclub in the heart of Little Odessa, Brooklyn. In these tapes, the mob boss, drunk, had boasted of a number of killings, as much to impress Tootskie as to frighten him and keep him in line, according to unidentified government sources. Tootskie knew where all the bodies were buried. Ilya was very afraid the other gangsters would find out about his thing for trannies, Tootskie testified. In court he/she had amused everyone but the accused by giving more information than asked for. The mob boss in question was not well-hung, he smelled bad, and he gave Tootskie a cat for a present when he/she didn't even like cats and had told Ilya this and would have much preferred some jewelry. On several occasions Ilya had threatened Tootskie's life. Oh, and if that wasn't bad enough, Ilya had killed some people, including a man Tootskie was fairly sure he/she loved.

Tootskie was now in the protective custody of the Federal Witness Protection program.

It was Crazy Anna.

Crazy Anna a man? Why hadn't I known, why hadn't I seen any tell-tale signs, Adam's apple, thick wrists? As shocking as that was, the idea of Crazy Anna in the Federal Witness Protection program was so much more nonplussing. Flamboyant Anna, trying to live quietly and secretly somewhere in suburban obscurity?

Who would Anna be in her new life?

Anna wasn't from Brazil, and probably hadn't been in a convent, probably didn't kneel for hours on dried corn kernels and bramble for penance. But whatever had happened to make Anna the way she was, it was probably equally as traumatic as the events she described, though the details were likely quite different. So it wasn't that she had lied, really, not in essence. She had merely used metaphor to tell the story. That's art, in a way, I guess.

'The front desk must have known something about this. Why wouldn't they tell me anything?' I said.

'Maybe they didn't know, maybe they were protecting her, maybe they don't trust you,' the brown-haired man said.

'Don't trust me?'

'You haven't lived there very long, you're a call girl, and you live on the third floor, aka, the Psycho Ward,' he explained matter-of-factly.

'I'm not a call girl and even though I live on the third floor, I'm not crazy.'

'I thought I heard Anna telling someone you were a call girl . . .'

'Bitch! I'm a writer.'

I introduced myself to him again, and he told me he was a math and physics teacher at the Steiner School, the experimental school where many of the hotel kids, children of artists, went to learn via the Steiner Method.

'You're not a drug dealer?'

'No!' he said. 'Did Anna tell you that?'

'Yes.'

'How well did you know Anna?' he said, still somewhat suspicious.

'I hardly knew her, as it turns out.'

There was a definite vibe between us, me and him. He invited me to his room for coffee and Italian cookies, and after I fed the cat, I went. He told me he was divorced and had a nineteen-year old daughter – you. I had always thought of math and physics as dull, egghead stuff, but he had a way of making it sound kind of romantic, with phrases like Physically Inspired Strange Attractors, stories about twin photons, separated for miles, reacting identically when one or the other was stimulated, poetic descriptions of Chaos Theory, seeming randomness that isn't random at all.

We stayed up all night, and started falling in love. We sat on his balcony, drank more coffee. The sun came up, and it was all so beautiful, like one of those candy-colored mornings from childhood.

That's how I got my cat Bastard, and how I met your father.

will self

....

anything goes airlines

'Gimme your slots, *goo*-on gimme them!' Oswald's choice of words may have been crudely unvarnished but his tone, as ever, was powerfully inveigling. As Cocteau so wisely remarked, charm is that quality that enables a person to solicit the answer 'yes', before even posing the question.

'Wat slats?' inadvertently rhymed Michael Donaldson – Mickey to his acquaintances, for he had no friends – who was one of those men whose avidity sat nicely in his chipmunk cheeks. If Mickey was in an Andean air crash, he would be able to eat his own cud before resorting to overt cannibalism.

'*Your* fucking slots, sweet penis, your bloody slots; your deep unfathomable, warmly thrilling bays; your slickly lubricious, oily pans. I want to tie your frilly apron strings tight round my scrawny arms and jack up your revenue . . .!' I sighed into my rough tweed napkin. Chez Shea, this still notionally hip Soho, Franco-Hibernian brasserie was, fittingly enough, as narrow as an aeroplane fuselage and tightly packed with tables. The diners sat in twos and fours, all bolted together, all facing the same-sized beech slabs. There were at least twenty club class people listening to this filth, whilst they dipped soda bread in tiny dishes of olive oil and sipped silver thimbles of potheen.

It would've been entirely counter-productive to draw Oswald's attention to the outrage he was provoking – after all, what did I know about the airline business anyway? I was simply along to make up the numbers – in both senses, for I was also the financial director of Oswald's latest enterprise.

'Even – and I mean totally *not* even – were it likely that I would offload my slats at all – and b'lieve me, brother, those slats are worth more than this entire fuckin' district, so-whatever—'

'—Ho.' I couldn't forbear from inserting.

'Issat so? Same as the States – tho', over here it's kind of a faggot ghetto, not so many slant-eyes around.' Conversations reignited around us as Mickey uttered this incendiary piece of racism. Truly, the evening had now been worthwhile for all of them. The sculpted, bijou and painfully expensive food; the wine list, from upon which the only affordable bottle had long since gugglingly departed; and the *placements* which would've been cramped for a party of Munchkins, all of this had now been validated by an authentically awful, obese, loud-mouthed American. Anecdotal bliss.

'Yeah, yeah,' Oswald pressed on, like all truly great salesmen he was absolutely devoid of even a trace of shame, 'but I'm not offering you anything like what they might be worth to an established operator. I can probably manage about ten per cent of it—'

'Ten-fuckin' – per cent!' Mickey guffaw-splattered the table with a fine spray of well-chewed *ceps*. 'Wat the fuck are you talkin' about, man? Issat all you made me come out, eat with you for?'

'Ah no, no – not at all—' Oswald broke off to summon one of the appalled waiters, who was so tightly bound into his apron that it looked like a winding sheet.

'Sir?' queried the upright corpse.

'I believe Ben,' (this was the *patron*, Oswald always knew the *patron* – another facet of his diamond sharp salesmanship) 'has a brandy in the cellar which was distilled during the General Strike – as nice a marriage between luxury and deprivation as can be conceived – would you be so kind as to bring us three huge snifters?'

When the waiter had departed to fulfill this bravura order, Oswald, who up until now had been merely flirting, cranked his legendary charisma up to full power, and turned it onto Mickey, so that the poor, venal, manipulative, airline tycoon was as paralysed as a fly shot full of neurotoxins by an arachnid with an eating disorder. 'I want those slots, Mickey – and I mean to have them; and let me tell you a really, really strange thing, within the next twenty minutes or so – it depends in part on how much of that rather frisky potheen you've had – you're going to want me to have them as well.'

'That "nyum-nyum",' Mickey was now exercising his hand-mouth-stomach coordination on a salad of smoked trout and foetal Romaine lettuce hearts, a house speciality, 'is the most ridiculous thing I've fuckin' ever "nyum-nyum" heard.' Oswald leant forward so as to bar at least a few of the earwiggers in the vicinity.

'Yeah, well, let me ask you something, Mickey – something sort of personal. You don't mind that, do you?'

' "Nyum-nyum" Well, hell – why not, this evening can't be much more of a non-event than it is already.'

'How d'jew like to get blown?' Oswald's tones were calm, his mien academic, he might have been enquiring as to whether Mickey was familiar with Spinoza's metaphysic of morals.

'Wat!' Another expectoration hit the beech – this time it was greenish shreds.

'Y'know – blown, gobbled, gone down on; what we term on this side of the pond – with, I feel, rather more accuracy – being "sucked off".'

'Are you serious?' Mickey had gone as red as the Etruscan-style tiles surmounting the bar. The ultra-sharp tines of his fork were levelled directly at Oswald's prominent Adam's apple – exactly at the point where smooth neck folded into smoother, Gieves & Hawkes silk.

'Oh totally, utterly, never-before-seriouser serious. Listen—' Oswald hunkered right forward and drew Mickey and me into a pyramid of visages '—now, of course, Jerry here knows this well already, but I'm certain you must be familiar with the case of Dowd as well, mm?'

'Wat, Dowd the Boeing guy, the VP in charge of aerofoil design?'

'The same.'

'He dropped out. Last year, wasn't it? Took a hike into the boonies.'

'That's right.'

'People said it was after the Paris show. He was walking round Seattle inna kind of a . . . blur.'

'I believe so.'

'Saying how he's had the best motherfucking blow job in his whole cock-sucking life and how the industry don't mean diddly-squat to him anymore, 'cos he's had the greatest motherfucking sexual experience he's ever gonna have and it's all over with him.'

'That,' Oswald pronounced solemnly, 'was me.'

The thing about Oswald – and I should know, by way of being his sidekick – is that he is most extraordinarily beautiful to look at, really easy on the eyes. He tells other people that he's half-Swiss, half-Italian – hence the jet black hair and the dark blue eyes; hence also the slim shoulders, snake hips and expressive gestures. All stirred in with milky skin and a peculiar robustness of constitution. In truth – as he'll freely admit to anyone if they second guess this papier mâché fantasy – his parents were both Irish and he was brought up in Crawley. But that's another thing about Oswald – he'll spin a line, any line ('Actually I'm diabetic'; 'My wife died last week'; 'I was a midget as a child but they gave me raw pituitary glands so I made up for lost growth . . .'), but the second it's called – his is a bluff no longer, simply a little *jeu d'esprit*: 'What!?' he'll exclaim. 'You didn't *believe* that – did you?' And the world, mysteriously flattered at being assumed so childlike, would ingurgitate its ire once again.

I daresay he could have pulled out at any stage – even once Mickey's penis was in his mouth – and still got away with such guileful credulity, but this time he had no need.

'You?'

'Me. I give the best fucking blow job in the world. The best. I tailor the suction, the palpation, the summation, all according to the subject's most intimate and secretly sought after desires. I seem to know this intuitively. I never cause embarrassment. I never fail.'

'You?' Mickey reiterated, eyes bulging, hamster cheeks billowing with air and almost flapping, like slack spinnakers. Now I realised why it was that Oswald was so sure of himself – Mickey, like so many fat little wannabe cocksmen, was obviously gay. Oswald, who didn't so much swing each way as describe the path that might be followed by a pendulum were it to be suspended inside a gyroscope carved from a single lodestone, was also expert at spotting people's larger preferences, the broad band of their attraction. So, Mickey fancied our Ossie – and who could blame him for that.

Mickey leant back, still feverishly goggling and paradoxically, obviously desirous of full osculation with Oswald. 'Yah – whaddya', some kind'uv a hooker? Issat it, Ossie, 're you a tart for slats? Can that be true?'

'Listen,' – to begin with Oswald was still hovering, chin above the cruets; yet, during the following speech, he somehow managed to fully retract and descend, near noiselessly, beneath the slab of beech – 'I happen to have a gift for sensuality – and that's what I want to promote with my airline. I've made good money in entertainment, in legal gambling, in dry goods and I've the DIY superstore chain, but what I've always wanted is to be the owner of a flagship international airline. Most successful entrepreneurs in this country – even the incomers – when they reach a certain point they want a football club. Premier League. That's their idea of having arrived. Me, I want an airline – and not just any airline, it's got to be a transatlantic. I want to be one of the great thrumming strings that connects your country with mine. I want to be a pulsing chord between two mighty nations. To do that I need your slots, but believe me, Mickey, if you're not satisfied just put your lips apart and say "no". You know how to do that Mickey, don't you?'

The final 'you' must have coincided as Oswald's ruby-red lips, already parted, fitted themselves neatly over the head of Mickey's penis, his deft fingers already having unlimbered the organ – which I pictured, for some reason, as antithetical to its owner: vivid pink, long, slim and curving – from its gun carriage of suiting and under-wear. How it could be that this act – whether decent or indecent is debatable – should've been allowed to happen in a confined yet public space, is nearly as much of a mystery as Mickey's compliance. I suppose it could've been Ben O'Shea's influence, however, I doubt it. No, I like to think that the twenty or so other diners responded both to the ludicrousness of the situation: 'Waiter! I believe that man over there is having oral sex performed upon him by someone underneath the table . . .' and its flat-out surrealism – as Oswald bent to his task the slab of beech began to buck as if it were a surfboard and Oswald a breaker below.

Who knows what it's like to be on the receiving end of one of Oswald's mind-blowingly expert acts of fellation – certainly not me. Not that he hasn't offered to give me one, it's just that I prefer to keep my distance from those perfidious red lips. And as I've never actually seen the act itself, Oswald being, as in the episode with Mickey, curiously efficient about concealing himself whilst blowing the straight sax, I think it would stretch your credulity for me to plunge beneath with bucking beech with him. I confined myself to the brandy – which was exemplary; and then paid the bill. I was, after all, the financial director.

The outfit was dubbed 'Anything Goes Airlines', and the gimmick was simple – but beautifully perverse. AGA would fly sixteen scheduled flights to New York each day; eight from Gatwick to Newark; eight from Heathrow to JFK. These were the slots previously occupied by Orbis Airlines before its chief executive, Michael Donaldson, retired into a Buddhist monastery outside of Reading.

AGA would operate bog standard Boeing 747s, the interiors of which were stripped back to the basics – no livery, no plastic mouldings, no antimacassars, no carpeting – and reinforced with steel plating. Steel plating, lead sheeting, and an injection-pumped inner sealing of a 100 per cent inflammable polymer mastic recently developed as part of the space programme. As Oswald so eloquently put it, 'You could let a fucking bomb off in one of these planes and it would keep right on flying on its wire, delivering its cargo of people purée to the land of the free.'

Not that AGA planes wouldn't have pilots – they'd have the best available. It's just that these operatives, like all the rest of AGA staff, would be insulated from what went on within the body of the planes they flew. Insulated by steel plating, lead sheeting and a 100 per cent inflammable polymer mastic.

There would be no 'classes' per se on AGA. Class was something which Oswald, very much Thatcher's child (and Blair's babe), vociferously objected to: 'We don't wanna even engage with that screweduptightassburning snob thing man,' was how he put it. 'On AGA you pay for space – that's all. Space. Not the opportunity to look down on some other poor keister. We're gonna elevate the little man here – in myriad ways.' So, each flight throughout the day would have progressively more space. Not more stewardesses, nor manicurists, nor movies, nor computer games, nor marked down booze, nor baby corn, nor nothing. Just space.

There would be four hundred spaces available on AGA Flight AG 301, out of Heathrow's Terminal 2 every morning at 7.30 a.m. Three hundred and fifty on AG 302 at 9.45 – and then so on until the four afternoon flights, the first three of which carried two hundred passengers and the fourth – the so called 'red body' flight (called by the punters, not by us) a mere hundred.

The 747s' interiors, stripped of dinky spiral staircases, depopulated of uniformed ex-convent girls from Farnborough, and devoid of aluminium mini-wheelie-bins full of vodka miniatures, were surprisingly cathedral spaces. Bulging manifolds of dully shining brushed steel, bellying out into plenitude, then tapering into detumescence.

In order to conform with safety standards, passengers were secured within hammocks of rubber straps during take-off, landing and turbulence. But throughout the flight these were stowed in the bulkheads. All that was left was the space and the passengers, and, to quote their Master of Revels, 'Their propensities. What they want to do. Their schtick. Their blag. Their *thing*. And here's the beauty of AGA – here's the thing that makes our

Standard & Poor rating actually perform frottage with my Fortune Five Hundred listing: We Don't Care.

'That's right, *anything goes*. Anything. They can fuck, fight, fulminate and fly off the handle; they can smoke, toke, then don a hood and rope. We don't mind if they jack off, shoot up, or slam dunk. They can bring any of the following on to the aircraft: sheep, rocket launchers, angel dust, unaccompanied children, surgical equipment. Anything, that is, which doesn't broach our – extremely generous – 100 kilo baggage allowance.'

As I've remarked before, Oswald was a broad brush man, it was left to me to fill in the details. It was left to me to jockey between the outrage of the media, the prurience of Parliament and the suspicions of the airport authorities. My tactics were low key. Rather than advertise the unique amoral selling point of the airline, I decided instead to market AGA as little more than an unusual low-cost operator, trusting to word of mouth and the paradoxically high ticket prices to do the rest.

I was on the first scheduled flight out of Heathrow and it's an experience I'll never forget. There was nothing about the appearance of my fellow three hundred and ninety-nine passengers as they gathered in the departure lounge by Gate 72 to indicate that they were embarking on a dirigible for the severely depraved. Granted, they were on the whole younger and fitter than the normal transatlantic crowd – and there were no children. But as we sat, pinioned 'twixt carpet tiling and strip lighting, there was the familiar atmosphere of terminal ennui. However, the second boarding was announced we all sprang to our feet and rushed towards the gate. In the

cantilevered corridors leading to the aircraft the passengers began lowing with anticipation, like kamikaze
cows lusting after the abattoir.

Once we'd debouched into the shiny interior of the
aircraft, the cabin doors closed automatically and hidden
speakers instructed us as to how to fasten our harnesses,
then ran brusquely through the safety check. With no
fixed seating this was mercifully short, merely a burble of
remonstration during which me and my fellow passengers eyed each other warily. After all, if AG 301 went
down, there would be no assistance for the fat or the old
or the lame; no luminescent arrows leading to an inflat-
able rubber rebirth. Oh no, Social Darwinism would
break out red in tooth and claw.

There was silence during taxiing and take-off save for
the engines. It reminded me of the time Oswald and I
found ourselves on the last flight out of Luanda before
the Angolan civil war turned medieval. The old cargo
plane groaning and juddering through the ascent, the
rivets in the wings audibly popping, whilst outside the
soft, grey florets of flak bloomed in the blue. And inside
all the bent antibiotic salesmen and anti-personnel
mining engineers sat in deep silence, anticipating the
noiselessness of the grave.

When AG 301 reached its cruising altitude our harnesses automatically unsnapped, stowed themselves and
there we all were.

Oswald had chosen this moment to make his final and
most personal announcement: 'Welcome everyone to
AGA Flight 301 from Heathrow...' the recording
purred – as ever, the more removed Oswald was, the
more present he seemed to be, '... to JFK. I won't be

bothering you with any flight information for the next seven hours or so, so here goes. We are currently cruising at thirty thousand feet and will shortly be crossing the Irish Sea. In approximately forty-five minutes, after leaving Irish air space, we will descend to 20,000 feet in order to rendezvous with AGA Flight 301A out of Novosibirsk. This is an ex-Soviet air force refuelling aircraft which has been specially adapted for our purposes, so that solid as well as liquid material may be transferred in mid-air.'

'You have forty minutes to write your requests down, seal them together with the correct hard currency in the envelope provided – we accept US dollars, sterling and deutschmarks, but regrettably not the euro – and then deposit it in one of the ten delivery system boxes positioned by the forward bulkheads. A list of available merchandise – from the finest Penang pink rocks of heroin, to the most refined bestial pornography, to the most advanced weaponry – is on display. After fuelling, passenger names will be called and deliveries received. Please ensure that you post your request in the box numbered on your boarding card.

'Not only cannot mistakes be rectified, but once the deliveries have been completed and we've regained our cruising altitude, there will be approximately five and a half hours until we commence our descent into New York, and during this time, as I'm sure all of you are well aware and keenly anticipating, *anything goes*. Thank you for flying AGA and in the immortal words of the Beast 666: "Do what thou wilt is the whole of the law!"' That last little flourish was pure Oswald; Charles Manson in lieu of Richard Branson.

Word of mouth and a discrete web site had been more than sufficient to enable the frequent AGA flyers of the future to self-select for this maiden voyage. This much became apparent within seconds of Oswald's recorded announcement. I'd been fearing a herd-like stampede towards the wilder shores of debauchery; passengers cramming their requests for pervy comestibles into the boxes, and then tearing each other's lungs out once the gear was delivered. Not so. This lot were an altogether more deliberative proposition.

They filled out their request sheets and patiently waited, sitting mostly cross legged on the floor chatting in a convivial fashion. The descent to the 'fuelling' rendezvous went off without a hitch, as did the 'fuelling' itself. Oswald may have bought former Soviet air force planes, and paid the Russian mafia generously for ground services in Novosibirsk, but he'd exercised extreme caution in hiring his pilots, who were Danes to a man.

When their package arrived, the two slight, whey-faced men squatting next to me unwrapped it to reveal ampoules of sodium amytal and a selection of surgical instruments. As I watched, the two men commenced performing surgery on each other; each inserting a slim, shiny catheter into his opposite number's cartoid artery, then neatly linking it to a five cc syringe primed with the barbiturate. They were now Siamese-twinned by plastic tubing.

'Um . . . I'm sorry to bother you . . .' I think my hesitation was more than called for, given the delicacy of the pseudo-operation ' . . . but would you mind awfully telling me what it is you two are doing?'

'Wada test,' said the one nearest me, a sharp-chinned

individual with restless maroon eyes behind red-tinted lenses. 'It's a perceptual experiment whereby half of the brain is put to sleep using sodium amytal. It enables neurologists to more accurately map the right/left brain divide.'

'But, why're you doing it?'

'Kicks,' said the other guy, while depressing the plunger on his syringe so that the left eyelid of his opposite number dipped, then closed. 'I put his left lobe to sleep, he puts my right. The result is that if we meditate while in this state, *we become fused as a curiously mismatched entire consciousness—*' The last part of this was uttered in unison. I began backing away.

'—I'm sorry to disturb you,' I said – although it was me who was profoundly disturbed.

'Don't go,' they called after me, 'we've got another set of equipment, we love doing threesomes!'

They weren't the only sadistic surgeons on board. Indeed, out of the four hundred I'd say at least a quarter were up there to strop their razors on human leather. By the time we touched down at JFK, all the surfaces of the stark cabin were slick with pink spume and actual rivulets of blood were flowing down a network of channels incised in the floor; channels which were – I now realized – designed expressly for that purpose. Oswald – he thought of everything.

But if the sadistic surgeons were plentiful they were also discrete and efficient. They cut themselves and each other; then sutured, sewed and bandaged. Even while they were doing the business they formed loose little huddles, like prudish bathers holding towels to protect each other's modesty. Not all of the rest were as retiring.

There were at least three large, distinctive groups of flamboyant sodomites who insisted on forming conga lines of buggery and then – as it were – stripping-the-willow with each other. But even though this was egregious in the extreme, it was impossible to get that offended, so jolly were they as they frolicked; a dancing daisy chain of bobbing bald heads, glinting oiled pecs and jiggling leather cache-sexes.

The druggies were, predictably, the least trouble of all. I suppose the received opinion is that near-psychotic individuals pumped full of mentally destabilising drugs have a tendency to fly off the handle, but really this applies mostly to young men on alcohol. Of course, AGA had hardly any of these folk, given that all the main carriers were only too happy to cater for them. No, our druggies were flying well off of anyone's handle already. Once they were irradiated with dimethyltriptamine, perfused with phenobarbital, and puffed up with crack smoke, the mere sight of one of their fellow passengers undergoing a more than averagely creative rhinoplasty was enough to cow them completely.

When the customs and immigration people swarmed on board at JFK, they were obviously expecting to mop up an emergency situation compounded from all the elements of an ebola outbreak, the Waco siege and the Christopher Street riots. They were all wearing full decontamination suits and body armour. What they found were file upon file of orderly, if wasted, passengers. Every last one of them had correctly completed their visa waiver. All drugs, weaponry, pornography and cutlery had been placed in the disposal bins provided, sealed, and dumped off of the Grand Banks in 10,000 fathoms.

After the passengers had been hosed down with disinfectant, maiden flight AG 301 was cleared for disembarkation and adjudged by everyone who flew on her to be an enormously violated success.

Not by Oswald, though. As soon as I was ushered into his suite at the Soho Grand, the CEO of AGA leapt up from a low coffee table where he'd been sculpting dinky, castellated ramparts from a pile of glittering white powder (Oswald never actually took drugs, but he liked to toy with them occasionally), and launched into a frenzied debriefing: 'Didjew see that boy at the front?'

'I'm sorry?'

'Jerry, Jerry – the boy at the front throughout the flight,' Oswald had monitored the course of AG 301 from his Manhattan hotel suite using a battery of satellite-linked cctv cameras, 'the one with the fucking purple Mohican.'

'Oh, him – yeah, I saw him. He didn't do anything much. Shot some smack, I think – whatever. But what about the guys doing the Wada test for ki—'

'—Exactly! He *didn't do anything much*! And d'jew know why? I do. I fucking do. He didn't do anything much because a posse of uptight, humanitarian, caring queers fucking *talked him out of it*! He was going to kill himself in a most spectacular fashion. He'd ordered up one of those itty-bitty carpet bombs, and his mate was going to implant it in his stomach. He was going to internally *liquefy*! – Before they ruined it.'

'Fair play to them, Ossie, I mean, they didn't want to go cup-a-soup alongside of him, now did they?'

'It wasn't that.' Oswald snarled, whilst employing a

dustpan and brush to clear up his coke castle. 'It was sheer bloody altruism. I heard them – talked him down they did. Told him there was no shame in being a fucking sicko. Told him they'd help him. Spooked him right out. Prevented *anything going*!'

'Ossie—Ossie—'

'—Don't you Ossie me – I'm not a fucking ostrich.'

'You are if you keep your head in the sand over this one. Look, in all good faith you've started an fantastically innovative airline; the first carrier in the world that's morally as well as commercially deregulated. But you have to accept the logic of the rubric you've lain down.'

'Meaning?'

'That if anything at all goes, it can be anything ordered, sagacious and cooperative; quite as much as it can be amoral, anomic and improvident. I mean to say – you can't legislate for anarchy, now can you?'

Nor could he. AGA was a great success: every seat filled on every flight; pre-booked well into the teens of the next century; and scalpers outside the terminals selling spaces on specific flights at anything up to a 4000 per cent mark up. Oh yes, business boomed, even if the DEA shot down a couple of our flights before we managed to get to the Right People. Business boomed and the twenty thousand odd early-corrupters who rapidly became AGA frequent flyers began to tailor the service to their own inimitable needs.

Communicating via the net, and coded messages on the passenger noticeboards, they began internally organising those forty daily flights. Sure, there were still plenty of AGA aircraft upon which anything did go, once Irish airspace was cleared, but in amongst them were numerous 'specialist' flights. As I've already mentioned the last and most expensive London–New York and New York–London flights quickly became known as the 'red body' services. Why it is exactly that so many wealthy and famous people should be so hooked on self-mutilation is beyond me. But that was their kick. It got so the ground staff could recognize these types as soon as they neared check-in. They all wore tightly-belted macs; they all wore shades; and they were all accompanied by inverted body-guards. Tough young men whose job it was to beat their wealthy clients senseless for the long hours it took to cross the Atlantic.

Then the sadistic surgeons got organized. Always the most methodical of perverts, it didn't take them long to secure – presumably through a buying cooperative – a majority of the spaces on the flights they favoured. The 1630 flight out of Newark became synonymous with their most creative activities, and dubbed, appropriately enough, the 'Airline of Dr Moreau'. AGA employees quipped – until their wages were docked – that it was one of the few ways there were of smuggling a pet into Britain. Success was guaranteed, as long as you didn't object to your dog's head being decapitated and replaced with that of a human psychopath.

Then there were the so-called 'Flights of the Living Dead'. Planeloads of genuine zombies, shipped across the pond, courtesy of AGA, on behalf of powerful witch doctors. These pre-programmed, heavily drugged, psychic mules were, with their blank stares and robotic movements, impossible to distinguish from the millions of ordinary travellers amidst whom they circulated, like retroviruses in the very body politic. Oswald was intensely proud of them. 'Without the Flights of the Living Dead and the 1001 Flights of Sodom and the occasional *Marie Celeste*, this airline would be about as dull as fucking British Midland. Christ! Even when you give the people what they fucking want, they still go right on and louse it up!'

The *Marie Celestes* were those sublime flights which departed Irish or American airspace with their full complement of passengers; but which when uncorked at their respective destinations, were found to be empty vessels. Devoid of anyone at all – or at least devoid of anyone living. Often there were charnel house remains, all the more grotesque for being neatly packaged, like the airline catering of Hannibal Lecter. Oswald savoured the aesthetics of the *Marie Celeste* flights, remarking to me that 'I doubt society will have ever found a more effective way of dealing with its self-annihilators. They're disposed of cleanly, efficiently, totally; *and*, in the process, they generate plenty of viable economic activity, rather than merely delaying the trains.'

Still, while there were these satisfactions, there were also far too many counter examples. Oswald had had high hopes for AGA flights becoming amazing free-fire zones. It was never clear to me whether he'd anticipated that the gun-toting passengers would all execute each other to the betterment of the world; but even so, he was dismayed to discover that not even the dumbest of boys, from the remotest of hoods, needed any help to understand that it was blindingly stupid to fire a weapon with a high muzzle velocity inside a steel box. Worse still was the realisation that passengers were getting together anyway

– either early in the flight or while still in the terminals –
to establish contractual agreements *among themselves* as to
what behaviour was permissible during the flights.

The trouble was that it wasn't an inert and uncritical
'society' which had noticed the impact of AGA, it was
an inquisitive, questing hydra of transatlantic academic
enquirers. These multidisciplinary hordes – like locusts
ravening for research – descended on our airborne
Arcadia in order to analyse it out of the sky. Or so it
seemed to Oswald when he found out that numerous
political scientists, philosophers and even serving politicians, were undertaking AGA flights in order to observe
humankind in the roughest and rawest of natural states.
Right behind them came others. Phalanxes of clinical
psychologists booked AGA spaces, seeking 'pure'
samples of the pathologies they'd invented. Armies of
anthropologists flew AGA in order to get in touch with
the mind set of bloodthirsty and deracinated traditional
peoples. Swarms of sociologists checked in for the AGA
experience, intent on discovering emergent trends.

But there was worse to come, far worse. Within
months of AGA getting in the air, academic papers were
being published with titles like 'Anything Goes Airlines:
A Blueprint for a New Social Contract in the Post-Super-
power Era?', and some of the wilder theorists were openly
propounding Oswald himself as a serious contender for
high office. What had begun as the most determined
example of laissez-faire, moral, libertarian capitalism,
was being subjected to lightning cooption by those established cohorts its creator loathed the most. 'D'jew
realise,' he screamed at me over the rental ether as I
walked up Old Compton Street, on my way for the anni-

versary AGA lunch at Chez Shea, 'that there are now some AGA flights that are non-fucking-smoking! I kid you not: flights where the passengers have all got together and agreed *not to smoke*! It's the last straw!' And he broke the connection. Leaving me with the plug of plastic rammed in my ear still pulsing.

The penultimate straw had been the news broken that morning that the Prime Minister's son had flown AGA to celebrate his eighteenth birthday. When the heir to the throne had flown AGA no one, least of all Oswald, had given a toss – but the Prime Minister's son! It made a mockery of everything we were trying to do. What had been intended as a bold strike against the most inner sanctums of conformity had become about as risqué as a strip-o-gram in a provincial steakhouse. Before long we'd be accepting birthday party bookings – for five-year-olds.

Outside Chez Shea squatted a pseudo-Buddhist monk, complete with off-the-peg orange robes and Tupperware begging bowl. I knew he was bogus because he was far too fat for someone dedicated one-pointedly to the elimination of all appetitive desire. His curiously familiar chipmunk cheeks puckered as he intoned: 'Got any spare change, guv?' in a peculiar, strangulated, Brooklyn/Cockney accent. It was Mickey Donaldson. 'Blimey,' I said, 'you've come down in the world. It's only a year since you gave up your slots and left Orbis. Yet here you are grovelling in the street. I bet you miss the days when you could cross the world as easily as a road.'

'Not at all,' he snapped back, 'I can fly even better now – and I don't even need a plane to do it with! Aha-ha! Ha-

ha-ha!' His demented loony chuckles followed me into the cramped fuselage of the once fashionable eatery.

Oswald was sitting together with Ben O'Shea at the back table of the restaurant. All the rest were empty. A year is a long time in restaurants. Both men had twelve-ounce glasses full of Black Bush in front of them. O'Shea was dressed as a failing, drunken restaurateur; Oswald was dressed as a German naval officer of *circa* 1940, complete with white-peaked cap, blue battledress, swastika epaulettes and regulation chin-strapping, close-cropped beard. I knew better than to remark on the costumes. 'That character Donaldson is outside begging for food money,' I said, by way of a conversational entrée.

'Tell him to come inside and eat,' O'Shea grunted, 'before we both starve.'

'Silly cunt,' Oswald slurred, 'left his monastery in Reading and follows me around. There's a whole posse of them.'

'Them?' I queried.

'The ones I've sucked off. They're fanatical. Worship me the way Warren Buffet's investors worship him. Fucking nuisance. I call 'em the stalk stalkers. Geddit.'

'At least you've got a clientele,' O'Shea broke in, 'a year ago this joint was heaving – and look at it now! I've had to subcontract Jean-Christophe to Spud-U-Like – it can't go on!'

'Ah Ben,' Oswald tottered to his feet, whiskey slopping from his tumbler, 'who gives a shit about your fucking food bar anyway – eh? There's only so many bourgeois cakeholes to stuff in this berg, no, what we should be mourning is the death of Anything Goes Airlines. It's a failure – I'm gonna sell the fucking thing. I was wrong. I dunno if it's that there isn't a long enough flight time, or if iss because people are too familiar with air travel, but iss not working, iss not working at all.

'Thass why I'm dressed up like this Jerry; thass why I got you along.' He turned back to the table and grasped the beechwood slab firmly in his elegant hands. He looked at me steadily with his dark blue eyes seductively scintillating. 'Now, Jerry,' he said, lifting his glass to eye level and staring through the whiskey at me, 'how much d'jew know about submarines?'

lana citron

....

the awakening chamber

I swam like a fish beneath the chlorine, water blue, orange rubber goggled that half masked my face. There in the murky depths of my thoughts, blurry limbs and half torsos until nearly choking with the want for breath, I'd emerge to gasp and splutter.

I, Oliver Steadfast, blond hair, button-nosed, pinky pale, rather adorable in that young boy pre-puberty way and in my element. H_2O. For every Tuesday and Friday after school, I would accompany my sister Paulette down to the local baths. A handsome red-brick Victorian building with cracked tiling and a generous selection of draughts, terribly basic, no private changing cubicles, communal showers but wonderful none the less.

Younger than Paulette, I was put in her charge and would follow her into the Ladies' Changing Room. My awakening chamber, for it was there I'd ogle goggle the ladies changing. That special place, perfume-scented, clothes strewn randomly, the L-shaped room was bereft of lockers and clothes were hung on pegs. If one had a distrusting nature, for a redeemable shilling one could avail oneself of a basket, much like a supermarket one and hand it out to the supervisor. This, however, meant going back out into the cold of the reception area and was, as far as we were concerned, not a necessity. So it was there I found myself all modest, with a towel around my middle, to hide my sometimes stirring prick and prying, I would undergarment peel off, ease my stripy trunks up those hairless legs of mine and come to learn the importance of that kinder phrase, 'I'll show you mine, if you show me yours.'

Ohh . . .

Yes, please.

My sister resented my presence. I tied her down. She wanted to frolic in the water with a couple of her best friends, Nadine Baker and Julie Summers. I recall Nadine as a plumpish girl who took the precaution of wearing her togs beneath her clothing and I would have to wait till after the swim to sneak a glance in her direction which, believe me, was something worth waiting for. Her skin a light caramel, was unblemished with a perfectly rotund bottom. Julie had a more boyish body. She was taller than the others with dark red hair and changed the swiftest of the lot. I had to be quick to catch her litheness and, just to assure you, I can honestly declare my sister held no personal interest, even though hers was the most advanced of the bodies. Ah, those water babes of puberty with burgeoning breasts and cherry-nippled, as prudish as myself, which in effect aroused my wonderment at the differences between us that had to be hidden.

How I loved to go swimming and how Paulette despised me. It was so unfair to have a little brother tugging at her side and perhaps if I had been in her swimming slippers, due to a ferocious verruca, I too would have felt the same but at that time, I felt her rejection profoundly and as a result annoyed her all the more, as only a sibling can.

In retrospect she must have suffered a crushing humiliation that day I pulled the towel from round her middle to expose her yellow-stained panties, chanting to her friends as a drummer boy, 'Piss Stain-er', my nickname for her and louder . . .

I hasten to add, this was not my usual behaviour. I had been provoked by one of her skin-stinging pinches. We'd been queuing for the baths, a small line of regulars when she squealed aloud, 'Stupid idiot,' as I had stumbled, unintentionally I assure you, on her toe and verruca. So she gripped my arm and as tiny a piece of my flesh as did fit between her forefinger and thumb was twisted any which way, till puce with the pain, my eyes smarted and her friends taunting, called me a pansy. So I was provoked into taking further action, thus my cries . . .

'Piss stain-er.'

I did not have to wait long for Paulette to retaliate, a terrifying deed which by default introduced me to another greater world.

Not as strong a swimmer as Paulette, she with all her friends would race the twenty-five metres up into the deep, most likely in an effort to avoid myself. But I would persist and splash wildly, lugging and heaving myself up along the metal bar.

On this occasion she was in the deep end luring me

further, out of my depth. Coaxing me with a drawn out 'OL-I-VER,' in that coy, sisterly whine.

'What?'

'I'm practising for my survival swimming test. Now you pretend you're drowning and I'll pretend I'm saving you.'

'No.'

'Do it.'

Her hand easing my fingers forcibly off the safety bar, so pretend was right. Her arm around my neck and instead of keeping me afloat, she was pulling me under.

She did indeed pass that test but in the pool as I splashed, spluttered my head beneath the water, my eyes bulging, she did dunk me till I near half drowned. The lifeguard calling out, 'No, keep his head up . . . up . . . up . . .' and she was then congratulated for her bravery on saving her brother as I was hauled out of the water, blue in the face, choking.

'Piss stainer.'

And whacked by the guard for my insolence!

I bore no immediate grudge and escaped a fear of water for already in my mind revenge bubbled and besides I had liked the weightless wetness of it all, from that position of submission.

Afterwards, Paulette left me alone and I put a lot of effort in, forced my head beneath and paddled as a dog. I became a stronger swimmer and underwater would annoy Paulette, open her bikini top, to pop my head up and gasp, 'Got you, Paulie.'

Could hold my breath for a minute, maybe two, dive

and wiggle. Oh, how I'd wiggle. 'Open wide for here I come,' I'd holler to Nadine or Julie and they'd both oblige. Legs astride and swim beneath and on my back, no small feat, to rub against, or wet glide, around the those trusting limbs. That was when I spied *him* and recoiled somewhat or just a little, for he a largish man and hairy, beneath the water too, his hands upon his tackle and staring at me from similar goggles.

I did not fancy the look of him, his brutish hairy largeness, leering and over-familiar.

Of course, I came to recognize the regulars as they did I. My favourite one being Mrs Hippopotamus, gargantuan but flexible and generous in her fleshy offerings with sagging breasts falling past her stomach. Oh, Mrs Hippo, how thirsty I was upon your beauty. She would lap the waters creating in her stride an undercurrent, her plastic flowered cap stuck on her head and huge rear, undulating upward, downward as she swam along in whale-like fashion. Her bulbous stomach, a mountain reflected beneath the shimmering water. Her companion was a skinny woman, all bones and red rashes with small empty chest sacs in comparison, and I never much bothered about her. She had hair on the back of her legs and under her arms, a scowl on her face and it was she who once remarked, 'Isn't it time you changed in the Men's?'

What had she to fear from me? . . . except I wouldn't give her the time of day and she caught me prying beneath the toilet gap to see her teeth clenched in concentration before spying my orange goggles.

'I dropped something, swear to you,' I lied. Her nose in

the air and mine, too, as she forced back the lock on the cubicle and dragged me inside to pull down my trunks and wallop me like I would never forget.

But to happier times standing beneath the shower. Cap in hand, the warmth of the water, not warm enough, for things would stand on end as I watched my sister and her friends change back into their clothes. Oh, how clumsy they were, towels dropping immodestly and sometimes even better . . . Best of the lot, Hippo would stand beside me in the showers, her togs decorticated, indeed as a rind from a ripened fruit. Right off, standing in her luscious flesh. I was small for my age and she did so lather herself and then the soap would slip from out of her fingers and fall in the drain below and she would bend over.

She did so bend.

Over.

Dear God, but there I saw the world.

She doted on me, I her darling pup, and gave me Fox's glacier mints to freshen up my mind.

After the swim Paulette with her group of giggly girls, chatted outside the pool house with the boys, throwing their hair back in the wind, wet and brash and laughing like instant retards. One time, I, spied emerging from that wondrous world, became the point of focus.

A youth named Victor had the audacity to say in a mocking tone, 'Are you a girl then?'

If only he knew.

Upon my heart-warmed glimpses that such an interest

grew. Indeed, I shrunk in awe of womanhood so that I might look younger and answer him.

'You're just jealous.'

Victor blushed as I tarnished his name.

Weeks after my dunking, timed precisely so my sister could not connect the incident to me, Paulette became ill.

Did you think I'd forgotten?

I, Oliver Steadfast and true to his word?

On a damp afternoon I snuck from the pool before the swimming session had finished and, oh deary me, pushed Paulette's clothes onto the floor, watching as they tumbled into a big wet puddle. Poor Paulette, for in those days we walked the mile and a half home and by the time we reached the hall door she was already complaining of fever.

It was the dead of winter, she caught a chill that landed on her chest and suffered a mild bout of pneumonia. The doctor left the strictest of orders, under no circumstances was she to go swimming till the summer. I began to feel guilty before I realised I had inadvertently sabotaged myself.

A hefty penance paid and I found myself up in the baths alone, my hand clasped around the Ladies' handle.

Stopped in my stride by an ignoramus of the most eminent type, 'Oi, that's the Ladies.'

Didn't I know it and he pointed out the Men's.

'I . . . I . . .' I followed his finger and blamed it on the darkening down gracing my upper lip. That is how it happened, my fault, for without Paulette I was suddenly on my own and old enough.

And I turned, turned never to grace that other place again.

I should have memorised each scent, each glimpse, oh Mrs Hippo, and she said to me, 'Well, well, aren't you growing into a fine wee man?' Dear Mrs Hippo to plunge upon my knees and wallow in my misery. The skinny one snarled with joy.

Did they tell me I'd be missed?

Not a bit of it and to top it all, to pour indignity upon indignity, in the Men's I changed role and became the focus of attention of that hairy male, who asked me if I'd like a rub down.

Pervert. Sick man.

See, I knew exactly where he was coming from, for occasionally Hippo would dry me off as I stood small and shivering, lift me on her knees and . . . end of an era.

I was shocked by his request, scared even, that I should witness such depravity and him making me shriek like a girl, like a high pitched howling dervish.

'You great big pansy!!'

Telling him quite plainly to keep his hands to himself.

In retrospect I was lucky, being small for my age and going on twelve before I had to change in the Men's.

Then as so happens, I gradually lost interest and crawled as an amphibian, to journey from phase to phase (the next one happened to be cricket) and evolve into adolescence.

john williams

the bosun

Mikey had always quite fancied management. Any fool could see it was where the money was. You look at them Spice Girls, Boyzone, all that shit, you could be damn sure it was the manager making the money, not the girls, bunch of game show hostess types in bra tops. He'd been thinking about it for a while, the way you do watching TV. It's Saturday night, you've not enough money in your pocket to go out, and you're stuck inside watching fucking Noel Edmonds, you got to be looking for an angle.

And how hard could it be? Find a bunch of fit-looking girls can sing a bit, get one of the boys to write a few songs for them, how could you go wrong? Nothing too tacky, of course, none of the teenybopper crap, something a bit classier, like 'Eternal', say. Mikey liked 'Eternal'. Nice looking girls too, which helped of course, even if you could see a mile off the kind of stuck-up church choir types they were. It might not exactly impress the boys to say you'd been listening to the new 'Eternal', but fair play to them he'd heard the new one on

Blue Peter the other day – watching with little Mikey, you know – and it wasn't bad. Yeah something like that would be ok.

As of the management side of things, Mikey figured it couldn't be too different from what a few of the blokes he knew did, looking after some girl who makes a living using her assets. He'd never got on too well in the pimping game himself, but he simply put that down to being too much of a decent bloke, too damn soft and, to be honest, none too keen on getting in a fight. Way he saw it, in the pop business, chances were your girls didn't pull a knife on you too often.

Only question really was where to start. School would be good, he thought, get a bunch of sixteen-year-olds, lot of enthusiasm, not too clever with contracts. Come to think of which he'd better have a word with his brief, see if he could sort him out with some kind of standard contract – as used by sharks everywhere, that kind of thing. Schoolgirls ought to be less chopsy too, with a bit of luck. Only problem, it was a right pain in the arse getting all the way over to the school. He'd popped round, asked Col if he'd mind driving him over Fitzalan and Col had given him a bit of a look, 'Jumping the cradle are we now?' he'd said, so what with one thing and another it took him a couple of days to get it together.

Course, minute he got there, he could see it was a bad idea. God knows what he was expecting to find. A bunch of girls standing on the corner by the sweetshop singing harmonies together? Well, surprise, surprise, it didn't quite work out like that. First thing happened was he walked straight into a girl named Donna who he'd had a little thing with a long, long time ago. She's standing by the gate waiting for her eleven-year-old to come out, take him to his karate lesson. And so he's stuck there talking to this Donna, who, frankly, the years have not been kind to, looking scrawny as fuck and still got the loudest voice he'd ever heard. Which is saying something in Cardiff where half the women seem to be in perpetual bloody foghorn practice. Eventually, thank Christ, her little boy comes out, a mouthy little bastard in a Man U top and Donna pisses off but by then it looks like Mikey's blown it. Started to feel like just another dad come to take his kids home, not a top-flight music biz entrepreneur looking for new talent.

Still, fair play to Mikey, he gave it a go anyway. Saw a bunch of fine looking sixth-form girls come out together, all lighting up at once, second they got to the school gates. He went up to the one in the middle, tall girl with braids.

'You ever done any singing, sweethearts?' he asked.

'Why, you fucking dance?' she said, and her mates all laughed like this was the funniest thing they'd ever heard.

'Look,' he said, 'I'm serious. I'm looking for some girls to join a group. Kind of All Saints type thing and I saw you beautiful young ladies together, and I reckoned you've got the looks for it.'

That stopped them for a moment. One thing with girls, you could never over-estimate their vanity. Flattery had always been a key weapon in Mikey's armoury. Lot of blokes couldn't do it, all that corny bullshit, your eyes are so beautiful, blah, blah, thought it was too stupid, but that was Mikey's strength. Nothing was beneath him, not if it worked.

'Oh yeah,' said another of the girls, little Asian-looking piece. 'And who are you then?'

'Me,' said Mikey, 'I'm . . . oh, I been around the music business for years, kind of a freelance talent scout and manager at the moment. Lot of contacts. It's all about who you knows, see, in this business. You know Cleopatra, yeah?'

The girls nodded.

'Well,' lied Mikey, 'It was me who discovered them.'

'No, it wasn't,' said the tall girl, 'I seen it on the telly, it was their mum. She's their manager.'

'Yeah, yeah, course,' said Mikey, 'lovely lady, too, but she didn't do all by herself, you know. That's just the way they put it out to the press like. No, she, um, the girls' mum, right, she had to have someone see her girls, spot the talent and take them to the right record company and stuff.' Mikey pointed to his chest, 'Mikey Thompson's the man.'

There was a pause.

'Mikey Thompson,' said another girl, light-skinned with freckles, 'I knows who you are. You knows my dad, innit. He never said you was in the music business.'

Bollocks. Mikey placed her now, Carlton's little girl, Shelley or something. Time to move things along.

'Anyway,' he said, 'question is, you girls sing or not?'

Then, before any of them could answer, he carried on, 'Silly question. Course you can. Tell you what, how about you come and audition for me tonight. Nine o'clock in the Community Centre.'

The girls looked at each other. Mikey could see vanity battling it out with cynicism. He relaxed, only one winner in that situation. The girls went into a little huddle, whispered furiously, then the freckled girl Shelley or whatever, turned to Mikey and said, 'Yeah, sounds like a laugh.'

'Great,' said Mikey, 'Great.'

It all started out promisingly enough that evening. First, Mikey nipped round the Community Centre and sweet-talked Ernestine into letting him use one of the offices for his audition. Even got Col round to play some piano. Then the girls turned up on time, well, half nine anyway. That's when things started going to hell.

First problem was finding a song the girls knew and Col could play. Col wanted to do some Motown, 'Heat wave', 'you keep me hanging on', something like that, but none of the girls seemed to know any of that old-style shit, as they put it. The girls fancied doing some TLC thing, 'Creep' or 'Waterfalls', but Col couldn't play either of those. Then the girls had a go at a cappella and, frankly, it sounded hideous. Mikey was no purist, he wasn't expecting the three tenors, but even so, it was horrible. Maybe they just needed the piano. At last, he had an idea.

'*Voulez-vous couchez avec moi?*'

'You wha?' said three of the girls, before the girl with braids, who was obviously the linguist of the group, weighed in with a hearty fuck off.

'No,' said Mikey, 'the song, yeah. All Saints, you know?'

The girls nodded. One of them had a go at the opening line.

Mikey looked at Col, raised his eyebrows.

'Yeah, yeah,' said Col, 'Lady Marmalade'. I can do that.'

Col basically had one piano part he played on everything, just a question of whether he knew the chords or not. And if he knew the chords well enough, like with this one, well, he could funk it up nicely, and Mikey suddenly had hopes. But then the girls started singing and they immediately dampened down again. There was just no way. None of them could sing a note. Well, the Asian girl wasn't too bad, had a sweet voice but the rest of them were just bloody painful.

After the second chorus, Col looked at Mikey and Mikey looked back, shaking his head, and Col took the hint and wound the song up.

'Well, what d'you think?' asked Shelley.

Mikey was right on the point of telling them when he caught the Asian-looking girl – Bella they called her – giving him a bit of a look, bit of an interested look, and he thought, sod it, bit of sugar-coating never did any harm.

'Nice, girls, nice,' he said, trying not to catch Col's eye. 'Needs a lot of work, of course, on the harmonies and shit. My man Col here will help you with all that.' He wasn't letting his eyes go anyway near Col now. 'And you,' he said, looking straight at Bella, 'you've definitely got something. I think we're gonna make you the lead singer, all right, girls?' The other girls just looked at each other and shrugged.

'So,' Mikey carried on, 'see you here tomorrow night same time?'

The girls looked at each other some more and giggled. Then the tall girl said. 'Yeah, all right,' and then they were off. The second they were outside the door Mikey and Col could hear their laughter ringing out down the corridor.

Ten o'clock the next evening and there was no sign of any of the girls. Mikey and Col were just sat in the office, smoking some of Col's finest. Col actually having quite a good time playing the piano, trying to get some jazz funk thing going, talking to Mikey about buying a sampler. That was one of those things Mikey had heard of, knew they used them on all the records these days, but he didn't have a clue what it was, when Bella popped her head round the door.

'What, they all gone already?' she asked.

'Nah,' said Mikey, 'you're the first one to get here.'

Bella shook her head, 'Fucking typical, all be round Shelley's watching *ER*.'

'So where've you been?' asked Mikey.

'Working, innit,' she said, 'shop only just closed now.' And then Mikey had her placed, she worked in the offie over Grangetown. Mum and Dad owned it he supposed. Still, this Bella wasn't one of them good little girls, all training to be chemists or something, she had her hair up in a top knot, Kappa tracksuit and some seriously big trainers. Nice, Mikey liked them sporty.

Bella stood there for a bit, looking unsure what to do next. 'So, bit of a waste of time, like, me being here then.'

'Nah,' said Mikey, then he lowered his voice conspiratorially, 'fact is, you're the only one can sing anyway.'

'Yeah, you think so?' she said, her face momentarily breaking into a smile. Then she frowned. 'Still not much point in carrying on now, is there?'

'Course there is,' said Mikey, 'C'mon, sit down. You like a little smoke?'

Bella smiled and nodded, and Col passed her the spliff.

'Look,' said Mikey, 'here's the plan. We do a little work now, figure out what sort of songs really suit your voice. Then I'll put some ads around like, audition some more girls, get a little bit of an act going and we'll be ready for the talent night.'

'Talent night?' said Col, as this was the first he'd heard of it.

'Yeah,' said Mikey, who'd half heard something about it on the radio, waiting in the Spar that afternoon, big thing up town, loads of TV people there and stuff. Big chance.

Col shook his head and started playing the piano, unmistakable Stevie Wonder chords this time, and Bella smiled, Col's skunk going straight to the spot. 'Yeah,' she said, 'I knows this one.' And then she started singing 'You are the sunshine of my life', sweet as anything, and for the first time Mikey thought he might be on to something.

Next few days, Mikey started looking around seriously for some more girls. He asked everyone he knew. He stuck posters up around the place; the Community Centre, all the shops around Butetown, even went up town and put one in Spillers. Put on the poster for anyone interested to show up the Community Centre nine o'clock next Tuesday. No phone number 'cause Col wouldn't let Mikey use his mobile number, and there was no way Mikey could risk putting his own phone number on it, Tina would kill him if a whole bunch of girls started phoning up, paranoid as she was. Course, paranoid wasn't exactly the word, Mikey had to admit.

Still, by the time Tuesday evening came around, Mikey

didn't have a clue what to expect. He made it round the Centre about half eight, had a quick pint of Labatts in the bar talking to a couple of the old boys, when the girls started to show up. By the time Col got there, about ten past, there were half a dozen of them. There were the Collins twins, dark-skinned girls, bit on the heavy side but Mikey liked the twins' angle. There was a white girl called Claire, big girl as well. There was another girl, Maxine, worked as a hairdresser up town, nice girl but never stopped talking. And there were two others.

Frankly, Mikey couldn't believe it. He knew he'd done the odd little thing out of line but what the hell had he done to deserve this? First off there was Bobby. Now what he was supposed to do with a gap-toothed lesbian pimp, must be in her thirties but still looked like a teenage boy, he couldn't begin to imagine. And then, for Christ's sake, there was Jan. Yeah, that Jan. His sister.

Now Mikey had nothing against Jan. It was just their worlds didn't collide much these days. He'd see her at work now and again when he had to go down the Health Centre, and they were always friendly, like, but her and Tina never hit it off much and, when it came down to it, he knew she disapproved of him, felt he could have done more. He'd got just as many exams as she had, how come she was the one with a job and he was a shoplifter? Still, it was a live and let live kind of thing.

So what the hell was she doing here? She always used to sing around the house and that, but here she was, thirty-two years old and a nurse, bit late for showbiz he'd have thought. Though, to be fair, stepping back a bit and trying to forget she was his sister like, she looked nice, little bit prim and proper but could be twenty-five, easy.

And anyway how old was that fat one who left from the Spice Girls? But, hang on, what was he thinking about – the last thing he needed was his bloody family getting stuck into his business.

Now chat was never something Mikey was usually short of, but the next five minutes, waiting for Col and Bella and God knows who else to show up, were bloody difficult by anybody's standards. Way Mikey played it was to give Jan a big smile, friendly but professional like, let her know he was serious, another one for Claire and Maxine who were busy gabbing together anyway, then he turned his attentions to the twins, gave them a bit of the old Mikey charm. Twins, he fancied that idea. Bobby he blanked totally for the while.

Finally, quarter past nine Col showed up with Bella, the pair of them coming through the door together, like.

'I was just over Grangetown,' Col said, 'doing a little bit of business, so I thought I'd stop by the shop, give our star a lift over, like.'

Mikey cut his eyes at Col suspiciously. It wasn't like Col to offer explanations. Col wasn't paying attention, though. His eyes were busy widening at the sight of the unlikely gathering he'd walked into.

Mikey decided it was time to take control.

'Right,' he said, 'Col here is going to play and you girls can take it in turns. We'll hear what you sound like one at a time and then try you out with Bella here who's already come through our previous round of auditions.'

Col went over to the piano, started fiddling about, and Mikey went over to the twins. The one on the left, Danielle – if he'd got them right – said they'd like to sing together, and could they do a gospel tune. So Mikey goes over to Col and Col starts banging out his usual part, this time using the chords to the Clark Sisters' 'You brought the sunshine', and the twins smile at each other and launch into it and they sound terrific, real spine-tingling stuff. Mikey found himself breaking out in a big grin, couldn't stop it. After a couple of verses he waved Bella over and she whispered in his ear she didn't know the song but then she had a go anyway and they sounded great. Bella had that Diana Ross sexy thing going and the twins had the big harmonies. All it needed, Mikey reckoned, was a soprano, someone with a nice Deniece Williams kind of a high voice and they'd be sorted.

Maxine went next. She whispered in Col's ear what she wanted to sing and he shuddered slightly. There was always going to be one wanted to sing 'The greatest love of all'. If you asked Col, there should be a law against it. It was like blokes with guitars in music shops doing 'Stairway to heaven', shouldn't be allowed. Then Maxine started singing and it was even worse than he expected. She murdered the high notes and hardly even bothered with the low notes. Worst thing was, you could see as she was doing it that, far as she was concerned, Whitney and Mariah could give up now, she – Maxine – was wiping the floor with them. Bella looked at Mikey, with a pleading expression on her face, as if to say are you going to make me try and harmonise with that? Mikey just shook his head. Handled it nicely, though, came over to Maxine, put his arm round her, told her she had too much personality to be in a group, she was one of those people born to be a solo act, and he'd certainly be in touch any time that's what he was looking for.

Claire was up next and just asked Col what he fancied

playing. Col says how about a little Luther Vandross. Claire smiles, says yeah, she loves her Luther and Col kicks into 'If only for one night' and the second Claire opens her mouth Mikey could tell she was perfect. Lovely high voice and she could really do all that Luther fancy stuff, playing around with the notes and that. Mikey motioned Bella over and Bella found a part and that was nice and then the twins came in two, but they couldn't find a part, so Col stopped the song and started again with the old Three Degrees' standard, 'When will I see you again?' Bella kicked it off, the twins came in next, then Claire added the high part and it was absolutely blinding. Mikey found himself hopping from leg to leg in excitement. The only cloud on the horizon, far as he could see, was he was going to have to bring in some kind of fitness trainer. One big girl in the group was ok, three was probably pushing it.

Then he was interrupted by his sister tapping him on the shoulder. Bollocks. He'd managed to blot Jan and Bobby out of his mind, still what could he do? All they had to do was listen to realise he'd already got himself a girl group. He was just about to give her a regretful shrug when the door opened and in walked the twins' grand-mother, Sister Lorraine to her fellow Congregationalists, Mrs Collins to Mikey.

Sister Lorraine was fierce. Always had been, and she'd never liked Mikey much. Still blamed him for knocking her favourite niece up, which must have been, Christ, getting on fifteen years ago. Mikey never understood why everyone always seemed to blame him. Fair enough, he knew he strayed around a bit, never knowingly turned

down a decent offer and all that, but it takes two to tango
and people seemed to forget that.

Anyway, ancient business, water under the bridge and
recycled half a dozen times far as he was concerned, but
Sister Lorraine took one look at Mikey, took a quick
listen to confirm her suspicion that the twins weren't
singing no gospel song and then appeared to blow up to
twice her normal size, which was formidable enough
to start out with. Even before she opened her mouth, Col
stopped playing and the girls all turned to face her.

'Danielle,' she said, 'Lavine. You call that singing the
Lord's praises?'

The twins looked shamefaced at their grandmother
and shook their heads.

'No,' said Sister Lorraine. 'Well, let's thank God I got
here in time. There is no good at all will come from
associating with this man.' She pointed her finger at
Mikey. 'Now pick up your coats, children. We going
home now.'

And that was that. Half Mikey's group walked straight
out the door. Danielle just managed to twist and give
Mikey a regretful smile but that was all.

Mikey turned and was just about to tell Bella and
Claire not to worry, he would set up some more auditions
for next week, replace the twins no trouble, when he saw
Jan walking up with a purposeful look on her face.

'Well,' she said.

Mikey shrugged, smiled weakly and Jan turned to Col.
'Wishing on a star,' she said, 'in C'.

Col nodded and started playing. Jan let him get into
the swing of it then started singing. And she was ok, not
great but perfectly fine. Claire came in after a little while

and did the high part beautifully. Then, before Mikey said a word, Bobby started in and after a couple of false starts found a low part. Bella couldn't find much to do, just sang along with Jan really, but once again it was sounding like a group.

Mikey looked across at Col. Col looked back and shrugged his shoulders as if to say it sounded all right with him. They tried out a couple more songs, an old Motown thing, 'Nowhere to run', that Col suggested and had to teach everybody, then 'Candle in the bloody wind' that Bella suggested and Col went along with which made Mikey even more certain that something was going on. Still, it sounded nice enough if you forgot what it was and Mikey was just about to call it a day when Jan pulled out a notebook and asked if they'd mind having a go at a song she'd written herself.

Mikey nearly had a hernia on the spot but the other girls all went, oh great and let's hear it, and so Jan sat down at the piano with Col for a little bit and played him the tune. Five minutes later, Col had managed to adapt his all-purpose piano part and the girls were picking up the harmonies. Mikey would have put money on it being some piece of save the trees nonsense, but instead it was some really sad thing about being dumped which made Mikey feel a bit guilty he didn't pay more attention to what was going on with her, him being the big brother and everything. And, fair play once again, the song wasn't bad at all. And after that they did all pack up and Mikey headed round to The Bosun for a quick one, feeling like he'd done a decent night's work after all, and doing his best not think about the fact that his group now had his sister in it. Not to mention Bobby.

Didn't last long, though, the trying not to think thing. He was only half way through his Labatts when Bobby came in The Bosun and sat down next to him.

'All right, Mikey boy?'

'All right, Bob,' said Mikey reluctantly.

'So how you liking the management game?'

Mikey scanned Bobby's face for signs of sarcasm. She knew as well as he did about his misadventures in the pimping game. Way Mikey saw it, the whole thing was screwed up. Girls always got chopsy about handing their money over to some bloke, who needed it for his legitimate expenses, like, paying the court fines, buying the finks, keeping the coppers sweet, all of that. Hustlers always acted like you were taking their money and sticking it straight up your nose. No sense of the responsibilities at all. But when it came to giving the money over to some other girl, one of the bloody lesbians down there, well, never a dicky bird. And the really ironic thing was they'd all go on like they were more afraid of some girl like Bobby here, five foot three if she was lucky, than they were of the blokes. Screwed up.

'All right,' he said cautiously.

'Safe,' said Bobby, ''cause, look, if you needs any help, I knows one or two people puts on shows and stuff round the clubs.'

Mikey laughed. 'It's not them kind of shows I'm thinking of. Never seen you as the lap-dancing type, anyway, Bob.'

Mikey broke off, expecting a laugh from Bobby, but she just frowned instead and Mikey realised she was dead serious about this.

'No,' she said, impatient like, 'it's the same people put

on regular shows. Like Bernie Walters, you know him right?'

Mikey knew of him as it happened. Bernie Walters had been around the scene since the bloody ark. Used to run the strippers down the Dowlais, but had some places up town and all. So he nodded.

'Yeah, well, Bernie's got this big talent night going. Up the Forum next week.'

Mikey nodded again. 'Yeah,' he said, 'I knows about that. I was thinking of putting the group in for it. If we're ready like.'

'Yeah,' said Bobby, and Mikey couldn't believe it, he could see this dreamy expression taking over Bobby's face. Like she really thought she was going to get up on stage and turn into Toni Braxton. Though, way things were going these days, anything was possible, far as Mikey could see. Look at that Björk. Fuck was that about, he'd like to know. Still, he was feeling better now he realised Bobby was right into it. Christ, people were easy once you figured out what they wanted.

'Yeah, Bob,' he said, 'that's the plan. Course there's a lot of work to do yet.'

Couple of days later, Mikey's in the Spar, minding his own business. Well, having a little chat with a girl he bumped into there. Just checking out whether she fancied giving the music industry a go, you know, when he gets a firm tap on the shoulder.

Mikey whirls round wondering which fucking copper's going to have a laugh going through the old what you got in your pockets routine. A person got reputation for something – playing football say, or shoplifting come to that – people never let you hear the last of it, even when you were a fully-fledged music biz professional.

So there's Mikey spinning round ready to go right off on one and then he freezes. Just like that.

'Hiya, Mum,' he says, wondering what the hell's going on. His mum lived over Whitchurch, no need to be in his local Spar. 'So what you doing over here? Come to see Jan?'

Mikey's mum glowered. She wasn't a big woman. You wouldn't have expected her to be, given the sawn-off size of Mikey. But she had presence, all right. In her younger days she'd been the spit of Eartha Kitt, same cats' eyes. Still had them, come to that. These days she had the raspy voice, too, courtesy of the old Embassy Regals.

'So why didn't you tell me?' she asked, eyes boring straight into Mikey's shiftless soul.

'Say what?'

'About this group of yours, darling?'

Mikey shuddered. She'd started the darling thing sometime in his teens. No one's mother called their kids 'darling'. She must have seen it in one of her films. He braced himself wondering what was coming next. 'Well, Mum,' he said, 'early days, you know what I'm saying.'

'Well,' she said, all smiles now. 'I think it's a fabulous idea. Jan's told me all about it and she agreed you need a little help on the presentation side, you knows.'

'Well, Mum . . .' Mikey attempted to butt in, but to no avail.

'All the dresses and make-up and stuff, styling they calls it. So I says to Jan, don't worry, your mum'll do it for you. So that's settled then?'

'What is?' asked Mikey, his head spinning.

And so it came to pass that on the day of the big talent night at the Forum Mikey was accompanied by his mother, his sister, a lesbian pimp and two teenage shop-girls. If it hadn't been for Col, Mikey would have gone insane days previously.

Still, funny thing was Mikey was feeling pretty optimistic. The last few days they'd been rehearsing every night and they'd got two songs really well nailed. They were going to do this old Supremes song, 'Up the ladder to the roof', and then they were going to do Jan's song and, to be honest, Mikey thought they had to be in with a chance. Didn't sound bad at all. Even his mum had turned out ok, done a lovely job on the make-up. Sorted out the outfits, too, which had looked like being a problem. Mikey had reckoned they should all dress the same, like those old-time groups, but that had never looked like working, you'd have had to shoot Bobby to get her in a dress. So Lena, Mikey's mum, had come through, said they should go with a Spice Girls kind of thing, give them all different images, like.

So Bella went street, in her tracksuit and big trainers. Jan went roots in some kind of African print thing and her hair in a turban. Claire was the tarty one. Nice big girl like you, Lena said, got to be proud of yourself, let them see what you got, and stuck her in a bra top she was practically exploding out of. Worked for Mikey anyway, he could hardly take his eyes off her. And then there was Bobby who was wearing some kind of karate outfit, looking mad as fuck, but what the hell.

Still, Mikey was feeling pretty hopeful on the way over to the Forum: him, Col, the four girls and Mikey's mum, who not to be outdone was wearing an outrageous leopard-look two-piece, all squeezed into Col's clapped-out Hyundai. They parked in some little staff car park, then trooped round the front attracting some pretty lively looks from the kids standing around outside the Odeon.

It was only when they were actually inside the club talking to the TV people organising the show that Mikey discovered the big screw-up.

'Hello,' says the woman, some kind of Nazi blonde in heels.

'Hiya,' says Mikey.

'Oh right, hi,' says the woman like she could give a shit. 'So who are you lot being?'

'What?' says Mikey.

'All Saints? Spice Girls? En Vogue?'

'No,' says Mikey, 'these here are called Tiger Princess.'

'Yes, I'm sure,' says the Nazi, 'but who are they *being*?'

Mikey looks baffled once more and the woman shakes her head and says, 'You do realise this is a "Stars in their eyes" audition, don't you? You know the idea is you impersonate a pop star? Yes?'

Mikey just stood there for a moment. 'Oh yeah, right.'

The woman sighed theatrically, 'Look,' she said, 'I've got other people to check in, why don't you sit over there and work out what you're doing.'

And with that she swivelled round, banishing Mikey utterly from her presence. Her gaze immediately fell on Mikey's mum. She beamed.

'Oh wonderful,' she said, 'Eartha Kitt.'

Ten minutes later Mikey accepted they were screwed. There never had been a girl group with two black girls, one Asian girl and a white girl, far as he knew. Funny thing was the girls themselves didn't seem too bothered.

'Look,' said Mikey, 'I'll go over, have a word, see if they'll let you have a shot at being the Spice Girls.' Desperate idea but there it was. So Mikey went over, had a word with the Nazi who practically laughed in his face, just pointed around the room where there were at least four sets of Spice Girls who actually looked the part. Crestfallen, Mikey headed back towards the bar, looking for his crew, who seemed to have disappeared. Eventually he found them out by the cloakroom, and immediately he smelled a rat.

Col was sat on the floor, his keyboard balanced on his lap, banging out the backing to 'Just an old-fashioned girl' while Mikey's mum, Lena, practised her purr and the girls did some oohs and aahs in the background.

Mikey looked at Jan and she looked back at him, doing her best to look innocent.

'It's a fucking set-up, innit?'

Jan did her best to look innocent but after a couple of seconds she just burst out laughing.

'Well,' said Jan, eventually, 'Mum always was a bit of a star. Best thing we give her a hand.'

And so half an hour later Mrs Lena Thompson, fifty-eight, of Whitchurch, was waiting next in line for her audition, flanked by Hell's own girl group and her devoted son, and accompanied by Col. She was wearing the same leopard-look two-piece she'd turned up to the show in. Coincidence? Mikey was definitely starting to wonder, but what the hell.

The bloke in front was wearing a black suit and heavy black shades. Had to be Roy Orbison and so he was, bloke had the voice down perfect and everything, only weird thing was after a couple of verses Mikey realised he was singing in Welsh. About the same time the TV people seemed to clock it, too, and the music stops and the clipboard Nazi came over.

'Lovely,' she said, 'perfect, only thing is what language was that you were singing in?'

'Cymraeg,' said the bloke and the TV woman went back and talked to her boss, came back a minute later and said she's sorry but you have to sing in English on this show. Bloke just looked her up and down, started cussing her out in Welsh and walked straight out the club. Respect, thought Mikey.

And then it was Lena's turn.

'Got your tape, dear?' asked the director.

'Tape?' said Lena, 'Eartha Kitt does not use backing tapes, Eartha Kitt has an accompanist!' and she waved at Col.

Col smiled and bowed.

Lena carried on. 'Meet my musical director, a gentleman of many talents.' She'd got the purr down to a T now, 'Mr Colin . . . Colin,' Lena looked at Col, having forgotten what his surname was. Col leaned over and whispered in her ear.

'Yes, my verry, verry good friend and accompanist, Mr Colin X. Now,' she held her hand out to the assistant director, 'lead me to the stage.'

It hardly needs saying what happened next. Lena was a knockout, of course. She got the best applause of the night, along with one of the sets of Spice Girls, but then the producer went into a huddle with the director, talking about the show's demographics and Saturday night wrinklies, and Lena was pronounced the winner. She'd made it through to the first of the TV rounds, shooting up in London in a couple of months.

Afterwards, Mikey went backstage to give the old girl his best.

'You'll be needing a manager then, Mum,' he said.

'Yes, Mikey,' she said, and then she turned round and waved to a heavily sun-tanned feller, about her own age, 'and here he is, Mr Bernie Walters.'

Still, it wasn't all bad. The Bernie feller turned out ok, said he'd seen Mikey's girls and he didn't know if he had any work for singers but if any of them fancied doing a bit of dancing down the Dowlais on a Wednesday night, specially the big girl, he'd see Mikey right for a cut.

Mikey said he'd see what he could do. Got to start at the bottom, after all.

nicholas blincoe

....

'voodoo ray', slight reprise

I met the woman by the river, just where the plastic pontoon slips into the Thames by the Royal Festival Hall. She leant against the embankment wall, the small of her back cradled by the edge of the stone top and started with her small talk. She asked me how long I'd lived in London.

I moved here with my mother, a year after my father's death. I didn't tell the woman that, though. I tend to be the quiet type, I don't know why. Sometimes I wish I spoke more. But in my own quiet way, I am always trying to make connections. It's what I do.

The woman said, 'What is it with you Mancunians? Why are you all so bloody taciturn?'

I shrugged. 'I'm from Stockport.'

'I know that.' She smiled suddenly. Then she handed me the ticket. 'This is going to be the easiest money you ever made. I'm paying you to listen to a concert. The Williams Fairey Brass Band.'

I couldn't hide the double-take, the quick check of the writing on the ticket. I couldn't believe that anyone would pay me fifty-an-hour to listen to my father's old band playing the Queen Elizabeth Hall.

The ticket said, Acid Brass.

'Is this a joke?'

She shook her head. 'Damned if I know.' Her wallet was open in her hand, she slipped out five twenties. 'I believe it lasts ninety minutes. But why not call it a round two hours, okay?'

An evening with the prize-winning Williams Fairey Brass Band, Stockport's finest. Perhaps even the best brass band in the country. And they were playing the hits of acid house and the summers of love, both I and II. I had no idea what to expect. I haven't listened to a full brass band since I was a child. Could be the last thing I heard was the 'Floral Dance'. I'm almost positive. But the lads just threw that in at the end, the very last encore of the afternoon. The tune I remember, the highspot of the event, was the track universally known as the Hovis Bread advert. I must have been eleven. My father was visiting the school, him and the rest of the Williams Fairey band. Now, twenty or more years later, I get paid to listen to the same guys and their successors chant and play through 'Voodoo Ray'. I could have sat there in my Queen Elizabeth seat, trying to imagine Dad among them, his cornet stuck to his bruised lips. Or I could let myself go, slip into the pauses between the mighty orchestration and swim.

But I'm rushing ahead.

Me and the lady took our seats and as she passed over the box of Maltesers, I tried to explain that I'm not a private detective. I deal in old books, what they call antiquarian books. Normally when I tell people that, they assume I'm also a collector. Some of them even try to spin out the word *bibliophile*, as though it's a word they use everyday, rather than a square term between their round lips. I just shake my head, tell them, *not me*. I'm not interested in the books. I don't like things, objects of any description. I just track them down. Like I say, I just like making connections. But I didn't think I could help this woman.

I told her, 'You want to find a record, go find a second-hand record dealer. I don't have the qualifications.'

'I know you have.'

Ahead of me, the lads were the size of toy soldiers, standing or sitting at attention. Their instruments cradled or shouldered, waiting to strike up the tunes. But first there were going to be introductions, courtesy of the special guest MC. I recognized him immediately he stepped out of the wings, stage right. Tony Wilson. He wasn't a member of the brass band, he was a TV newsreader and, more famously, the head of Factory Records. Tony spoke for only a few moments. He had a strong confident voice but he was a professional. The guy had a Stockport accent, he would never lose that.

Why do I think of him as Tony? It's not as though I know him. Maybe he doesn't even use the name Tony. He might be an Anthony, an An-*th*-ony even, where the 'th' is lisped in the American-style. How would I know? Just because I saw him on television every night, back when I was a kid watching the local evening news, or read about him in the music papers when I was a little older and following the bands that reminded me of Manchester, like New Order or MeatMouth or The Happy Mondays. It doesn't mean that I have any special insight into the man. Just because we come from the same town: me and Tony and the lads of the Williams Fairey Brass Band.

They sounded fantastic at the Queen Elizabeth Hall. I only wanted to sit there, listen, hope that the woman next to me couldn't see me crying. Remember those tracks: 'Pacific 202' by 808 State, 'Strings of Life' by Rhythim is Rhythim, the beautiful 'Voodoo Ray' by A Guy Called Gerald. I knew them all, tunes I first heard ten or more years ago and would stay with me forever. True, most of their actual titles had slipped away. The only reason I can list them now, Tony Wilson came back on stage between each song and reeled off the credits, wrapping them around little anecdotes. I took a sideways look at the woman, then. When the band was playing, she seemed distracted, even a little bored. But the moment Tony came back on stage, she was riveted.

The band was playing 'Let's Get Brutal' by Nitro Deluxe when the woman nudged me. I held up my hand. I couldn't eat another Malteser, the honeycomb centre soaked up my tears until they were so swollen, I couldn't swallow. But then I realized she was trying to pass me a note. I flashed my pen torch across the typed words and saw that she had set down some details of the record she wanted me to find.

'What's an acetate?' I asked.

She hissed, 'It's a kind of record, but instead of being pressed in a factory, it's cut directly from the original tapes, on a special lathe.'

The band was tapping into the almost percussive song, fuelling the beat with handclaps and hard military drumming. As a result, the brass wasn't as deafening as it had been on the earlier tunes. I surprised myself when my voice came out louder than I expected.

'You say an acetate looks like a normal record?'

'Yes, approximately. They tend to be thicker and only have grooves on the one side. Also, they are more fragile, so don't go frisbeeing it about, ok?'

She knew I was taking the job but I turned my voice down, struggling to keep a flat and dull tone. Not letting her read past the words.

'You think I can find an amateur recording, made sometime circa the late 1970s?' I flicked the paper between my thumb and finger so it cracked in the air. 'You've not left me much to go on.'

One typed sheet. Plenty of white space.

She said, 'If it was recorded in Stockport, then it was probably at Strawberry Studios. And if it used brass, then there must have been a local session musician.'

I said, 'Ian Delamere.'

She said, 'See, you're already cooking. You know the area, you've got the leads. It's no different from tracking down a rare book.'

I took the job.

The soprano cornet in the Williams Fairey version of 'Let's get brutal' has an almost comic quack. Not comic *ha ha*. It has a comic book edge, something eerie-freaky. From the sound, I was sure it had to be Ian Delamere but I scanned the faces on the Queen Elizabeth stage without seeing him. I recognised some of the others, older now, of course. Back when my father was in the band, Ian Delamere would have been among the youngest, midway between my age and my father's. He was always the go-ahead band member, playing with enthusiasm but interested in a wider world of brass: the Philly sound, Blue Beat, even Miles Davis. He used to tease my Dad, who always said there were only two types of music: marching and sitting. I don't know what Dad would have made of the house sound, the music I first discovered in fields, mixed with sunrise and dry ice, seeping into skin made porous by ecstasy.

Acid Brass. On my way out I found an information sheet that explained how the original idea grew out of a pub conversation between a man called Jeremy Deller and his friends. It was a joke, but then Deller got it off the ground. As it was his concept and Deller was an artist, I guess that makes the whole affair a conceptual artwork. If so, it's fine with me. I'm no philistine. If I ever under-value art, it's because I don't like stuff and clutter: objets d'art, pots and paintings, figurines, even books and furniture. Any kind of knick-knack. If anyone asks, I'd say let's have more conceptual art: it's the art for me. A concept doesn't demand shelf space, Lottery funding, export orders or structurally sound museums. At bottom, it's nothing but a connection. Certainly as far as Deller's original input goes, that's all Acid Brass is: two words, 'Acid' and 'Brass', placed together so they spark off each other. The guy had even drawn a diagram, charting the connections he'd made between the words. He'd managed to make quite a number, filling a page with phrases like 'the North' and 'open air festivals' as well as longer terms like 'deindustrialisation'. He traced arrows that linked these words with both 'Acid' and 'Brass', so the connections couldn't be missed. I wondered if I should add another one, in personal biro. The connection between me and my father, spinning out of the word I love and one that meant so much to him. ACID stroke BRASS.

Of course, once the concept leaves the artist's hands, then it's a different matter. Imagine, for instance, a twenty-eight-year-old antiquarian bookseller, sitting on the Manchester train with a borrowed Sony discman on the flipdown table in front of him, listening to a CD of an earlier Acid Brass performance, recorded last month in Liverpool. Once the music's juicing through me, I find it hard to think of it in pure conceptual terms. It's still a connection between alternate viewpoints, but now it's more like a wire stretched between two pegs. It sets up reverberations, sometimes beautiful, serene, or else it is pumped up with bombast, with the grandiose, with the very small and the occasionally silent. In the quietest moments, I think I hear Ian Delamere's soprano cornet, trembling like it did at my father's funeral.

I bought the CD of the band's Liverpool concert for the sleevenotes. I read them carefully but couldn't see any sign of Ian Delamere's name. When I called Stockport, a PR man from Williams plc left me hanging for twenty minutes before confirming that Mr Delamere left the company and the band almost twenty years ago. Word was he'd moved on to bigger things, seduced by bright lights etc. At any rate, he'd moved to Manchester. Another few telephone calls gave me his new address and number.

The London–Manchester train stops at Stockport. Two minutes later it whizzes through Heaton Chapel at high speed and, in a further two minutes fifty approx. arrives at Manchester Piccadilly. Reduced to bare minutes and seconds, there doesn't seem much difference between Stockport and Manchester. There are enormous differences in other ways. Stockport is somehow the posher of the two, which in Manchester's eyes also makes it the funnier, because how can the smaller town seriously believe it has an edge over the big city? Of course, it's all relative, depending which way you're looking down the track.

If you're in Heaton Chapel, which is where Ian Delamere's from, it is doubly confusing. Do you look north to Manchester? After all, Heaton Chapel is right on the Manchester/Stockport border, which is also the Lancashire/Cheshire border. Heaton Chapel fades into Manchester's inner-outer core of Burnage and Levenshulme. In both geographical and spiritual terms, it is closer to Manchester than it is to Stockport town centre. Coming from Heaton Chapel, you would think you had every right to call yourself a Mancunian. But what if you looked south to Stockport and the Cheshire Plain, which a friend once accidentally but tellingly called the Pleasure Chain? Stockport soon blends into Alderley Edge and Knutsford, where anyone with serious money soon moves. And Manchester Airport is actually in Stockport which somehow gives the smaller town the more cosmopolitan air. So why settle for Manchester's hardbitten sardonic suspiciousness when you could have the money and the contacts and the easy escape route to softer climes that Stockport offers?

It's a tough one.

Doubly so for Ian Delamere, who was Catholic so went to the Xaverian college which is well inside Manchester. Throughout the major part of his schooldays he travelled to the city to be educated a stone's throw from Maine Road, the ground of Manchester City FC. Only, he couldn't support them, he had to support United. Manchester's Catholics, like Noel Gallagher for instance, might put loyalty to place over loyalty to a colour. But a Catholic from Stockport would always support the Reds.

It was a schizophrenic way to grow up, there was pressure from all sides, or so I would imagine. It could be the making or the breaking of you. The kind of circumstances that might turn you into a Tony Wilson (as indeed they did) or into an Ian Delamere.

I had asked Ian to meet me at Piccadilly station. He was waiting on the platform, his comb-over lifting slightly in the breeze coming off the cooling engines of diesel locomotives. These days, even Bobby Charlton knows enough to keep his hair short and neat and not try and hide the shine by plastering his hair from one side to the other. Ian Delamere's loyalty to the style would make him an oddity. The fact that Ian is a white Rasta puts him in a league of his own: the first white dread comb-over merchant.

'How's runnings?' he said.

'Okay.'

'Irie, mate.'

He took me to a club in a cellar, just off Princess Street. I was surprised the place was open so early in the evening. Ian told me it was cool, he was playing with his band later on.

He said, 'I gotta be early to set things up, seen?'

I nodded.

He didn't do much setting up, he did more sitting down, rolling a cornet-shaped spliff. While we smoked he told me he heard the brass band were doing a few acid trax. He thought it was a brilliant idea, he could get into that. At least, he could but he had his own thing.

'You know what I'm saying?'

'Not really, Ian, no.'

'You got to stay true to your thing, man. Listen up.'

The DJ was spinning a song I knew, 'Hard man fe dead' by Prince Buster. The lyrics told about a man who was being carried to the graveyard in his coffin when he yells out, 'Don't bury me!', and the mourners have to set him down again. As the song says, 'He's a hard man fe dead'.

The reason I know the song, Ian played it at my father's funeral. And once again, just as he did back then, he laid down his cornet-shaped spliff and picked up his cornet-shaped lump of brass and played along with the solo, quietly weaving in and out of the twin saxes of the old Jamaican session musicians.

I buried my eyes in the top of a pint of Guinness. When Ian finished, he nodded and said, 'Seen.'

'I'm fine, mate,' I sniffled.

'No problem, mate.'

Ian had stayed true to reggae ever since my father's funeral. I never knew why. All he said now was that he was not promiscuous. This was his *t'ing*, he was sticking with it. No more brass bands, no more session work, just ska, rock steady and reggae.

'So how's it going?' I asked.

'Tough, man. But I survive.'

He had the spliff back between his lips. I could barely see him through the smoke but his face was a sunless grey sheen. He looked like a poor man.

I told him, 'You know, I pay for information. It's a legitimate expense.'

'Yeah? Well, maybe get me a drink.'

'How about the price of a couple of bottles of whiskey, mate? The woman who hired me, she's got to be loaded.'

I laid it on thick, I wanted Ian to feel good about taking a fifty off me. That it wasn't anything to do with charity. And once I was sure he'd accept the money, I told him the story.

He said, 'You joking, mate?'

I shook my head, 'Straight up. You know anything about the session, did you play on it?'

'Not me.'

'But you know about it?'

He nodded. 'I couldn't take the gig, I was jamming with some guys I know.'

I started asking who did play on it but I suddenly realised I knew the answer. It was my father.

Ian said, 'They asked if I could recommend someone. I gave them his name. It was supposed to be a joke . . . I only found out later, your dad went for it. I still don't know why.'

My father was returning home late one night. He must have smelled something wrong with his motor but it was so late and it was a cold night, he probably thought it would keep for just another few miles. But his engine was spraying oil, the wiring was shot and the petrol hose was worn through. The fire brigade brought an expert witness to the inquest who compared the car to a home-made bomb, a lit fuse allied with a quantity of combustible material. It was no wonder there was so little left of my dad. Basically just bits of car and cornet, steel and brass.

'He died coming home from that session?' I asked.

Ian nodded. 'All because I couldn't do it. I wanted to try my hand at reggae music.'

And I realised, then, that Ian had stayed true to reggae because of my father's death. It wasn't out of love but out of melancholy. Once, he would use his cornet to step outside the brass band and explore. Now he used his horn to dig a hole and lie in it.

Some time during the fourth or fifth pint, I asked him, 'You know where I can get a copy of the recording? Maybe an acetate.'

'You're kidding. You know whose session it was, don't you?'

I had no idea. 'Some amateur, it's what I heard.'

'It was Tony Wilson, the Factory meister himself. The call came in the middle of the night, the guy wanted to record immediately. Any expense, it didn't matter.'

I was thinking, Tony Wilson? Tony Wilson killed my father?

'So it was a Factory recording?'

Ian shook his head. 'No. Personal. Just him and a few session guys. But it was never recorded. What I heard, Tony had a tin ear. Maybe it's not true, but that was the rumour.'

I sat there, taking it in. Could it be true that from Factory Records through to acid house, all the music that meant the most to me, as far as Tony Wilson was concerned they were just concepts? Connections he made in his own head but could never truly hear.

'What was the song?'

'A love song he'd written himself. The story goes, Tony was having woman trouble and was trying to woo this chick back.'

I wondered if the song was written for the woman who hired me. It would make sense. But, equally, she could have been a crazed newscaster-stalker, desperate for a rare and personal memento of the man off *Granada Reports*. I didn't know. What I did know, my father was sacrificed on the bonfire of Tony Wilson's passion. And there was nothing left to prove it, no final lasting object to stand as a testimony to his sacrifice.

I preferred it that way.

lynne tillman

ode to le petomane

I shuddered. I seemed. I wanted. I tried. I loved. I proposed. I discovered. I knew. I studied. I dug. I needed. I imitated. I believed. I was. I realized. I wanted. I had. I became. I initiated. I gushed. I declared. I recorded. I recognized.

I shuffled the deck. It was given to me, but I colored the cards. I dealt a hand. I threw the cards in the air. They fell on the floor. I picked them up in no special order. Failure hung around, pale, shapeless, ready.

I fox fate, it's a daily routine.

The wind's crazy. People walk, their umbrellas collapse. I can't fight the elements. I'm alone, watching. Another ugly brown shoe was lying at the back door this morning. It matches the one that dropped there last week in the middle of a wet, dark, wild night. I wasn't waiting for the other shoe to drop, then it did. My expectations are my own, sometimes I share them. Sometimes I'm disappointed or surprised. Expectations are secrets. I play with mine, them. It's a tricky business.

Fourteen ugly brown shoes could be sitting at the back

door tomorrow. Maybe there was a party. Everyone took
off their shoes. The shoes fell from the roof and landed at
the back door. If fourteen bodies were lying there, dead,
I'd need other explanations. A seance on the roof; they
left their bodies behind. Or a mass suicide. I'd want to
scream 'Murder', call the cops, if death was skulking at
my door.

The shiny bags of garbage scattered in the backyard
shimmer in the occasional sunlight. They sometimes
look like a novel form of aboveground burial. The wind
blows the bags everywhere. They've always been there.
No one removes them, and I'm not going to touch them.
I hate garbage, full of morbid ideas, crap.

Now a thin, tall guy is walking down the street, bent by
the wind. He has to go to the post office and stand on
line, negotiate with people who hate their jobs. The way
he sees it, it makes him a kind of human retrospective –
writing letters, walking to the post office, being willing to
stand and wait patiently.

I engage with things as much as people. But I usually
don't have fantasies about them. That probably isn't
true. I watch television, I talk to it, it's not only talking to
me. I'm not a sieve. It isn't, either. Something else could
be there but that doesn't mean what's there isn't conclu-
sive, in its way. Inconclusive, too.

This tall, thin guy liked envelopes. Envelopes enveloped, and usually words were incommensurate. He
folded the letter into three equal parts, the way nothing
ever is, with definite edges, and stuffed it perfectly into
the envelope. He sealed it up. He didn't hate licking glue.
It reminded him he had a tongue like other animals who

use it more. Letters usually reach their destination, and unseen by others, are read in private. Often the recipient doesn't really get the message. He knew that. It was a more controlled exchange even with the interference of the post office. If it's not the post office, it's the telephone company. He couldn't control that.

I don't come to any conclusions alone, even when I'm held in my own silly, irrelevant isolation. I think my isolation isn't solitary, it's a concoction – you're in it, so is he, she, they are, too. You might have other ideas. You and I can appear to be interchangeable, easy to substitute. Like pronouns, just as deceptive. I can believe, pretend I'm volunteering. I renew myself, things. If I tremble, it's a disease. Nostalgia for the new.

The thin guy wrote his longtime fiancée: 'We share heaven and hell. Hell's being right and wrong. You think I betray you by my indecision. It's how you think. What can I say. I'm vanishing imperceptibly.'

A cranky magic act. The guy in the post office often disappeared behind the horizon between himself and others. He couldn't tell where the edge was for somebody else. For her. He pushed at her limits regularly. Cunning, silent, he demolished raw feelings which arrived from a purple nothing, a needy non-place. They rushed out in clumps and wanted something to hang on to. Finders, keepers, weepers, his words were held responsible.

Now he was almost at the head of the line, worried about how he'd written her. He knew there was trouble ahead. He inevitably thought that, a record stuck in its own, ancient groove.

Your cover songs and mine could be danceable, fast, slow, permeable, intransigent, opaque, accessible, beautiful, reluctant, funny, tough, different from what's in store. I want to go far and still stay in touch, on line. I don't have a dog, but I could walk one mentally if I decided to. No one would know I was just walking the dog. I can more easily do the laundry dramatically. In the laundromat, MTV's on, I see other people's clothes, I watch their eyes, mouths, how they fold their shirts, they notice me or don't, smile, don't. Music caresses, pounds, a rhythm for everything. We're doing laundry in the same time, even if we're in different cycles. It's intimate and alien. Underpants flop around in dryers. That's anonymity. Signs hang on walls and doors. I always forget which dispenser is for the bleach. I approach the attendant, a woman with sweat on her lip, annoyance on her tongue, acid in her stomach. I smile, tame her fury temporarily, find out, pour in the bleach, go home, come back.

He thought hard about what to say, how to put it, what shapes and colors to use when he tried to draw it out for her, even how to sign the letter. His effort exposed him. When Dorothy Parker was restless, or lonely, she hung a one-word sign on her office door: MEN. Men walked in, thought it was the men's room. She laughed probably, enlivened. He had never thought of that – WOMEN. On his door. And he wouldn't, ever. He was surprised by what was immediate to him, but wasn't to other people. Same way around, them to him, her to him. His jaw ached sometimes, explaining, and he hated the sound of his own voice, repeating himself in different settings. All the words in his universe taunted him, pictures multiplied forever in a series of mirrors. Even his reasoning was an image of itself, feeding back. He was often, he was now, frightened for no reason. Outside, the wind blew indifferently.

I change, don't, can't, have habits, am a habit, want to make everything flip into another register, can't find the register. Someone I knew once worked at the reception desk at Claridge's. A man called up and said, 'There's a bomb in the hotel,' and my friend opened the hotel register and looked for the name and answered, 'I'm sorry, there's no Mr Ahbomb in the hotel.' Then he hung up. Later he realized it was a bomb threat.

You try to reach me, with reflections and illuminations, and I might not find what's evident to you. It's scary, this strangled distance between us, worrying about agreeing to agree even about the terms of agreement. Something may be avoided in the contract. It may be implicit, elusive, but necessary.

Sometimes I think that's all I can do – leave room. I build a room. I paint it, wallpaper it, furnish it, sleep in it, leave it, return to it, hope the room's still there. There's litter in it. I don't mean to return to garbage, but there's a lot of waste in my life.

The guy was staring at a man in the post office who had twenty packages to mail and was holding up the line. A robber stealing time. At least he was next. He wondered if his letter was to her or for her, or for someone else. Or for no one. He glanced back at the long snake of people with envelopes in their hands. Their vulnerability was on display. In that instant, he understood that a letter stands for something which has many letters in it. He wasn't sure if he was standing for himself and others, or not.

In the nineteenth century a French performer named *Le Petomane* farted for the public. He set his farts on fire, too, to give the audience a good show, an olfactory night on the town. I have a picture of *Le Petomane*, ass sticking out, long unlit wooden match in his hand. There must be a slit or opening in his trousers so he won't get burned. Hell of an entertainer. I wonder how he got the idea to go public.

The guy listened to his stomach growl. At home he let his body go, heard it compose a soundtrack – groans, sighs, moans, farts. He took painful, heavy breaths. He belched, chomped, chewed, slurped, smacked. No one compared slurps, belches, and groans, the beauty of life's secret, disgusting moments. His turn finally came. The postal worker he liked whispered, 'Did you hear about the crash? Everyone was killed.'

If weirdness was usual, expected, I'd be forced to think on my feet and sitting down. Make things up on the spot – dialogue, ways to walk, look, relationships. Nothing would correspond to anything for long. In a private arena, I'd have my own agenda. I wouldn't hurt anyone. See, I'm walking to the point, along the edge, where a fantasy of doing whatever I like and a drive to be liked compete. I'm not unique, so I don't have to worry. But in the present, I can't decide how many people I should speak to.

The guy shook his head, just grunted to the postal worker who had whispered about the devastating crash. Strangers share the grotesque. A shadow crossed over the envelope, it was the postal worker's hand. But the guy felt darkness, a gap, in the middle of his brain. She could've been killed on that flight. It was possible. Maybe he wanted her to die. He enjoyed the fantasy and tasted the sensation, bittersweet loss. Anguish and relief played a wistful song in him.

He mailed the letter. He wouldn't know how beautiful flesh was, he realized, until he couldn't touch hers anymore. He couldn't know how beautiful flesh was. He recorded all of this and more, and he wrote her again and again, 'I can't. I won't.' He invented a virtual reality game – a funeral home and cemetery for love. He stole and was stolen from, he deceived and was deceived. Don't try to contact me, she wrote back. Ever. She thought he was crazy.

I listen to Archbishop Desmond Tutu on the radio. He admits, sheepishly, 'I love to be loved.' I'm amazed by how many ways there are to go and how many dead ends. I can't try everything. I want to. I'm improvising, everything's provisonal.

By now the thin guy was such a wreck, his gums were bleeding. He finished work at the insurance company. He locked the doors, turned on the burglar alarm, looked down the street, and glanced warily at some other men who stared vacantly at him. He turned his back. He saw the ocean, sullen and green. The grey sky was perpetually monotonous. Then the ocean roared. A huge flock of birds, thousands of black marks, dark ideas, streaked across the sky. He watched them swirl and dart. They flew in unison. They broke away from each other. They swelled and dropped and swooned. They rushed, scrambled, and took their shape again. Then they abandoned it and separated. They went on and on. He wondered why they did that. Things never total up. They never stay still.

Yesterday morning a man with a red nose and a face cut from too many close shaves removed the shiny garbage bags from the backyard. He had to climb through a window to get outside because the door wouldn't open. It wasn't locked, but it was stuck. When he couldn't get the door open, he cursed it. Then he turned and shot me a creepy, even sinister, half-smile. He said, 'I don't know what you're doing. But you've jinxed the place.' I didn't say a word. If that's what he wants to think, let him. There are a million other explanations, but he must like the idea, be invested in it. It's not my bank, but I could begin to appreciate, investigate, his characterization, throw a party for it – a bad recognition is better than none at all, distorted mirrors still reflect an image. I have my illusions, he has his. I would stop celebrating loss, if I could figure out what replaces it.

The plumber has just left. He said he told the man with the red nose months ago that the door was stuck, the faucet needed to be fixed, the toilet seat was broken. I didn't jinx the place. It was already jinxed. I arrived, saw the damage, demanded repairs, got them. There are promises and mistakes everywhere. It's hard to tell them apart. I keep going.

matt thorne

....

bridge class

Their relationship so far had progressed as a series of dares. Monica set the challenges, and Sam accepted them, amazed they were still together. Coming from a long line of cuckolds, Sam had been brought up to believe that betrayal was his birthright, an inescapable part of his DNA. He'd come to terms with this at an early age, thinking of it as a kind of hereditary heart disease. Resigned, he'd decided to see how far he could get before his luck ran out, taking a bitter pleasure in trying to outlast his elders. His great-grandfather held exclusive rights over his wife's insides for twelve years. His grand-father managed only eight. As far as he knew, Sam had already bested his father, who notched up a pathetic six months. Part of the reason why he made so little fuss about Monica's demands was his belief that every time he gave in, he bought himself a few more months of loyalty.

In spite of his fears, Monica appeared to have stayed constant throughout their four years of marriage, becoming less and less interested in the outside world, and now rarely spending an evening away from their small house in Cherry Hinton. Three weeks before their wedding, Sam had held his wife's hot, exhausted body and marvelled that a woman once so independent had now become eager to take on the trappings of out-dated traditions, insisting that 'love, honour *and* obey' remained in the marriage vows and telling everyone how much she was looking forward to authorising a cheque with her husband's surname. She seemed so different to the way his father had told him Sam's mother behaved in the run-up to their wedding, and as excited as he was, he couldn't help fearing that her enthusiasm would soon give way to frustration. After all, he had seen how even relatively luxurious surroundings had driven his mother into depression, and although he'd given up on his ambitions and taken a reasonably lucrative job designing websites, he knew he'd never be able to match the life-style she'd grown used to with her parents. He also knew that no matter how hard he tried to fit in with the com-munity she'd chosen for them, there'd always be something unorthodox about him. He just didn't seem capable of making things legitimate, and although he was a well-paid, happily married man, his neighbours didn't look to him for help in the way they did with other members of their village.

Monica had taken almost a year to decide on a job. It was a period her parents observed with great interest. To begin with she maintained that she wanted to be a housewife, making derisive comments about former uni-versity friends who communicated their career advancements in faux-modest missives. Although Sam had no problem with her staying at home (save for the fear that it might speed her inevitable slide into infidelity), he sensed that this uncharacteristic pusilla-nimity was her way of hiding the fear that she wouldn't be able to find a job equal to those of her friends. When Monica first met Sam, she'd been about to give up on men altogether, believing that friendship offered much more satisfying rewards. Grateful to be proved wrong, she'd felt that she should thank fate for bringing Sam to her by reversing her vow and giving up on friends instead.

There'd been no formal break. Moving away meant that all but the most ardent of her former companions forgot about her, and although those who didn't kept sending letters, they made no physical attempt to get in contact. Knowing that Monica couldn't get a job worthy of her talents without their help, Sam did his best to persuade her to write back.

'But I like being in charge,' she protested, midway through one of their many rows. 'Looking after you gives me much more satisfaction than any job could bring.'

'You'll still be in charge. I'm just offering to help out. I feel guilty sitting back and doing nothing.'

'How can you feel guilty? You support me.'

'Your parents support you. I'm lucky if I can pay the phone bill.'

She stroked Sam's hair from his forehead. 'Do you want me to work?'

'All I'm saying is asking for help is nothing to be ashamed of. That's how I got my job.'

Although the conversation ended with Monica in tears and Sam retracting all that he'd said, they both knew she'd have to get a job. They'd never disagreed about anything serious before, and this new conflict stiffened their limbs when they slept, making it painful to share the same bed. Sam knew his victory wouldn't be absolute. Monica'd always compared her friends' careers to swimming in a cesspool, and he knew there wouldn't be a complete volte-face. Nevertheless, he was surprised when she told him she'd accepted a position in a small antiquarian bookshop. He'd assumed they'd abandoned their old pretensions when they got married, and now felt threatened by her movement back into a circle in which he'd never felt comfortable. Monica's mother (a former academic who'd moved into radio after the birth of her child) was delighted by her decision. It was left to her father to share Sam's concern, instructing his son-in-law to keep a close eye on her.

Sam's first attempt at infidelity proved a disaster. A tall, talkative temp had fallen for him, and made it obvious that she'd be delighted if he took an afternoon off and accompanied her to her flat. He held out for two months and then gave in, only to find he'd compromised himself for a woman with plastic-wrapped sheets and a rebellious bladder-muscle which dictated that although she was happy to fellate him, and, should he have the stomach for it, felt eager to engage in sodomy, any vaginal activity was strictly off-limits. Although he found her frankness an exciting change from his wife's coy compliance, Sam considered these restrictions too literal a confirmation that what he was doing was, at some basic level, *not right*, and contented himself with ejaculating over her feet, rubbing the sperm between her toes and taking some small satisfaction from the fact that, technically, he'd yet to betray his wife.

For the next few months, Sam thought that this false

start might've ended his desire for extra-marital activity. He'd only been seeking an insurance policy, something to make it easier should Monica ever stray. There was nothing more damaging to a relationship than self-righteousness, and he wanted to remove that option as early as possible. He'd done that now, with the added bonus that he hadn't really endangered the sanctity of their marriage. This happy period ended when Monica informed Sam that she wanted to learn Italian at night class. Frantic at the new danger to her fidelity, Sam got so upset that the only way she could reassure him was to suggest he accompanied her. Embarrassed by his weakness, Sam told Monica such an arrangement would be demeaning, but if she insisted on having a night away from him every week, he would find a class of his own. Monica seemed pleased by this compromise and returned from the library with prospectuses for all the nearby colleges, schools and folk centres. After lengthy consideration, Sam decided he'd take up bridge, partly for its recherché appeal and partly because it was being taught at a school several miles from the one Monica had chosen. He also had a foolish idea, gleaned from old American literature and movies, that bridge was a more respectable version of seventies key-parties, and thought that if his wife was learning the language of love, he could permit himself the thrill of making up a four.

Sam's first class took place two days after Monica's. He got through his evening alone by working late, eating out and avoiding alcohol while he watched TV and waited for his wife to come back. Monica managed not to aggravate him when she returned, claiming the teacher favoured people who already knew Italian over absolute beginners and that she wasn't sure how long she'd keep going. She also told Sam that the class was populated exclusively by housewives, apart from one guy called Marcel who was probably gay. Sam smiled and took her to bed and they made love more energetically than they had for weeks, although he found it hard to shake off the churlish belief that Monica's actions were prompted by an urge to keep the peace rather than genuine arousal.

Although he'd spent weeks arguing that he had no interest in spending a night away from Monica, when the evening arrived Sam found he felt excited about going to his class, thinking that as he had already suffered, he might as well enjoy his reward. The class was being held at a small comprehensive school several miles outside Cambridge. Even with a map and directions, it took him almost an hour to find it, and once he'd located the building he couldn't believe so small a shack could be running classes. It looked more like a scout hut than a school, and there was only one other car in the car park. A woman in a brown cord jacket and black leggings sat on the stone steps by the front entrance, looking at him.

Sam walked across. 'You here for the bridge class?'

'I'm the teacher,' she replied, grinning at him.

He looked at the padlock. 'Date mix-up?'

'The class has been cancelled, I'm afraid. There wasn't a big enough response.'

'How many did you get?'

'Two, including you. Not even enough to make up a four.'

'Where's the other guy?'

'He must've got the letter. Didn't you get the letter?'

Sam shook his head.

'They're not very reliable. That's why I came across.'

'You gonna wait till he turns up?'

'What time is it?'

'Ten past. I had trouble finding the place.'

She stood up. 'I don't suppose he's going to come. Do you fancy a quick drink?'

'Why not?' Sam smiled. 'Shall we go in my car?'

She laughed. 'Unless you want to walk.'

He drove her into Cambridge and they went to The Castle Inn, a pub he knew from experience wouldn't be full of students. It was still early September so the town was empty anyway, but he didn't want to risk spoiling the evening by taking her somewhere too loud for them to talk. He bought her a Jim Beam and a pint for himself. She thanked him and asked, 'So why bridge?'

He looked at her. 'I studied American literature at university.'

She giggled. 'And?'

'And it seemed like part of that life.'

'What life?'

'Marriage, morality, repressed desires.'

She looked at him. 'I don't understand. That's what you want?'

'Yeah.'

'Why?'

'So I can feel potential.'

'What sort of potential?'

'I want to be an adult. No one wants to be an adult any more. All the time I was growing up, I'd look at my parents and think one day I'll be like them.'

'And your parents played bridge?'

'No, but they did other things, adult things like keeping secrets and being optimistic. All that stuff no one does any more.'

'I think people still keep secrets.'

'Yeah, but you know what I mean.'

She looked confused. 'And what's that got to do with American literature?'

Sam laughed. 'Sorry, I don't know why I'm going on like this. I've just been looking forward to tonight.'

'I can tell. I feel really guilty now. I had no idea I'd be meeting someone who'd built bridge into their personal philosophy.'

'Let's slow down, shall we? I'm Sam Emmett.'

'I know, they got your cheque. They can post it back to you if you want.'

'No, don't worry, just tell them to tear it up.' He swallowed. 'I know your surname's Peters and your initial's K, but . . .'

'Kelly,' she told him.

'So why do you teach bridge, Kelly?'

'I suppose my reasons aren't that different from yours. My Dad used to play bridge at his club all the time, but refused to teach me. He said I was too stupid to understand.'

'So you learnt in secret, challenged him, and won.'

'No, he doesn't even know I can play. He'd certainly never give me a game. I think he thinks there'd be something unseemly about playing bridge with his daughter. It's weird because he doesn't mind playing chess or backgammon, even poker with me. It's only bridge he's odd about.'

'Your family likes games then?'

'Yeah, my Mum prefers word things, Scrabble and stuff like that. She's always winning crossword competitions, but Dad just sneers at her. He thinks that stuff is for kids.'

'Is he into maths?'

She nods. 'It's that sort of mind, isn't it? He likes logic puzzles as well.'

'What about you?'

'A bit of both, although as far as they're concerned I'm too flippant about the whole thing. Mum might ask me for help with the odd clue, and Dad likes to explain puzzles to me, but they don't take me seriously. My sister deals with them much better than I do. She thinks they're both crazy.'

'Do you live with your parents?'

'No, my sister. We're both teachers at the same school. The place you came tonight.'

'It looked too small to be a school.'

'It's only an infants' school. It's amazing it's still open.'

'I didn't realise infant schools did night classes.'

'They don't usually. We've got a weird headmistress.' She paused. 'My mother.'

He laughed. 'I suppose I'm a bit of both as well. I got into my job through playing computer games.'

'Do you like games?'

'Yeah, I think so. I'm an only child so I haven't had much practice, but I'd like to learn.'

'Maybe I could still teach you the basics of bridge, if you're interested. I won't charge.'

'I'd like that. Same time next week?'

'Ok, but come to my house. My sister goes out on

Thursdays so we'll have the place to ourselves. I'll show you where it is on the way back.'

Monica was still awake when he got back. This surprised Sam. Staying up past nine was unusual for her, and they'd long since given up trying to synchronise their sleeping patterns. She sat with her legs tucked up beneath her, watching the television. Each Christmas Sam watched Monica unwrap the same presents from her mother: dark turtle-necks, black tights and plain kneelength skirts. Until recently, these clothes had remained piled in her wardrobe, but since taking the bookshop job she'd been wearing them every day, adopting the gifts as her work uniform.

'Good class?' she asked.

'Much like yours, I imagine, only with old people instead of housewives.'

'Did you play then?'

'No, the experienced people did, but I was put in a four with the other amateurs and the teacher talked us through the rules.'

'Is it really that complex? It seems strange to have to go to school to learn a game.'

'It's not so much its complexity, more to do with the playing conditions. You need four people who are all committed, and . . .' He stopped, realising Monica was staring at him. 'Does it sound stupid?'

'No, go on, I'm interested.'

'Is this how we're going to end up? Two oddballs wittering on about their hobbies.'

'It's nice,' she smiled.

'Really?' He sat down next to her, turning off the television. 'Well, shall we see if my outside interest has had the same effect on me as yours did on you?'

She laughed, and he put his arm around her, burying his face in her hair.

'I'm sorry I wasn't more understanding,' Monica said later, fluttering the thin sheet that covered them.

'About what?'

'When you were upset about me going to night class. I didn't think you were being serious.'

'Why not?'

'I didn't think one night apart would be such a big deal. But I felt really lonely tonight. You don't notice it when you're doing something, but when you're here alone . . .'

He looked at her. 'I don't have to go again.'

'No, that's not fair. I want to carry on with Italian and it'd be unfair of me to stop you. I just want you to know I appreciate the sacrifice, that's all.'

He cuddled her. 'Still, it was nice just now, wasn't it?'

'Yeah, it was lovely, but I don't want you to think it was connected to us being apart.'

'I was only joking.'

'I know, but you realise I like being with you, don't you? I'm not going to Italian to escape.'

'I understand. I love you, Monica.'

'I love you, too.'

Sam wore a suit to his next bridge class. He had long enough to change between finishing work and setting off, but liked the idea of retaining a slight formality. It made him feel less awkward, as if he was carrying a little of his work confidence with him when he went to Kelly's house.

In the inside pocket of his suit jacket were two packets of playing cards. The weight against his chest felt comforting, like a detective's gun.

Kelly's sister had yet to leave when Sam arrived. She answered the door and invited him in, saying Kelly was on the phone to their mother. Sam smiled at the sister and asked her name. She told him she was Karen, explaining how their mother had a thing for names beginning with K. Sam tried to be polite, knowing that getting her on side would prove useful later. Before Monica, every woman he'd dated had been the older one of two sisters, and he recognised the concern behind Karen's casual conversation. Sam supposed she already knew he was married, and wondered what she thought about that. He answered her questions with jokes and flattery, wanting her to like him but knowing unconditional approval would be unlikely.

He heard Kelly coming downstairs and wished he'd brought something. He hadn't wanted to bring wine or flowers because he worried it'd be inappropriate, but sitting on the settee waiting he realised he could've got away with a box of chocolates.

'Hi, Sam,' she said, walking over behind her sister, 'did she get you a drink?'

Karen turned to him. 'What would you like?'

'A beer,' he replied, hoping he'd said the right thing. Karen nodded and went out to the kitchen. Kelly slipped in where her sister had been, the springs of the settee bouncing her against Sam.

'Don't worry, she'll be gone in a minute,' Kelly whispered. 'I asked her to stay because I wasn't sure how long I'd be on the phone.'

Karen returned with the drinks and then said goodbye. Kelly waited until she'd gone before walking across and turning off the television. Sam could see Kelly hadn't exaggerated her interest in games. Beneath the TV was a huge stack of jigsaw puzzles, along with Scrabble, Monopoly and Trivial Pursuit.

'So where d'you want to start?' she asked.

'I don't mind. I brought some cards,' he told her, placing the packets on the table. Kelly examined them closely before biting a hole in the cellophane and tearing it off.

'I've got some *How to Play Bridge* videos we can watch. Or if you want we can go through some puzzles I've clipped from the paper. That's probably the best way of learning.'

'I don't mind. Either of those is fine.'

They didn't spend much time on bridge that evening, instead continuing the conversation they'd begun the week before. Sam skirted round any personal questions, not wanting Kelly to think he was coming on to her. She responded by keeping the talk light, referring back to bridge after any tricky silence. At ten thirty Sam excused himself and drove home, relieved to find Monica already asleep.

Several weeks later, Monica told Sam she was going to the wedding of an old college friend.

'But two months ago you wouldn't even call them.'

'That was before I got my job. Things are different now.'

'Why?'

'Because I don't need to feel embarrassed. It'll be fun to see their faces when I tell them what I'm doing.'

He reached for her hand. 'But you'll be gone for three days.'

'I have to stay that long. It's impossible to do all the driving in one go. Besides, it's an old-fashioned wedding, with all the pre-ceremony dinners and stuff. You'll be okay. Thursday's your bridge night.'

'I thought you understood how I don't like being here alone.'

'I do understand, but you encouraged me to keep in contact with my friends. Come, if you like, the invitation's for two. I only didn't say anything because I assumed you wouldn't want to go.'

Sam thought about Kelly. 'No, you're right. I'm being stupid. I'll just miss you.'

'I know. But it won't be long.'

Sam called Kelly on the evening Monica left. He said he was only phoning to check she'd be able to see him the next day, but he managed to mention that his wife would be away for the next three days. If Kelly wondered why he was sharing this with her, she didn't say anything, keeping up a steady flow of small talk. They spoke for thirty minutes, then Sam thanked her and hung up.

Kelly was wearing tight blue jeans with a black jumper. Her lightly hennaed hair looked good against the dark wool. He'd been there two hours when Kelly said it was about time they played a game.

'Of bridge?'

'No, a different game.' She stood up and walked through to the kitchen. 'But I think you'll like it.'

Sam studied his fingernails, waiting for her to return. She walked back carrying a bottle of whisky on a tray with two tumblers.

'A drinking game?' he asked, amused.

'Partly. Although it's also a truth game. It's called three fingers.'

'Never played it.'

'Good.' She poured out two full glasses. 'You can ask me any question you want. If it's a relatively innocent one, it's worth one finger.' She wrapped one finger around the glass. 'That means if I don't want to answer it, I've got to drink that much whisky. If it's a little more intimate, it's worth two fingers. And if it's really bad, then that counts for three. Does that make sense?'

Sam nodded. 'Who starts?'

'You.'

'Okay, for two fingers, do you like living with your sister?'

'Yeah. I didn't to begin with, and saw it as a real urgency to get out of here, but now I find it quite comforting.'

'Your turn.'

'For three fingers, why did you tell me your wife's gone away?'

'Three fingers. You mean I've got to drink all that?'

'Or answer the question.'

Sam squeezed his fingers as close together as possible and drank the measure.

'My turn. For two fingers, why d'you want to play this game?'

Kelly looked at the whisky, wrapped two fingers around the glass and downed it.

'That wasn't that bad a question,' Sam said. 'Why did you drink?'

'That's another question. And it's not your turn.'

It was Sam who suggested calling an end to the game. Kelly had just confessed that she'd wanted him since their first meeting and would like to sleep with him. He told her that if he had any more to drink that'd prove impossible and she smiled sympathetically. Then she said, 'Just one more question.'

'Okay.'

'For three fingers, is this going to be a one off?'

He downed the drink.

That was Sam's last bridge class. He sent Kelly a letter and a box of chocolates, writing that he wished he was a better man. She didn't reply. He threw away her address and phone number, hoping it wouldn't take him long to forget it. Once or twice he found himself dialling the first few digits by mistake, quickly replacing the receiver before he could complete it. Although he'd never been a fan of drunken sex, he'd been scared by how good it'd been with Kelly, and didn't want to risk making love to her sober. Monica had already given up her Italian, and instead of being irritated that they suddenly had lots more time together, the couple became more considerate to one another, both trying to compensate for their partner's loss. One evening, Monica asked Sam, 'Do you miss playing bridge?'

'A bit.'

'Is it the sort of thing you can teach me?'

'Not really. But there is another game we can play.'

'With cards?'

'No, something different. I'll fix it for tonight.'

Monica smiled at him, interested. 'Ok.'

Sam bought the whisky in his lunch hour. He had his suspicions about the weekend Monica had spent away, and felt eager to get through their mutual confessions. He sensed a recent change in their relationship and couldn't be bothered to feel angry. It wasn't until he got back to his office that he remembered how scared he'd once been about Monica betraying him and realised his new insouciance was a real achievement. He drove home feeling pleased with himself, looking forward to his evening with Monica.

'Ready for our game?' he asked, after she'd finished watching the news.

'Ok,' she smiled.

Sam went out into the kitchen for a tray and some glasses. Monica watched him place the tray on the coffee table and take the whisky from the off-licence carrier.

'Whisky?' she asked, looking up at him.

He nodded. 'It's a drinking game.'

'I don't want to play a drinking game. I thought we were going to play cards.'

'Give me a chance to explain. It's a proper game.'

'I don't even like whisky. This is ridiculous.'

Sam ignored her and started filling the glasses. 'You can ask me any question you like.'

'Do you love me?'

'No, wait, listen.'

'Sam, this is stupid. If you want to get me drunk, let me have a drink I like. There's some Stella in the fridge.'

'No, it's not about drinking.'

'What then?'

'Asking questions. You have to ask questions.'

'You can ask me anything you like. I don't have any secrets from you.'

'Please, let me explain.'

'I really don't want to play, ok? Let's watch some TV.' She picked up the remote. Sam glared at her. 'All right, all right,' she said, 'explain.'

He ran through the rules, and told Monica she could go first.

'For two fingers,' she said, 'what's your favourite thing I do?'

'Sucking me off. Same question.'

'What's my favourite thing? Sex, I guess.'

'Not head?'

'Head's ok. But I prefer sex. My turn. When were you happiest with me?'

'Our reception.'

'Really? Why then?'

'Because I felt proud of you.'

Monica stared at him. 'I didn't realise I was on show.'

'Of course you were on show,' Sam laughed, 'it was a wedding. For two fingers, when were you least happy with me?'

'When you thought you had cancer.'

Sam swallowed. 'You never said anything.'

'Of course not, you'd have been furious. But it was so ridiculous. Only old men get bowel cancer.'

He kept his voice even. 'Your question?'

'For three fingers, have you ever been unfaithful?'

He drank three fingers. Holding Monica's gaze, he said, 'Three fingers. Same question.'

She drank her whisky.

Sam stood up. 'I'm going for a drive.'

Sam started the engine. He might not have Kelly's address any more, but he could remember how to get there. He looked back at the house, telling himself he should go. He waited thirty seconds, wondering if Monica would come after him. He turned off the engine. The curtain twitched. He waited. Monica opened the door.

She looked nervous. Sam stared straight ahead, waiting until she reached the car. She tapped on the window. He pressed a button and the smooth glass slid down.

'Come inside, Sam.'

'No.'

'Let me in, then.'

Sam opened the door and she squeezed herself on top of him. He wondered if the steering-wheel was digging into her back.

'Where did you learn that game?' she whispered.

'School. We used to play it with sixth-form girls.'

'That's sweet. I'm touched you wanted to play it with me.'

'It's stupid.'

She kissed him. 'Maybe we should've played one of my games instead.'

'You don't know any games.'

'I do.'

'What?'

'Strip Poker.'

He laughed, and she looked up hopefully. Sam couldn't stop himself smiling. He put his arms around her and she burrowed into his lap. He held Monica and stroked her hair, staying in the same position until his legs went numb.

paul charles

....

she thought she could fly

A Detective Inspector Christy Kennedy Short Story

Francis Bucher ran out into the courtyard at the front of his house. He was screaming and hollering at the top of his lungs, something you just didn't do in this neighbourhood. The other four inhabitants of the courtyard, which was just off England's Lane, between the borders of Primrose Hill and Belsize Park, figured that if they could afford to buy one of the five properties in this very exclusive (million pound plus) cul-de-sac, they should at the least be assured of a little peace and quiet.

Each of the five houses were uniquely converted homes and usually the owners respected each other's space. Francis Bucher, however, was not your regular rich type; he was a member of the new swanky.

'Oh please,' he pleaded at the top of his lungs, 'for God's sake, please don't jump, Susan!' He cared little whether his neighbours heard him or not, as hear him they must. He was creating as much disturbance as one of his clients would on his regular late-night slot on Channel Four.

'Please don't jump, Susie. I need you. Don't do this to us!' Francis continued, if anything louder than before.

Francis appeared to be looking towards a sky lit by a true blue moon; a starry starry moonlit night. His eyes appeared to be out of focus, but he just might have been able to make out the form of his wife Susan, sitting precariously, four storeys up, at the edge of their flat top roof. It had been the flat top roof of the house, and ideas of a roof garden which had first attracted Francis Bucher to this converted school house. He saw the potential for amazing BBQs with spectular panoramic views across Primrose Hill, Camden Town, and Regent's Park down to Trafalgar Square on one side and up to the new Alexandra Palace on the other.

You see, Francis, in his professional capacity as a public relations representative, liked to entertain and to be entertained. This was borne out by his disproportionately large belly which was greatly exaggerated by the fact that he always wore tight-fitting T-shirts. The T-shirts were always crisp clean, worn only on the inaugural occasion, and advertising one of his current clients or products. This evening Action Man was dancing in the moonlight; dancing because each and every time Francis wretched his rotund stomach to draw breath for another scream, the thirty-year-old, fifteen-inch, scarred warrior would quiver in tandem. Francis Bucher's black, Nike trousers suffered from not having a waist to cling to, thus ensuring the well-paid, and even better fed, publicist continuously and unconsciously, hoisted his trousers up to avoid embarrassment.

He had furnished their flat roof with garden furniture from the nearby Swiss Cottage branch of Habitat. One large oblong table, under canvas canopy, and several little islands with a few wicker chairs carefully positioned, highlighted the various sizes and colours of potted plants. In one corner he had the most up-to-the-minute essentials (again, the products of one of his clients) at the ready for his next barbecue. This was the only sheltered area on the roof, benefiting from a chimney shaft on one side and a weathered wicker fence unit on the other. The roof garden was framed by a two-foot high red-brick wall. His wife was now sitting on this wall at the front of the house, close to one of the little islands of furniture, feet dangling over the outside edge.

'Susan! PL-EA-SE! DON'T!' the home counties voice called out once more.

Gradually the lights of the neighbouring houses were being turned on as, one by one, they were awoken from their midnight-hour slumber. They were used to hearing late night noises from the Buchers, but rarely on a midweek night.

Mrs Alexandra Faix, the lady from the house directly beside the Buchers, was first on the scene, flying out through her front door, pink-slippered feet barely touching the gravel as she tried to tie up her dressing gown, which was flying about her like curtains on a clothesline on a windy day. The Buchers and the Faixs, although separated by a ten-foot gap between their houses, shared one side of the courtyard. The remaining neighbours, Green, Browne and Black (a freaky coincidence admittedly, but the truth nonetheless) enjoyed the luxury and privacy of a side of the courtyard each.

Mrs Faix immediately looked up, following the direction of Francis' gaze. When she recognised her friend and neighbour perched on the edge, she too joined in shouting skyward.

Susan Bucher showed no acknowledgement whatsoever of her husband and neighbour's concert.

Francis walked away from Mrs Faix and closer to his house, his leather Harrods-monogrammed slippers crunching on the grey and light brown gravel as he moved.

'Susan, don't do this!' he called out, somewhat quieter than before.

Alexandra Faix didn't know whether to stand her ground, wait for her husband, or rush into the Buchers' house and climb the stairs as quickly as her legs would carry her. Would her bursting out onto the roof garden startle Susan Bucher and prompt her to jump? When she reached the roof, would she look stupid as Susan revealed that, in fact, she was only playing a game with her husband? One didn't want to look stupid in front of the Buchers. She decided to stay where she was, at least until her husband joined her.

The next neighbour to emerge was Michelle Browne, a single woman in her mid-thirties. Michelle didn't even try to tie up her white flannel dressing gown, letting it fly out behind her like Superman's cape, exposing a flimsy pair of ice-blue pyjamas. She rushed towards Alexandra, whom she grabbed for comfort as they stared up at the Buchers' roof top.

'Susan, please come down, we've got our friends out with us now, Michelle and Alexandra. Won't you please

come down? Go back from the edge please . . . we
need . . .'

'Ple. . . .!'

Whatever it was Francis was about to say was either
forgotten or lost in the harmonic screams of Alexandra
and Michelle as Susan Bucher lurched off the edge and
appeared to be falling directly towards her husband. All
three stood, synchronised dropped jaws, speechless. The
only sound heard was the sound of the wind as it rustled
through Susan's clothes.

The entire fall seemed to be happening in slow motion
as Susan apparently floated towards the ground,
appearing to take forever. Then . . . splat! There was the
sound of a dampened thud. Most of the noise came from
the gravel stones rearranging themselves to accommodate the projectile's final resting place.

The screaming in the courtyard started up again as
mysteriously as it had stopped. Only this time the sound
of desperation had been replaced by an eerier sound of
regret.

Francis ran towards his wife and leaned over her and
appeared, to Michelle and Alexandra, to put his ear to
her heart, apparently searching for a heartbeat. His
efforts appeared to be in vain and he remained in that
position for a minute or so, very close to her, hugging her
and gently rocking back and forth.

'Susan!' Francis cried.

He turned and looked back across the courtyard seemingly unaware that the blood from his wife's various head
wounds was staining his Action Man T-shirt. He saw
Alexandra and Michelle still locked in embrace, staring
at him in disbelief, and still screaming uncontrollably.

'It's over,' Francis said calmly. 'I was too late. I never thought she'd do it. I thought she was just bluffing.'

He paused and looked at them, his face merely suggesting a smile. His eyes beseeching them with a 'What shall I do?' look. Eventually, just before the tears came he said plaintively, 'You know, she said she thought she could fly!'

Detective Inspector Christy Kennedy tuned in to the crunching sound his feet were making on the gravel as he walked across the courtyard. He was bemused by the different 'crunches' made by the various feet. As far as he could make out, the crunch sounds depended on: size of shoe; type of shoe; weight and sex of the owner. He wasn't quite so bemused as he approached the body of Susan Bucher. The blood of her departing life had tainted the gravel about her head a brilliant red. A brilliant red stain which, like the memory of her existence, would fade with the passing of time.

He felt a heave in the pit of his stomach.

A shiver ran the entire length of his spine; he felt chilled to his very bones. It was not long after midnight on a spring evening and he shouldn't have felt so cold, Blue Moon or not.

'She didn't land that way, sir.' A Scottish voice advised him. Kennedy was relieved the voice had interrupted his dark thoughts of death.

'Sorry, James?' he replied in a voice not much above a whisper.

'The lady, sir,' DS James Irvine continued, 'she didn't actually land like that when she fell.'

'Ah. How so?'

'Her husband, a Francis Bucher, you can't miss him, he's wearing an Action Man T-shirt. He's back in the house, sir, being comforted by WPC Coles. He found her, sir. Apparently, he straightened her out. Apparently, she was a sorry sight.'

'And why would Mr Bucher have done that, do you think?' Kennedy continued. He was still speaking in a quiet voice, a voice so quiet that DS Irvine had to strain to hear him against the continual crunching on the gravel by the members of the SOCO team.

'Well sir, you see, Susan Bucher jumped.'

The DS paused and pointed to the flat roof above them. 'That's their house and according to Mr Bucher, and confirmed by two of the neighbours, Mrs Alexandra Faix and Ms Michelle Browne, he tried to talk her down. He failed. The neighbours were out in the courtyard with Mr Bucher when his wife jumped.'

'Really?' Kennedy said, raising his voice a little in an expression just somewhat short of disbelief.

'Yes,' Irvine confirmed as he averted his eyes from the roof top and back to the corpse, 'and then Mr Bucher rushed over here to see if there was anything he could do and realising it was too late, simply straightened out her contorted limbs and hugged her. Mrs Faix and Ms Browne tried to pull him away but, they claim, he continued to cling to her as if his life depended on it. Ms Browne, sir, she's the sister of Peter O' Browne – she dropped the 'O' – do you remember he's the record company guy who was murdered in that bizarre ritual murder some time back?'

'Of course,' Kennedy replied, looking at the property

directly across the courtyard from the Buchers, 'I remember the house.'

Kennedy looked once more at the corpse, this time studying it closely.

He guessed the woman was about thirty-three to thirty-five. She was dressed in white, figure-hugging slacks, and wore a white (unsponsored) T-shirt under a white man's shirt (unbuttoned). All the white fabric, like the ground about her, was stained with her blood. One of her black flip-flop canvas shoes had obviously become dislodged on her final descent and lay beside her, motionless, like a pet primed and waiting to be entertained by its owner. She wore no jewellery, excepting a white-gold wedding ring which seemed to have become embedded in the skin near the knuckle of her finger.

Kennedy knelt closer to the body. He could do that now. It wasn't that he was more comfortable with corpses the longer he was around them; no, it was more down to the fact that he had started his work. He had been able to set aside his grief at the loss of life and his brain was now working overtime on possible theories as to what had happened. The body of Mrs Susan Bucher had now become a piece of evidence for him to examine.

He looked closely at the fingers. Using a pencil he lifted the hand. The wedding ring had definitely been moved. Clearly visible, even to the naked eye, was a valley circumnavigating the finger where the ring had once rested. The ring had been moved about a half an inch closer to the knuckle in what Kennedy guessed had been an unsuccessful attempt to dislodge it.

Susan Bucher had shaggy, badly-kept brown hair. Her

face was bloated and now offered only a passing clue to its once well-defined and beautiful features.

Dr Leonard Taylor was next to arrive on the scene and showed some surprise at the number of police officers already present.

'I say,' he began with a bit of a chuckle, 'a great turn-out from Camden's finest and all for a jumper.'

'Someone called this in as a domestic disturbance and then a second call came in a few minutes later saying we better get here quickly, someone was dead,' Irvine advised the pathologist.

Kennedy, who appeared to be ignoring this exchange, said, 'Mmmm'. His attention had now moved to the corpse's wrist. As he raised the pencil, supporting the hand even higher, the open-cuffed shirt sleeve fell down the arm revealing a red, blue and black mark around the wrist.

Kennedy's curiosity got the better of Taylor and he knelt down beside the detective.

'A watch strap perhaps?' he offered, nodding at the centre of Kennedy's attention.

'I doubt it, Leonard,' Kennedy began as he lowered the pencil, and consequently the arm, to where he'd found it on the gravel. 'If it was a watch strap, the mark would be a lot older than this. Could it have anything to do with drug administration?'

'No, a tourniquet wouldn't do you much good there, you'd have to be closer to the elbow.' Taylor raised the lifeless limb now for closer inspection, 'And you're absol-utely correct about the wrist mark, it is recent, very recent in fact, I'd say just before death.'

'Look, we'll leave you to your job, Leonard. I wouldn't

be so sure she's a jumper, though. Careful how you go, eh?'

'Enough said, old chap. I'll see what I can turn up for you.'

'Shall we go and talk to Francis Bucher, sir?' Irvine inquired, tonally co-equal with the original, and still the best, Bond. Both he and Kennedy stood back from the corpse giving Taylor his space.

'No,' Kennedy replied quickly with resolve, 'let's have a chat with the neighbours; those first on the scene. What were their names again?'

'Alexandra Faix and Michelle Browne, sir. They're both still in a bit of shock, sir. They're in the Faixs' house and the husband, Jacques, is looking after them.'

A few gravel-crunching moments later Kennedy and Irvine knocked on the stained oak front door of the Faix residence. Jacques, small, full-figured and dignified, answered the door. There's something about English spoken with a French accent that is very appealing . . .

When Kennedy had been growing up and Brigitte Bardot was all the rage, he and all his mates just used to scour the tourist packed streets of Portrush in search of that accent. If you managed to discover and date such a girl, you had already amassed quite a few brownie points without even having to lay a finger on her. Hell, even the memory of the way they said 'No!' to you could send you to sleep contentedly each and every night for the rest of the summer.

Jacques Faix greeted the police officers warmly and invited them into his rustic-looking house. The minute he closed the door behind them they could have sworn they were in a cottage somewhere in the wilds of the countryside rather than pretty close to the centre of London. Alexandra and Michelle were sitting on the couch together hugging, not each other any more, but steaming hot cups of tea.

God bless the French, Kennedy was thinking a few seconds later, not only do they make you a cup of tea when you come to see them about some unpleasant business, but they make a darned fine cup.

'I'm sorry for what both of you have been through tonight,' Kennedy started, placing his empty china cup onto the asymmetrical pine coffee table and signalling that the small chat was over. 'I've just a few questions for you both and then we'll be out of your hair and allow you to get back to bed.'

Jacques seemed to welcome this news but his wife said, 'I couldn't possibly try to sleep after that, I'd be scared of the nightmares.' Alexandra paused. She didn't share her husband's accent; not quite a Londoner but somewhere close Kennedy thought. 'And Michelle, we couldn't possibly send you home to an empty house after this. You'll stay here, of course.'

Michelle Browne began to utter some words of protest but they fell on deaf ears.

'No, no, we insist, don't we Jacques,' Alexandra started and continued, oblivious to her husband's reply, 'now, Inspector, what are your questions?'

'I hate to put you through this again, but both of you were in the courtyard when Mrs Bucher fell?' Kennedy began.

'*Jumped*, Inspector. Both myself and Michelle were in

the courtyard when Susan jumped,' Alexandra corrected the detective.

'Tell me,' Kennedy continued, appearing to choose to ignore the correction, 'did she say anything when she was up there on the ledge?'

Both women thought for a few moments. Michelle was first to speak. Kennedy recognised the Liffey lilt immediately. 'Now I don't remember Susan actually saying anything. We three, Francis, Alex and myself, were certainly shouting and screaming but I don't actually remember Susan saying anything, do you, Alex?'

'No,' Alexandra replied immediately. She then paused for a few seconds before making that a definite confirmation, 'No, she didn't say a word.'

'How long were you out in the courtyard before she . . . before the incident?' Kennedy continued.

'It wouldn't have been more than a couple of minutes.' Alexandra replied, 'I'd not long gone to bed. Jacques was sound asleep as ever. You could sleep through the sinking of the *Titanic*, couldn't you, dear?' They were not words of reproachment but spoken (and meant) affectionately. She held out her hand to her husband and he took it in one hand and stroked it with the other. At that moment in time they reminded Kennedy of Serge Gainsbourg and Jane Birkin, the 'Je t'aime' couple; the beautiful English rose and the rugged, but sophisticated Frenchman. Kennedy's thoughts were disturbed as Alexandra continued, 'All of a sudden I heard this screaming out in the courtyard . . .'

'Sorry to interrupt you, madam, but could we go back a bit? I'm thinking about earlier in the evening when you were in bed and you first heard the screaming. I was wondering whether or not you heard anything from Mrs Bucher then?' Kennedy enquired, happy that Jacques had chosen to pour another cup of tea.

Alexandra considered the question for a few seconds before replying, 'No, just Francis, but then he was wailing at the top of his voice so perhaps he could have drowned Susan out. Anyway, as I was saying, I heard all this screaming and shouting and I just grabbed my dressing gown and ran out into the courtyard.'

Kennedy now looked at Michelle Browne.

'I pretty much heard the same thing, you know, the racket out in the courtyard. I just put on my dressing gown,' she said as she noticed that her dressing gown had fallen away from her knees to reveal her gossamer fine pyjamas. She quickly drew the dressing gown over her knees, making herself decent again. No one noticed the gesture except Kennedy. 'I ran out into the courtyard to see both Francis and Alex calling up to Susan. I didn't hear Susan say anything either.'

'Tell me,' Kennedy began changing tack somewhat, 'was there always a lot of noise from their house?'

'You mean, were they fighting all the time, don't you?' Alexandra replied.

'Well . . .' Kennedy began.

'The answer is no,' Alexandra offered on behalf of the England's Lane trio.

'They were being quite civil about it.' This time the conversation was spiced with a French accent for the first time.

'Civil? Civil about what, sir?' Irvine enquired, throwing a little Scots into the mix.

'Why, the divorce, of course. They were divorcing,' Jacques replied innocently.

'Francis and Susan Bucher were divorcing each other?' Irvine asked incredulously.

'Yes, but as my husband says, they were being extremely civil about it all.'

'Yes. Susan had told us only last weekend at one of their dos that she couldn't believe how generous Francis was being. She said that he was agreeing to every single demand she and her solicitor were making. Her solicitor was with her, in fact,' Michelle offered, as she and Alexandra stole a glance at each other.

Jacques merely pursed his lips and delivered the French version of tut tut.

'Oh, come on, Jacques,' his wife reprimanded him, 'he's got his new woman, she's entitled. I'd say Francis came out best. He found himself a model. You'll know her, Inspector, she works under the name of *La Baule*. She'd done fabulously well out of modelling but now she's launching a pop career. That's how she met Francis, he does all her promotion and publicity. Poor Susan, on the other hand, got this Columbo-type character, a solicitor, originally from Liverpool.

'Oh, looks can be deceptive. I think Susan's had a much more successful visit to the well,' Jacques said with a faraway look in his eye.

'Not any more, dear, poor Susan's dea . . .' Alexandra started. She failed to finish the word as she raised her other hand and offered it to her husband as well.

'Francis seems to think that the incident happened . . . was due to some kind of hallucinatory drug. Do you know if Susan indulged?'

'Oh, Inspector,' Alexandra replied, with a tone which implied, 'you don't expect us to go snitching on our friends, do you?' She looked first at Michelle and then her husband before replying, 'I personally thought she'd cleaned up her act. I think they both used to indulge. But I understand she was trying to leave that part of her life behind.'

The other two nodded copiously in agreement.

'One final thing, and I apologise in advance for having to ask you this.' Kennedy now began acting a little restless, 'Susan Bucher, just before she . . . just before she left the ledge, did she jump out feet first, did she fall off, or did she leap out?'

Michelle was the one who chose to answer that question and she replied immediately.

'Well, it's funny, really. None of the ways you've described. She kinda tumbled off, more like a sack of potatoes falling than a human.'

Three and one half minutes later, Kennedy and Irvine were in the Bucher household. Kennedy left Irvine with Francis and, following the owner's directions, he and WPC Anne Coles found their way up on to the roof top.

'Has Mr Bucher been up here since you arrived?' Kennedy asked as they walked out into the cold night air.

'No sir,' Coles began replacing a vagabond wisp of blonde hair back into her complicated hair arrangement. 'When I arrived in the courtyard, he was still on the gravel holding his wife's body in his arms. Mr and Mrs Faix and Ms Browne were standing by offering words of comfort.'

'Was he saying anything?'

'Not really anything very coherent, just muttering on and on about the fact that she shouldn't have done it,' Coles replied.

'So then what happened?'

'Well, the rest of the SOCO team arrived with DS Irvine and he organised them to start their work and told me to bring Bucher in here and stay with him,' Coles replied.

'Did he say anything?'

'No, just asked me to make him a cup of tea.'

'Did you leave him to do that?'

'No, I brought him into the kitchen with me while I made it,' the resourceful WPC replied.

'Good,' Kennedy said as they walked towards the ledge of the roof. 'Tell me, was Francis Bucher unaccompanied at any time?'

'No . . .' Coles began and then hesitated. It was only for a split second but Kennedy immediately picked up on it.

'What? What have you remembered?' he pushed his WPC, not the slightest trace of annoyance in his voice. In fact, if anything, it appeared he wanted Coles to tell him that she had left Bucher alone. They had now reached the ledge and found a large wooden chair close to the edge. It seemed oddly out of place. Kennedy noticed the island of table and chairs closest to that position had only three chairs whereas all the rest had four. As he clocked all this, he was still waiting for Coles to answer.

'Yes, sorry, sir, I mean no,' she replied hesistantly. 'No, he wasn't in my view all the time. He went to the toilet, the one to the left as you come in the front door. I'm sorry, I didn't think. I thought he'd be okay . . . I thought she'd jumped.'

'It's perfectly ok. Perfectly ok. At least now we know where he hid the vital piece of evidence.' Kennedy replied, staring up at the Blue Moon. 'We're done up here. Let's retreat to the warmth.'

As they returned down the stairwell, they noticed the numerous photographs of Francis Bucher with various celebrities: stars of stage, screen, radio and children's toy packaging.

'I say, did you see the position Susan jumped from when you were up there?' Francis asked as Coles and Kennedy returned to the living area. 'I haven't had the heart to go up there again myself since. Did she leave a note or anything? She'd always be a bit crazed when she was high, you know. She was one of the few people around who still consistently took LSD, she loved to trip. I kept telling her that there's a cumulative damage factor going on there. She wouldn't listen to me, though. It used to happen a lot in the seventies, you know. People jumping out of windows, claiming that they could fly. I thought we'd all grown up since then, didn't you?'

'Sorry, sir, I wonder, could you excuse me for a moment?' Kennedy began, apparently ignoring Bucher's spiel. 'I need to visit the toilet. Could I use yours, please?'

'Why, yes,' Bucher began, slightly taken back. 'Of course you can, it's on the first floor at the back.'

'Isn't there a closer one?' Kennedy began, looking first at Bucher and then at Coles.

'Um, yes, it's just, ah, the one on the first floor is ah, more suitable for guests, if you know what I mean,' Bucher replied, confused to the degree he looked at each of the police officers in turn implying, 'What's going on here?'

Kennedy made his way to the ground floor toilet and locked the door behind him. He searched around for a few minutes for his prize which he eventually found in the back of the medicine cabinet. Flushing the toilet, he returned to the living room with a lift to his step.

'Very clever, Mr Bucher. Very, very clever,' Kennedy began, as he sank back down into the hi-tech, very industrial, extremely uncomfortable sofa – a grey affair with a few hints of blue scattered about. At least it bore testament to the fact that the Buchers hadn't shopped exclusively at Habitat.

'Sorry? What? What are you talking about?' Bucher replied, twisting in his swivel chair.

'Very, very clever. You just made one mistake, really. Maybe two. The first you would have got away with if you hadn't made the second,' Kennedy said as he crossed his legs, clasped his hands in front of his knee and sank back into the sofa.

'What the feck are you on about?' Bucher screamed.

'I mean, the chair up on the roof, you used the back of the chair to support her while she *sat* on the edge of the roof. You couldn't be sure that in her drugged comatose state she'd remain on the edge for you, could you? So you trailed the chair across to the edge and rested her against it until you were ready to complete your plan,' Kennedy said quietly, the calm to Bucher's storm.

'What are you on about? She was on drugs. Michelle and Alexandra saw it. They saw Susan jump. I was down in the yard. They were beside me when she jumped. It's that simple, there are witnesses. It couldn't possibly have been me. Why are you doing this to me? I tried to stop her. Didn't they tell you that?'

'Then we get to your second mistake,' Kennedy continued, pretending to ignore Bucher completely. 'Now that *was* a bad mistake. The mark on your wife's wrist. It would have been so easy to avoid that. You could simply have attached the string to her belt, or at least put some kind of padding around her wrist. That way you'd have avoided the telltale marks on her wrist.'

'I haven't got the slightest idea what you're on about,' Bucher said, somewhat resigned.

Coles and Irvine looked on with great interest.

'Perhaps this will help your memory a little,' Kennedy began as he removed a large coil of nylon picture string from his pocket.

This time Bucher said nothing, he merely rearranged his overblown stomach into a more comfortable position.

'I'd say that you'd met this model, *La Baule* I believe is her name,' Kennedy began. 'You decided to divorce the old model, as it were. She, in turn, met a canny solicitor who advised her exactly what she was entitled to. You surprised everyone by agreeing to all her demands. But that was only because you'd never planned to give her anything. I wouldn't even be surprised if there's a juicy little life insurance policy. You needed her dead. You plied her with drink and drugs, trailed her up onto the roof and tied this nylon string to her wrist. It's very strong this string, isn't it, and it's not very bulky.

'You dropped the end of the string over the ledge, returned to the courtyard, grabbed the dangling end of the string and started to shout at the top of your lungs, raising quite a racket. Your neighbours came out to see what was going on. When they were close to you in the courtyard, you pulled the string and Susan rolled off the ledge and fell to her death. You then ran over to your wife, appearing to Michelle and Alexandra to comfort her, but what you were in fact doing was untying the string from her wrist and stuffing it into your pocket.

'When you were back in your house, at the first available opportunity, you visited the toilet in order to hide the evidence. I would bet money now that we will find particles of this string in and about the mark on your wife's wrist.' It appeared as though the detective was finished, because Bucher exhaled a large sigh. But, there was more. Only a little more.

'You also tried, unsuccessfully, to remove your wife's wedding ring. I must admit I found that a bit tacky and it was the first thing that made me think that perhaps your wife didn't, in fact, jump. I assume it must be worth a lot of money?'

'Yes,' was Bucher's immediate one-word reply. He then tried to expand on it. 'But I . . . How could you . . . She didn't und . . .' Bucher tried unsuccessfully to say what what was on his mind. He started his sentence several different ways, but it was very noticeable that none of the ways were to include the phrase, 'I didn't do it.'

stella duffy

....

cancer man and the lady in the moon

The best time to catch a crab is in full moonlight, on the beach. This will be the stretch of shore he has already decided belongs to him – and woe betide the trespassers. The crab is both fish and fowl – he swims in the sea, but he lives on the land. He is lunar-driven and follows the moon. But if the crab diverts his gaze from the moon to you and decides to make you the object of his pursuit, there is no backing off. Once the diffident, backwards and forwards, sideways running crab has hold of your toe, it won't let go in a hurry. Or ever.

It started slowly, small. A slight twinge. The feeling not quite pain, yet not easy to describe as actual pleasure. More just a tiny cellular alteration. Inside, not detected through face or body change, barely discernible even when naked. Luisa didn't notice it to be an actual change, until it was too late. She didn't understand his intent – even that he had any – until it was too late. But by then it was all too far gone to remedy, the only cure to cut and burn. Her cancer man.

Luisa met Charles through her work. She was important there, at the office, in charge of a team of twenty – sometimes more. She'd made the big leap to boss five years ago and more than rewarded the faith of her superiors. Her workforce were superlative creatives all, but it was Luisa who made the final decisions. And, if necessary, she was just as willing to take the fall for any big mistakes. There had never yet been any big mistakes. And still fewer small ones. People spoke about Luisa as one might a champion thoroughbred, discovered by accident. Self-trained and silver-spoon free, and all the better for it.

Luisa started off with the company straight out of school, in at the very bottom as an office junior. In those days there were plenty of jobs in advertising for bright young things with minds of their own – and mouths they knew how to keep shut. Do the job, put up with the hours, take the shit, offer up your own ideas for the further gratification of the boss, and never complain when he steals your ideas. (Back then – all of fifteen years ago – the boss was highly unlikely to have been a she.) This was long before all the degrees in media and marketing had crept into her surroundings. Before her workplace was taken over by foreign academics and world-market analysis. In the beginning Luisa simply learnt from those who employed her, copied those who let her. Intended to keep doing so until she became a boss herself. And, in time, she became a damn good one herself. Hard work, a few well-placed fucks, prized discretion and, at the base of it all, an astonishing degree of inherent ability.

Luisa did not have the expected qualifications, it was true. She did not carry degrees with her as an armour against the vagaries of the working world. But she had experience and strength and learnt knowledge. She had an understanding of her craft, burnt into her bones by late nights and early mornings. And if, late at night, her five hours' pressured sleep was occasionally disturbed by a wind of concern rippling across her unlined face, there were no signs of worry in the morning. Sure, plenty of people were made redundant these days, colleagues were hired and fired within weeks. And actual qualifications made no difference at all. Luisa was not book-learnt, but she had been born with native cunning and an astonishing ability to labour until she dropped. And whenever she caught herself worrying that perhaps someone with extra letters to their name might possibly look down on her, Luisa reminded herself of the strength of her bank account and the accolades of her peers and superiors. At thirty-two, she sometimes felt she had only just begun. Luisa had always known she was meant to go far. Then she met Charles. And went too far.

Work and money are important to the crab. Family is important to the crab. The outside trappings that are his hard shell are what he shows to the world. The pink flesh is what he shows to you. But only if you're really very lucky. If you're chosen.

Charles Strongman was the new guy, all the way from New York and imported as hot-shot, bright boy, the new big gun. Destined to slaughter the opposition, set things straight, wipe out the competition. Destined to end up wiping her eyes. Only Luisa didn't know that in the beginning. She was to work alongside him. Introduce him to the place, the people – help him understand the company ethos. Eventually, once he knew how things worked, Charles would take over a department of his own. Her department. His joining the firm was intended to give Luisa the opportunity she had been craving for three years or more – an opening she had been actively lobbying for even longer. Charles' appointment to take over more than half of Luisa's existing clients would free her to concentrate on her own baby, the development side of the company. A new and exciting proposal that had the full backing of not only the whole board but pretty much everyone else, from the cleaners up to the CEO. Everything was all agreed long before Charles arrived, his office space was booked and cleared the minute his left hand finished signing the contract, all the way across the sea in Manhattan. Luisa started preparing for Charles at work months before they first met. Without knowing it, she'd also started preparing herself for Charles.

The week he arrived she was completely on top of it all. His workspace was sorted, his assistants had been ready and willing for a fortnight, five different lunches and introductory dinners were booked. Luisa had finalised the perfect schedule, she had the new guy all arranged. Almost. What Luisa didn't realise was that Charles came with an agenda of his own.

The Cancer man is proud of his family, holds them tight.

*Would keep them all forever under his shell if he could. They
swim only in his rock pool, in his wake.*

Charles had one wife and two children. His wife was
beautiful, elegant, intelligent and, unlike Luisa,
supremely well-educated. She ran her own consultancy
business and was delighted at the opportunity to relocate
and diversify into new markets. Perfect woman. Charles'
son Adam was thirteen. Bright and charming, he had his
mother's good looks and his father's winning ways. Ideal
boy. Their daughter Marina had suffered a shock attack
of polio as a tiny baby. Consequently she was slow to talk,
slower to walk. But now she was almost ten and showing
every sign of catching up and possibly even overtaking
her brother. Her withered left leg would never grow as
strong or as supple as her right one but, in some strange
way, her miniature imperfection in a family of extreme
flawlessness, made her all the more attractive. Ideal girl.
Charles mentioned the suggestion of leaving America
one night at dinner. Wife glowed with admiration for her
clever man and offered all the support he could have
hoped for, children smiled adoring at perfect Papa.
Made-for-TV family, they would follow him anywhere,
fifties values gorgeously cloaked in millennial chic.
Charles considered himself an old-fashioned man with
modern virtues. From old money himself, he valued
wealth. Took it seriously. But he took care never to over-
estimate its importance to his life. (He didn't have to –
he'd always had plenty.) Money may have been his
bedrock, but family was what turned his house into
home. And wherever he went, Charles took his home
with him. The whole family – Australian nanny and new

kitten included – skipped from their Manhattan apartment without a backward glance. Daddy called and the other three followed, quick scuttle sideways across the Atlantic.

Luisa met the family at the airport herself. Ordered cabs for the nanny and children and kitten, drove Charles and his wife to the house in her own car. Luisa shook hands with Charles, was not surprised when the wife leaned in to kiss her on both cheeks, feigned interest in the kitten. She showed the happy family around the beautiful house, and then, while Charles showered and dressed again, Luisa was forced into small talk with the wife which left her feeling physically short and intellectually shrunk. She left the house in relief and drove him, fashion-plate fine, to his first meeting.

'I'm sorry to hurry you away like this.'

Luisa was polite and professional. So far, she felt nothing. Which is not to say nothing was happening. Charles smiled, nodded, lifted his left hand towards her, pulled it back again, then reached it out to lay on her arm, 'Really, Luisa, I expected to have to work today. What I didn't expect was that I'd get such personal attention. From you of all people. I know how very valuable your time must be.'

Charles left his hand on her arm a moment longer than necessary and Luisa was surprised when he moved it away. Surprised to be disappointed.

For the remainder of the journey Charles entertained Luisa with an account of his life. His strong family background, his years at college, meeting his wife, the birth of his first child, his career progress, his enthusiastic acceptance of the challenge of this new job. None of this was news to Luisa, she had, after all, been instrumental in choosing Charles as her semi-replacement, anyway. What was new was his attention to detail in the retelling. His concern that she should understand exactly what he meant when he explained his abiding affection for his late mother. His minute delight in the intricate details of both his town and summer houses. What was new was that Luisa did not expect to care. Did not pay that much attention to her own private life, was surprised anyone else did. Although she was aware that Charles was giving her an edited highlights version of his life, selected pieces so as to seem open and giving, while at exactly the same time holding close any information he did not wish to divulge. Luisa could see it was a useful technique – eagerly offer some details, quite a wide variety even, thereby forestalling the asking of any difficult questions.

Didn't your wife mind leaving her own work?

Aren't you worried about interrupting your children's education?

Why do you talk about your mother so much?

How is it that your home is so very important to you?

In their first proper meeting, Luisa realised Charles needed careful handling – very careful if she was to maintain any power and not end up being handled herself. In their first meeting, Luisa was still detached enough to notice this. But by the time she dropped Charles off at his own office, he'd already dug in one claw, draining her initial reserve of discernment. By the time she picked him up for drinks with the Board, she was already becoming attached to him and didn't even know it. But she would.

The Cancer man knows what he wants. He doesn't always show it, shout his intentions out loud, he is not Leo or Aquarius, after all. His is not a race that just anyone is welcome to applaud from the sidelines. But once he makes his mind up, his side-step dance becomes a tight grip hold, impossible to run away, even before you know you're caught.

When the disease takes hold, really takes hold, there is a choice. To fight and destroy, or to roll over and give in. Sometimes the destruction of the disease also involves a degree of destruction of the self. Sometimes giving in can be the best answer, the only real answer in the end – fighting uses up so much energy, and if there is no time left and nothing there but the disease, then why continue to fight it? Why not give in and learn to live with it rather than dying to live without it? And sometimes the disease creates a need to follow both patterns, one day giving in and giving up, ceding the self to what is bigger and stronger, other days fierce and unyielding, fighting to the last, rooting out and obliterating every last drop ·of the enemy within. Cancerous love – Charles is the opposite of the oncologist; the medical specialist who meets new people every day, people coming to her with hope of cure or, if not, then release. Charles meets new people every day, but this Cancer man picks his perfect individuals. Chooses himself a new victim, not always the most likely, not always the easiest either – but he knows her the minute he sees her. She is the Cancer man's dream – happy homemaker who will move into his life and arrange and take care and shine in moonlight. Be the perfect girl. Perhaps she reminds him of his mother, his original hard-shell soft woman. Perhaps she simply reminds him of himself – and from the moment he sees her Charles knows he wants her dark meat, means to have her, crack her open. He means to get in.

Charles took his time. Moved in, backwards again, soft sidle sideways, neat steps, clean. This man was born in the middle of the year, he straddles both halves, not quite starting, not quite ending. Of the sea and the shore, he is ebb and flow at the same time. Moves in and backs off while his shell-painted smile remains the same. He cannot be judged from where he rests in his perfect home with the perfect wife and delicious life – but neither can he ever be ignored, dismissed, he is too dangerous for that. Luisa did not notice the danger, simply saw the glinting sunlight sparkling diamonds from the back of his bright, salt-encrusted shell. He is beautiful. He knows it. He expects her to know it too. Charles took his time, but when he launched himself at her, there was no retreat to be had. For either of them. He is a man who knows his own mind. Unfortunately for Luisa, he knew hers too.

The Cancer man is adept at the art of flattery, understands when a woman wants hearts and flowers, desires serious passion or moon-lunatic laughter. He knows how to ration his secrets so that when she has finally finished unburdening her heart, the prospective lover will now realise that the Cancer man knows all of her mysteries and yet he has only just begun to intimate the truths of his own troubled soul. The crab is a fine fisherman.

Charles grabbed her in a pincer movement. One minute it was all hard shell and hard-working businessman and the next he was soft underbelly, take-me, make-me, break me open and please climb in.

Luisa was not used to the attention. She was small, dark, sallow-skinned. Not unattractive – just nothing all that special, really. Not noticeable. No reason for men to notice her. But Charles did. Charles smiled when he came into the office in the morning. Smiled at everyone, sidling down corridors, in and out of offices, grabbing hands and arms, scuttling through the building, making himself known. Every single day, making himself known, making his presence felt. And then he'd pop into Luisa's office, special smile, just for her. A sideways glance, a wink, a sly pinch on the back of her hand. It looked like the same greeting he gave everyone else, but there was that little bit more to it. Sometimes when she wasn't there, he'd leave a note on her desk. Nothing revealing, nothing incriminating. Just a 'Hi, hope you're well this morning.' Nothing at all, except that he got in. Except that he found his way far in. And once he was in deep enough, Charles started his real work.

The crab carries his home with him. He will not be invaded if he can possibly help it. His is the armour and the movement of attack. It is he who decides the moment.

They began the affair. Always at her apartment, never his house of course. And not obvious in the office either – his job, her job, both too important. But in private, on the hot beach of her sheets, there they crash-landed a desire that surprised them both. Tsunami lust. Charles had made plays for women before, maintained polite little affairs, discrete ways to let off the steam of his otherwise perfect life. Even he was surprised at how deep Luisa got into him. Dug herself right down, churned and then settled. But Charles could control himself. Was all control. Knew what he wanted, was deliciously pleased at the excess he received. Took it all in, looked carefully at his reactions, saw himself dangerously close to going in too deep and then stepped back, held it in, side-stepping crab, he neatly resettled himself. Now he had everything he wanted. All tidy, all perfect, and if both he and Luisa had been surprised by the extent of the lust, the extremes of desire, then Charles, at least, was well practised in reining in his emotions, taking what was necessary, and stepping back from the rest. He came close to the boiling passion, tested the steamy water, and jumped back. Not Luisa.

What could she do? She was a single career girl, just reaching the body-screaming stage. And delighted though she was with her career and her prospects, playing with Charles did too much to remind her of what else there might be, outside the office, beyond the company. How much more business could she do before it was all she was? Charles had the perfect family – she knew, she had met them. He had the beautiful home – she knew, she had found it for him before he'd even arrived. And he had the amazing job – Luisa knew that only too well. It was the job she'd handed over to him. Of course, the new part of the company was going well, it was her creation, her own new nest, painstakingly put together step by step, garnering more approval each day. But meeting Charles simply reminded Luisa that until now, with the brief exception of a few, doomed office flings – as often as not designed simply to move her one rung further up the ladder – she was all job. And it wasn't that she didn't want to be the hard-working woman, she just wanted all the rest as well.

Because Luisa was Cancer girl too. She wanted home and safety to hide in beneath her shell. Wanted to carry the perfect home with her always, but she discovered, as had so many other women of her age, that the mothers of sixties' change had forgotten to mention this to the powers that be, forgotten to let the big bosses know that the young women might also want what the men took for granted. Luisa had no picture-perfect wife waiting at home, with dinner on the table, body on the bed. She had the office and the career and far below in the priority list, she had her desires. And she wanted what he had. Once she was in under his shell, under his spell, she had a taste of what it might be like – the love and the life and the career. And it tasted too good to pass up on. But not immediately. Initially it was all the taste of him.

Cancer girl is mad woman, moon woman, happy smiling crying woman. And so very clever. She is looking for a rock to anchor herself on. It is work or home or brave self or him. She would be fine and intelligent and beautiful and artistic, the charming moon goddess beaming gorgeous smiles of creative joy. But only from a position of safety. A position of mutual safety. And she is easily rocked by the waves.

And Charles knew what he was looking at when he saw Luisa, Charles had the same desires himself. Got in. Charles found his way into her soft underbelly, showed her his, she showed him hers. He grabbed her close and held her heart sharp in his tight claws. Charles got in.

And stayed there. When he was not close, Luisa could still feel him. When she rattled around her small apartment alone, all she could see were the body-map lines on walls they had fallen against kissing, the wet towels which he let fall having showered the scent of her from his skin, the dent in her bed where his body should have been. Because his clothes must always be perfect, he took to leaving clean shirts at her apartment, something fresh to wear before he returned to his home. Charles' home was kept fresh and perfect, while Luisa left behind all pretence that her apartment was anything like a home and acknowledged it had become simply a dry pit that she kept ready for the man. Waiting for the tide of him to rush in and fill her up again.

Charles decided he should come home with Luisa on Friday nights. They could leave the office together perfectly amicably. She was taking him home, his house was on her way, it saved on petrol and was greener after all, better for the environment, more economical all round. Though they never used his car. More economical for Charles' environment. He came back to Luisa just for one hundred and fifty exact minutes and then he left her to return to his family for their weekend treats. Once Luisa left his coffee cup unwashed for two days when he went away to the ocean with the family. Left the cup on her bedside table, took it to work with her. Held it to her mouth where his lips had been. Charles took the family to the beach for the weekend and they played in rock pools and fished for shrimps. Luisa worked at the office all weekend to stave off the pain and held his cup to her lips. Breathing in the had-been-him.

Cancer is taken by the tides, affected always by the ebb and flow of the moon. It is truly consistent only in the constancy of its changes. It is the time sign, tidal sign, where suffering is an art form and tears true beauty. It can howl and laugh out loud at the moon in the same breath, on the same upbeat backbeat.

Charles was her disease. Luisa suffered from him. For him, in him, without him. When she initially diagnosed her excessive need, she was shocked. And then delighted. This was what she had been longing for. Often without even knowing. What her would-be-star soul desired. She was silent movie heroine and basking in his lust, shining with returned passion. Without him Luisa languished – and watched herself doing so – and thought it looked good. With him she shone. It was delicious, it tasted perfect. It was in the beginning. New disease, new wardrobe of desires. She was the tragic heroine and she loved herself for it. Though not for long. All too soon it began to hurt. Charles could not speak to her in the evenings, the weekend, would not return her calls to his mobile phone on a lonely Sunday night. Practically ignored her in the office – just in case. Except for the occasional stolen kisses, the one dangerous fuck on her desk, the grope in the lift. And then it was that most days she felt the stabbing pain of wanting what she could not have. Could have some of, was welcome to partake in pieces of, but was never allowed to devour whole. Luisa could not have all of her chosen one, the one who had chosen her, and it was beginning to eat her up. Charles was her beautiful disease and she only realised that he was making her sick once he was already inside and growing.

The Cancer woman will heroically sacrifice herself for a partner, a child, a project she believes in. She chooses her course of action and sticks to it, sticks through it to the end. Bitter or not.

Lisa did not neglect her office job, was too well-trained, too ingrained in the task of being the business girl, to ever allow her workday life to slip. Being the successful one in the sharpest suit was all she had wanted since she first entered the cool chrome foyer of the building. There was no way, not even with the rolling waves he was creating in her life, that Charles could affect the consummate, creative efficiency she brought to the building with every breath. Charles was there, in the office, in the reconditioned air swirling around her. He was a part of everything she did. She continued to be successful, thrusting forward, taking the company higher and higher. Partly she was such a dynamic whirlwind because Charles was there. Because his being close energised her. Luisa did not neglect her office job. She neglected her life. Luisa tidied and smoothed her home every Friday before dawn. Rose at five in the morning so that everything would be perfect for the two and a half hours Charles spent in her apartment on the Friday evening. Shopped at lunchtime and took home the most perfect sweetmeats, most tempting wines. On Friday evening between six and eight thirty her home was paradise shore. The rest of the time it was dried-up desert. Mud flats of wasteland, waste Luisa, what a waste. She was a paragon of vital strengths at the office, fantastic professional for whom no task was too great, no small duty too mundane. But Luisa found she forgot to eat when

Charles was not with her, forgot to drink when she was not pouring for him. Forgot to be when he was not close.

The Cancer woman follows a moonbeam direction. Will walk purposely along it, even when the deceptive silver light leads her into the deepest, most dangerous waters.

Luisa wanted all of Charles. Charles did not have all of himself to give. And even if he had, he was not prepared to give it. He already had the wife who demanded all of him, the children who demanded all of him, the job that demanded all of him. There was no more all for Luisa to claim. She knew this was not good. Even from within the whirlwind of desire, she knew this was not good. Luisa the businesswoman developed a new strategy. Had one, single, glaring moment of blinding awareness and knew better. She would make Charles a project just like any other. When he was not around, she would dismiss him from her thoughts. He would be a workplace dream. It was a beautiful idea, but impossibly impractical. And it was also too late. Even when she started, Luisa was aware she was fooling herself. Charles had burrowed in and was growing inside her.

The crab is furious in its tenacity. It is unlikely to let go without a fight. It would rather lose its own claw than set you free. After all, it can always grow another one.

When she tried to cut him out, her Cancer man proved he had already found another way in. Cutting him out of her life – not calling for three days, not answering her phone for two, did not help. There were always manufac-

tured work reasons for Charles to make contact and
anyway, not talking to him just made her want to do it
more. Deciding not to think about him, made him part of
every thought. She was hungry, she thought of him
eating, laughing, lunching in the office canteen that she
avoided. She was thirsty, and she thought of drinking
with him. Cool wine, hot coffee. Sipping from his lips,
drinking him into her, feeling the cool of him slip down
her throat. She was sleeping and she'd wake hoping
Charles was sleeping beside her, dreaming he slept sound
beside her. She cried and the tears ran hot and salty
down the back of her throat, branding her tender flesh
with the idea of him. Every time she tried to pretend that
Charles was not constantly there with her, the image of
him burned itself deeper onto the back of her eyelids.
Every time she tried to dig him out, he pushed the ten-
drils of desire in deeper still. Because she had invited
them to. He was her Cancer man and she had made him
part of her cellular structure, willingly invited him into
her life. Luisa knew that she had encouraged him to
become part of her – had hoped Charles might become
her escape, when even she now saw that he was her dead
end. And Charles loved it. Every moment.

*It is, of course, important never to push the Cancer woman too
far. The girl crab, too, has a fierce and vicious pinch. She may
scuttle out of harm's way whenever possible, she may find
herself the victim of her own changing moods more often than
not but, when cornered – or when the moon is just too damn
full – she will attack. To the end.*

At the end of another long week, after the two and a half

hour limit of their passion, after Charles had gone and left her apartment cold and empty, Luisa woke up and looked around her. Saw the desolation, recognised the shipwreck she had become. And quick, clever, perceptive crab, she knew then that it was time to make an end. Now she knew she was going to have to cut him out. Quit. Cold turkey. Stop, just like that. Make it be over. There was no other way, the disease had spread too far. Cut and burn. Charles had Luisa, held her fast in his pincer grip. She would have to force him to let her go.

Dressed crab, potted crab, crab salad. Kanisu – Japanese crab and cucumber rolls, crab and cucumber salad. Filo pastry rolls filled with crab and coriander. Crab cakes. Crab chowder. Crab cannelloni with tomato sauce. Crab, orange and avocado salad. Crab marinated with sweet peppers, baked in a light pastry tart. Crab omelette. Crab rösti. Fresh crab salad with balsamic vinaigrette.

But first, catch your crab.

Catch the crab in a fresh rock pool, at the shore, where it is most at home, where it feels safe.

Luisa made her careful way into Charles' safe house. Masquerading as the temporary nanny while the real nanny was ill. Hungry Australian girl laid low with food poisoning from the crab sandwich Luisa had sold her on the street the night before – Nanny Janet's appetite had always been her undoing. Just as Charles' over-eager desires were his. Sensible wife, then, to employ a fat and homely nanny.

Isolate the disease so that treatment may be directed at the area most at risk, minimising the chances of affecting surrounding areas.

Luisa collected the children from their driver and saw them off to school. She had met them just the once at the airport when the family first arrived and the two little ones had been far too excited about the new land, new life, to recognise her again now. Luisa knew the wife was away on business for three days. She had picked her time very carefully. Luisa settled herself in Charles' study.

Do not bother trying to catch your crab when it is still and quiet. It will always see you coming. You are actually more likely to successfully hunt your prey when still waters are agitated, when the crab is preoccupied with other matters.

The 'temporary nanny' did not arrive after school to pick up the children, Charles was called out from a major meeting at work to fetch them, Luisa had not even called into the office to explain her absence and, for once, he was not able to dump his troubles on her desk. By the time Charles finally dropped the children off with his wife's new friend and her own two small ones, rushed back to the office to take care of the last of his business, and made it home alone, he was more than flustered. And Luisa had not returned any of his calls. He was agitated and furious. And not careful.

Taking care of your own delicate fingers and sensitive big toes, grab the crab's shell, hold it high above the ground. Beneath the strong, red shell you will see its delicate, pale, soft flesh. Delicious flesh.

'Hello, Charles.'

As soon as is humanly possible, plunge the crab into boiling water. Do not waste any time. The salted water should be hot enough to be on a bubbling, rolling boil.

Luisa threw herself across the room to Charles, kissed him hard and fast, took him by surprise. Took him. In his own home, for the first time ever. Charles broke his own cardinal rule. But Luisa was too strong for him, too much for him, too powerful for him. And anyway, this was what he really wanted. To have her here, in his house, in the holy of holies. To be daring enough, just once, to break his own rules. She knew that.

Keep the water boiling hard and fast.

Luisa was still taking him, taking him in, when his beautiful and perfect wife walked into her own bedroom. Luisa had been in the study beside the answerphone when the wife left Charles a message. The wife had also heard from the school, she would be on the first train home. She would be extremely anxious about the children's safety. The young and impressionable children stood at the door and watched their mother confront their father.

Lift the crab carefully from the boiling water.

The wife and children returned to New York. They took the nanny with them. And the cat. But not Charles.

Then plunge the still hot crab into iced water, bringing the temperature down immediately.

Charles could not cope without the beautiful wife, the kiss of the pretty children. His work began to suffer.

With both chemo- and radiotherapy there is a risk of collateral damage to surrounding tissue, other organs. Most cancer patients recognise that this potential damage is an acceptable danger when dealing with the greater problem.

There was nothing they could do, he was clearly not coping. It had all become too much for him – the company was forced to let Charles go. Luisa had to abandon her new project and return to her original position. She found she felt little regret. And she willingly accepted Charles' greater rate of pay. And his bigger office. And his nicer company car.

Using a small fork, carefully dig out the soft crab flesh. The claws are easily cracked with a nutcracker or small hammer – the flesh here is often sweeter.

Luisa wasn't all that interested in Charles' newly appointed pretty little secretary. She was interested in skills. And timekeeping. And complete loyalty. The secretary left quite quickly.

The juiciest flesh is always worth the trouble.

Charles scuttled back across the Atlantic to attempt happy families one more time. He knew it might be hard work but he was tough. And willing. And running very scared.

A clean bill of health may take up to five years. But with care and a sensible routine, most people go on to enjoy a long and fruitful life.

Luisa chose then to dedicate herself to work for a while. She still bore the marks of Charles' claws. And really, scraping her own nails over the scars was pleasant enough. For now.

The flesh should be fresh. And meltingly delicious. Enjoy the fruits of your own hard work.

Eventually, Luisa replaced the secretary with an assistant. A charming young man. With no other ties. And a fine array of skills. Not all of them office-based.

It is never wise to disturb the sleeping crab. She may seem terribly sensitive, and it is true, the Cancer woman is a tender and delicate soul. Just like the moon, though, she can turn overnight. Beware the lady in the moon.

patrick mccabe

....

they didn't come from barntrosna

There was a time if you'd said: 'There were cyborgs in this town one time, you know,' they'd have looked at you as if you were mad. But not any more, not by a long shot. That was a lesson they had to learn the hard way. I was sitting in my local enjoying a quiet drink as I usually do when I'm finished work at the library, when Barney Filkin, a neighbour of mine, and a part-time fitter/welder by trade, came in and said, to nobody in particular, it seemed to me at the time: 'You know, the strangest thing just happened.'

By all accounts, he had been out at the Foster place which is a big spread just outside of Barntrosna on the Conageehy Road, and was making his way home when some kind of a strange light appeared just up ahead of him, like a rectangular sheet of purest luminescence just hanging there in front of him. He was quite distressed as he continued his story, sipping intermittently from a glass held by what was incontrovertibly an extremely unsteady hand. 'The first thing I thought of straightaway, of course, was aliens,' he continued, 'and kind of half-expected to be transported to the ship, wherever they had it, for experiments or whatever.' He paled as he recollected there in the late evening gloom of the quiet bar – the factory hooter had not yet sounded and the double doors had yet to be flung open to admit the red-cheeked, white-capped men of *Barntrosna Tasty Meats* in single-minded search of any number of well-earned, thirst-quenching beverages – the pressure of his single prominent front tooth forming a thin white tapeworm on the soft pink flesh of his lower lip as he endeavoured valiantly to quell his anxieties, turning to me to stare, drawn-cheeked, and say: 'But, Pats! It was nothing like that at all, you see!' Such was the level of his tension that his pupils seemed enlarged almost to a degree that the very bar itself would be incapable of containing them. It took the best part of an hour and any number of calming libations before he returned to even what might be considered an approximation of himself. As I recall that evening beneath the pixillated, tyre-circled dartboard, the words which come to my mind again and again are those he tremulously spoke each time the glittering rim of the glass touched his lips: 'Never in a million years did I think it would be like that, Pats. In a million years – not ever!'

I am well regarded in this, the town of Barntrosna, and I expect that is why a lot of the inhabitants are prepared to wholeheartedly put their trust in me. There is a heartening, olde-worlde respect for learning in these parts, and it would be little but spurious false modesty to disavow that my reputation as something of a scholar and fascinating teller of tales (which of course has been something of a family tradition down through the years – my Uncle Maurice, a fabled local historian before his tragic death in his Morris Minor in 1963, to this day spoken of in terms which can only be described as 'hushed', due to his awesome stature) has something to do with it.

Even I, however, despite my many years' experience – albeit part-time – as a novelist, crime and science-fiction writer of some distinction (I rarely allude to my historical biographies in this context as it is a genre in which I have not toiled in any significant way for many years, but *Seamus Charps – Conscience of A Liberator*, chronicling the life and times of a Barntrosna native who worked for some time in Daniel O'Connell's house, and *Stabbed To Death*, an inventory of the deaths which took place throughout the turbulent years of the 1790s and *Jack McGush – A Life*, are still available from any good bookshop – certainly from our local library where there are at least seventy-five copies of each title) had never heard anything quite like my neighbour's story; or in the wildest of my dreams anticipated that within a matter of days, what had seemed to be a slightly worrying tale of one man's experiences and his own personal perceptions of what Mr Joyce in his writings has described as the 'ineluctable modality of the visible', proved to be for him little short of an emotion and temporal maelstrom into which not only he had found himself unwittingly pitched, but as we soon discovered, I too, and practically everybody domiciled within a three-mile radius of our town!

The first indication I had that these events were going to involve me – indeed, that I was to become a major figure, I suppose you could call it – in the inexorable movement of the drama (although of course I did not realise it at the time) – that had already begun to significantly gather momentum. Not that there was anything untoward to be perceived as I took my dog Pongo for a walk that evening on the Cloanaboghey Road, as I always do, instinctively greeting my neighbours as I made my way past the sunheaded rows of wild flowers and intricate brambles arrayed all along the bird-chirping banks. Pongo, as a rule, is widely considered to be among the most placid of creatures – by all but the most irascible of our citizens – so when he began to bark loudly and strain fiercely at his lead, I naturally was consumed by a strange combination of pure, undiluted fear and untramelled, eager curiosity. But at no time did these words cross my mind: 'Pongo is barking because he knows there are cyborgs in this area!' In fact, I attributed his excitement to the presence of nothing more unusual than a freshwater rat furtively scurrying along the bank beneath the stone parapets of the nearby bridge, or even less spectacular, a passing insect, such as a dragonfly or wasp, perhaps, which had escaped my notice. 'Perhaps,' I found myself considering, 'his state of heightened sensitivity is attributable to a lack of calcium in his diet, for recent reading in *Pet News* had alerted me to the fact that there had of late been a disquieting amount of concern with regard to *Bounce*, the particular brand of dogfood to which he was accustomed and had been part of his staple diet right from his very early years as a small pup. The more consideration I gave to this particular possibility, the more I became convinced that I had identified the source of the animal's by now fur-tautening tension.

Such was the degree of certainty with which I drew this conclusion that I felt my whitened knuckles bunch into a fist about the weatherbeaten leather of my favourite pet's leash. 'Of course!' I repeated excitedly, 'After all, what other explanation could there be for it!' Rarely have I been so resolute in a conviction as I was upon that midge-ridden sun-dappled day.

I was wrong.

For, only minutes later, about the branches of a large chestnut tree which rose up before my trusty hound and I as we turned the corner, an eerie light began to gather, disparate strains of the cloud which was forming seeming to converge just directly up ahead of us and beneath the wig-like entanglements of majestic green foliage, the power of its glare becoming such that I could no longer discern the location of the small animal who for many years has been my pride and joy. Within a matter of seconds finding myself propelled forward, my safety ensured only by the presence of a privet hedge close by the five-barred gate above which the shimmering con-figuration – now suffusing the entire stretch of roadway back as far as Tom McConnie's – trembled ominously like so many strung elastic bands composed entirely of light. I could think of nothing to say and without due consideration cried out: 'Who are you? What do you want?' as Pongo continued to bark furiously, at once advancing and retreating, his staccatoed ejaculations as so many tiny arrows consumed without effort by the seemingly bottomless maw of the ever-enlarging living magnesium-flare of the light-sheet which now – to my horror – enveloped him. It is incumbent upon us all as citizens of what has often been termed this island earth and inhabitants of he universe in this infinitesimal stratosphere in which we find ourselves, to extend the hand of friendship to any extra-terrestrials or their associates who might take it upon themselves to visit us. In less enlightened times, perhaps through fear or insecurity or a combination of both, this was not the attitude. If a metallic, silver, cigar-shaped module was seen to be flying in the sky, it was not the instinct – and never has been, in living memory – either of the military or those in government charged by us to act on our behalf, to engage our visitors in calm, reasoned, exploratory dialogue designed ultimately to lead to a deeper understanding between us all. Rather, almost without exception, their response has been to cry: 'Fire!' and 'Blow them out of the fucking sky, men!'

For many years, I have held such unenlightened, essentially parochial ideas in contempt. I pleaded consistently for 'understanding' and 'interplanetary cultural exchange'. But, as I enjoined the clandestine travellers located somewhere within this shape-shifting aurora borealis now grown so it hung between two trees like a giant hammock, consistently receiving no response, not even the slightest acknowledgement for my efforts, I began to feel within me the first discomfiting needle-prickings of what can only be called impatience. I, as a citizen both of Barntrosna and earth, respected unquestionably and without reservation, their right to visit my planet, but surely I too was entitled to some measure of courtesy. 'Who are you!' I cried anew as Pongo – having been located at last, whimpering behind a dock leaf – with renewed, heartening vigour, took runs and flying leaps at the continuously metamorphosing chimera that seemed to fluctuate forever just beyond the reach of his nose. Once again I requested some measure of social acknowledgement, and again found myself ignored. It was not my intention to irritate our visitors or indeed give them any excuse whereby they might feel themselves entitled to justifiably take umbrage and thus possibly endanger relations between us, but I really think that – for any individual – there is a level of good manners and simple honest-to-goodness courtesy which simply has to be preserved and if that is not there then it just cannot be considered acceptable. And which was why I cried out: 'Ah for Christ's sake, can't you answer the question!' and later, 'I'll ask you one more time, do you hear me? One more time!' For that reason and that alone.

There have been many versions of this particular incident circulating in the environs of Barntrosna since its occurrence, including that favoured by Josie Gurk who claims he was shortcutting through the fields on his way to the Bridge Bar when he saw me 'kicking and punching nothing' and 'roaring at the top of my voice'. To which allegation – persistently repeated in various hostelries to the point of tedium, of course, and Mr Gurk enjoying the sophisticated timbre of no one's voice quite so much as his own – I can only reply that perhaps a good idea might be if this same gentleman took it upon himself to attend to his farming duties once in a while, and graced the slop-dappled, morbid interior of The Bridge Bar with his presence a little less.

For – regardless of what idle chatter the idiot goes on with – at no time did I become abusive. I simply asked a few questions. Certainly I was peeved – that I have never denied. But to descend to the level of physical abuse – it simply never happened. I am not a physical person. Never have been. And the idea that I would willingly assault a visitor to our shores is completely and utterly abhorrent to me. The fact is that any difficulty which transpired was, I assure, not of my making. If the cyborgs wished to be made welcome, perhaps it might have been an idea for them, before they considered embarking on an epoch-making journey anywhere, to devote a little time to the study of the social code and mores of earth in general and our town in particular, and then, presumably, they might have a more successful 'fact-finding' mission, or whatever ill-planned, hare-brained idea it was brought the cheeky fuckers down here in the first place. Which was a question I put to their leader, when at last he did decide to honour me with an appearance and pay some acknowledgement to the fact that I had been trying to attract his attention for almost three quarters of an hour. At that time of course I had no idea that he and his inter-galactic travelling companions were cyborgs, for, despite my considerably voluminous writings peripherally connected with this field, I pretend to be no expert and for me one alien is pretty much the same as another. But, let me tell you, I was soon left in no doubt as to the exact definitions of the generic status when, emerging from within the plume of smoke which at that moment discharged itself from the heart of the by now quite dazzling machine, a large half-man, half-machine informed me in a tinny, mechanical-sounding voice that he was Trygon, leader of the cyborgs. I extended my hand but he declined, insisting that it wasn't the custom on his planet as most of its inhabitants didn't have hands. 'The great majority of cyborgs have either steel claws or three-

pronged hooks for the purposes of motor tasks,' he
declared. 'Hands as you know them are unknown in our
part of the galaxy.' It was the first time I had ever
encountered anyone from further away than thirty miles
from the Barntrosna district, and I was certainly taken by
the sight which now presented itself before me and there
is no doubt about that. I suppose Trygon was in the
region of seven foot three or thereabouts, in many ways
resembling the earthling as we know him only quite a
good deal taller, of course, and possessing a lot more
mechanical parts than we ever would. I noticed that the
backs of his legs were entirely constructed from wire and
a complex arrangement of intersecting metal coils, and
that the base of his jaw was fashioned from the brightest
shining steel. He had no eyes, of course, as very few
cyborgs apparently have, their function performed, it
would seem, by a six-inch refracting visor of black glass
or perspex, of about one-and-a-half inches in width and
six in length, which he could rotate at will by means of a
computer memory bank stored in his brain, and with
which he could see around corners. Emblazoned in
beautifully-calligraphed letters across the flesh-coloured
plate he had bolted to his chest was the single word
Trygon in bold capitals. It was while I gave my full attention to this that there followed a potentially disastrous
moment when Pongo, prompted by the sudden whirring
of the rotating visor, leaped forward and sank his teeth
into the cyborg's multi-riveted heel. I had but time to cry
out: 'Pongo!' Before the strange visitor from a distant
star's defensive laser beam – which of course was acti-
vated straightaway – completely obliterated a conifer tree
directly behind me. Terrified as I was, I hurled myself

forward and scooped up the idiotic animal, shielding both of us as best I could as I cried: 'Don't shoot! Don't shoot!' The alerted semi-mechanical juggernaut was on the verge of unleashing another death-dealing sword of lethal light when it dawned on him exactly what was happening and in his memory bank, the dot matrix scanner formed the words: *Threat eliminated.* I have to admit that it was a nasty moment, though, and there can be no doubt about the alarming levels of anxiety experienced by both of us – my trusty but headstrong pet and I – but after that, relations between myself and my strange companion improved somewhat. In answer to my questions, he responded that as it was expected that the natural mineral resources of their own planet were expected to practically disappear in an unspecified number of years – studies by their most respected scientists were still ongoing – it had been decided that he, Trygon, and a selected few trusted and respected men-machines would travel to other galaxies and solar systems and investigate the possible existence of other locations where resources might be available, with a view to establishing trade links which would be of mutual benefit to both parties. The longer we engaged in explanatory discourse, the greater my sympathies for him and the plight of his clearly inevitably-doomed world became. And when he inquired as to whether I would be in a position to be of assistance to them, essentially because of my knowledge of the terrain – which is considerable, thanks to my work as secretary of the county-wide Literary and Historical Society – I had no hesitation whatsoever in responding in the most positive terms. Whereupon I was invited into the interior of the ship, which of course was, as it transpired, a metallic silver cigar-shaped module, and for a single fleeting moment found myself overwhelmed by the erratic symphony of lights and assorted coloured bulbs which assailed my vision, not to mention the bank of television monitors which played havoc with Pongo's natural instincts, reducing him to a state of nostril-sweating fever and irrational behaviour, ultimately culminating in his advance towards a seemingly innocuous lever which, when firmly in the grip of the terrier's teeth, proceeded to have the effect of disgorging seemingly interminable yards of white computer paper containing a myriad of inexplicable codes and symbols, within seconds engulfing the howling, perplexed animal. It was only with the assistance of two cyborgs that I succeeded in liberating the unfortunate creature from his paper prison.

It was then time for us to set off for the town and after a moment or two's discussion, it was considered that it might be prudent to employ the use of the ship's teleporter, what with all the labyrinthine explanations we would be at pains to give if we were, as we undoubtedly would, to encounter some of the local citizenry along the road. Not to mention veiled hostility, which even in these enlightened times, is still very much a part of life in the town of Barntrosna. I had no great wish to find myself in a situation whereby I would be compelled to explain to Trygon what is meant by the term 'blow-ins' and similar would-be euphemistic terms of disapproval. Knowing the town as I do, I have to confess that I harboured some anxieties that we might find ourselves in even more unpleasant situations. What, for example, would I say to Trygon if we were to encounter Jimmy Skutch from

Billagalawna Villas, whose sociopathic tendencies were well known in the town, but could be deeply troubling, if not totally and utterly mystifying to those from outside its boundaries. An image of his drooling, brandy-suffused face as he emerged from The Congo Arms came into my mind and I stiffened with horror as I perceived him acquiring the equilibrium he sought with the aid of the petrol pump which was located nearby, removing the thin streak of stout which had drawn itself across his upper lip and, with a logic-defying, devastatingly effective sweep of his forearm, crying: 'Go on cyborg! Youse'll get no water about here! Get water on youser own fucking planet if you want it! What do youse think we are? The St Vincent de Paul? Out to fuck, youse crowd of clanky bastards!'

I cold feel the blood drain from my face as at once I cried: 'To the teleporter! Now!'

On first entering the cell-displacement machine, Pongo was again uneasy, as I could discern from the rising hairs upon his back and the sharp dart of his hazel eyes about their sockets. But he need not have worried, for the transportation of protean matter across a small area such as was our requirement is but a matter of seconds and before we knew it, we were standing in the lounge of The Bridge Bar, beneath the photograph of the All-Ireland team which had scooped the Sam Maguire cup in 1962. The barman, whose name is Peter, and is a long-standing friend of mine, was delighted to see us and beckoned us over with his customary good nature. He flipped table mats onto the counter in front of us and said cheerfully: 'God, lads! I didn't see youse standing there at all!'

'Peter,' I said, 'these are some friends of mine. Trygon,

this is Peter. They're from outside the town – here on business.'

Peter grinned as he shook Trygon's hand, a quizzical frown forming as he remarked: 'God bless us! That's a queer kind of hand! If I didn't know, I'd say it was flesh-coloured metal!'

'It is flesh-coloured metal, Peter,' I said. 'Trygon was in a car accident some years ago. He was deprived of all his extremeties.'

'I'm sorry to hear that,' Peter said. 'The sooner this new drink-driving bill is introduced the better. The quality of driving in this county is cat altogether. Cat now and that's a fact! Anyhow, gents – what'll it be?'

As we received our foaming pints, a warm glow settled over us and it was with some pride I viewed my new companions. By my side Pongo relished the trayful of salted peanuts and crisps generously provided for him by the warm-hearted barman, and I gave my full attention to Trygon who, in that odd Dalek-like mechanical voice of his, was explaining to me how glad he was that they had had the good fortune to come to earth, and particularly Barntrosna, on their what to all intents and purposes was a life-or-death mission. It was a great source of pride to me to hear that such an auspicious traveller and evidently highly-regarded physicist should hold our town in such high regard and it is to my eternal shame that I did not act sooner to prevent the decline of the evening which, had I been perceptive enough, I would have seen as inevitable. I had been aware for some time of a certain disgruntled presence located in the vicinity – directly below the butcher's calendar on the south-facing wall, in fact – but had not succeeded, due to the dimness of the light and the harsh, uncompromising design of the flock wallpaper, in identifying this as the figure of Ed Squires, a local journalist and noted curmudgeon, who compiled the greater percentage of his material for his column *Squireye* in *The Barntrosna Standard* in that very corner, and who was now approaching us with his steel-grey brow knitted in a firm knot of unmistakable hostility. The corners of his mouth resembled two fangs of flesh and I could tell by the glazed patina that filmed his eyes that he had an amount of drink consumed. As might be expected, he addressed himself in the first instance to myself, resting his hand on my shoulder and slowly releasing the words from his mouth like some steady, deliberate, slow-acting poison.

'So, McElhinney,' he began, 'who's this you have with you today?' A few new recruits for the Barntrosna Literary and Historical Society perhaps?'

I flushed deeply, shamed before my companions by the sour note struck by the interlocutor, and the inevitably dispiriting effect it was having on the proceedings. Pongo fixed the unsteady with a canine glare that left no room for ambiguity.

'No,' I began, 'they're not, actually. They're visitors to Barntrosna, in fact.'

When Squires heard this, a gleam unmistakably signifying extreme interest came into his eye and he seated himself beside me, calling to Peter for a quintuplet Hennessy brandy on the rocks, and producing from the inside pocket of his sports coat the standard-sized spiral bound notebook and eraser-headed pencil. 'Well now,' he continued as he gingerly licked the lead of the pencil, 'what exactly is it that brings you here to our little town?' I was about to cry out – I could feel the words forming on the tip of my tongue with an acidic tingle – 'Don't tell him anything! Lie through your teeth, Trygon! But give him no information!' – but I was momentarily distracted by the sudden crash of the opening door and the ensuing blinding flash of sunlight, out of which emerged the aforementioned Jimmy Skutch, standing before us with his Fair Isle sweater in tatters, the fly of his stonewashed jeans open wide and a murderous glare in his eye. After an initial burst of what can only be described as a surreal-istic, infantilistic babble, his words began to make a kind of sense and it could be gleaned from his continuing disseminations that he had been unfairly evicted from the nearby premises of Dano Beggs, an establishment known as The Stoop Your Head. His cheeks flushed a fierce crimson as he fixed Peter with an unrepentant stare, as if the barman by nature of his calling was somehow impli-cated in this recent act of defenestrative treachery, and growled: 'Beggs'll pay! Make no mistake! Beggs'll pay for the day he tossed out Jimmy Skutch!'

Perhaps if I had followed my instincts and my bur-geoning sense of unease and incipient truculence, what transpired within the next few moments and which led ultimately to the damning indictment of our town and its long-touted *cead mile failte* (i.e. hundred thousand welcomes) which it purported to extend towards strangers, might never have happened. But, whether through cowardice or embarrassment or perhaps a com-bination of both, I held my tongue and must accept my undoubted share of the blame for what led to the sad events which followed and which now, without any of us realising it, began to unfold. The first indication that there was a possibility that things might go awry manifested itself when Ed Squires, addressing himself to Trygon in a most forthright manner, inquired of him as to what the purpose of his visit might be. Trygon, although initially taken aback somewhat by what he would have considered the sheer brazenness of the question (Trygons abhorring social indiscretions of any sort), regained his composure quite quickly, presenting himself in the half-light with remarkable insouciance, even when Squires, raising the cigarette to his lips, out of the side of his mouth snidely suggested that the purpose of their quest might be a search for 'spare parts'. The reporter was then assailed by a wracking bout of cigarette-induced coughing that seemed in its ferocity like the relentless tearing in some back-street grocery store of so many brown paper bags. The effect of this was to double him over, simultaneously provoking from the lewdly-attired Jimmy Skutch the comment that such afflictions were they to continue would 'not do him any harm' and might serve, as he put it, to encourage him to 'shut his mouth and give his arse a chance once in a while'. A remark to which it appeared the journalist was about to react in the strongest possible way when the door once more opened to admit a local fisherman of some renown, The Red Killeen, who without a word settled himself at the bar counter and in total silence proceeded to roll himself a cigarette. A silence however which was soon significantly pierced by the raucous interlocutions of Jimmy Skutch who, steadying himself against a pillar directly underneath a poster announcing to the people of Barntrosna a circus which had been and gone many years before, invited all present to raise their glasses to 'the meanest

shitehawk who ever trod shoe leather in Barntrosna –
ladies and gentlemen, the one and only Red Killeen!'

With this, he burst into uncontrollable laughter and
cried anew, jabbing the air with an index finger remi-
niscent not so much of sausages as black puddings: 'Look
at him! Pretends he doesn't hear me! Do you not hear
me? Not hear me, do you not, Mr Ride-the-Crabs-in-
the-Skillet?'

What perhaps unsettled me not a little was the fact that
I was conversant with the knowledge that the object of
Mr Skutch's derision was not renowned in the locality for
his temperate and restrained nature. That and the words
which then came drifting past my eyes, as Trygon's visor
trawled the gloom of the public house in order to glean
from my expression some indication as to how best interpret the by now exhaustively persistent interrogations of
Ed Squires, who was not only glaring into the rotating
rectangle of black glass of the Trygon, but poking him
incessantly with his pencil and forcibly demanding information which the cyborg was clearly reluctant to divulge.
'If you were in an accident, then why don't you just say
that! Why don't you tell me! How else do you explain
why one half of you is wires and screws and Jesus Mary
and Joseph knows what and the rest of you is ordinary
plasma? For the love of Christ it's not too much of a
question to answer is it? Huh? Huh, my friend?'

How Squires came to work himself up into quite such a
state, to this day I have not quite fathomed, but clearly
what he had decided to interpret as the cyborg's obstinate
refusal to co-operate with the media had produced the
effect of suffusing his cheeks with a deep red glow and
the pencil was attacking the air with a renewed fervour.

'You think just because you're with this bollocks you don't have to answer my questions, is that it?' he snarled and to my eternal shame, I could restrain myself no longer. 'Shut up, Squires, you hopeless excuse for a smalltown hack! He's under no obligation to talk to you or answer any of your so-called questions!'

At this point, it is incumbent upon me to reveal that there has been a long-standing spleen between Squires and me, dating back to the time when I replaced him as chairperson of the Barntrosna L&H Society. Slowly he turned and, facing me with a spiteful, malevolent gaze, spat shards of distilled, almost solidified hate in my direction. 'Well, well. If it isn't Pats McElhinney, nancy boy of all time with his famous books! All tough now, are we, since we got in with the men-machines!'

'Shut up!' barked an unmistakable voice from the bar and the copperheaded bulk of The Red Killeen shot a scowl towards the lizard-faced reporter. This appeared to act as a spur to Jimmy Skutch who up until that moment had been silent, as if lost in contemplation, perhaps considering his next move, but who now opened his mouth to reveal a black-toothed crevasse not unlike a long-since disused mining shaft from which rang out the words: 'Shut up, Killeen! You effing bastard of a crab-riding son of a prostitute-soliciting sailor! What good are you and what good were you ever, you useless fish-stinking scrapings of an eskimo's barrel!

It is a truism in the area that to confront The Red Killeen in any manner, however coded or circumlocutory, is at the very least unwise and, within a matter of seconds, Jimmy Skutch found himself regretting his intemperate musings as the fingers of The Red Killeen

closed tightly about the waist of a beer barrel. Unbeliev-
ably, however, Ed Squires continued with his – as he
would see them – 'necessary investigations' and, by dint
of his ceaseless pencil-prodding, had succeeded in
extracting from the head cyborg, the information that
they were on a mission to find water, any quantities whatsoever of the natural mineral that they could succeed in
locating, due to the fact that the supplies of that 'elixir of
life which is not valued' had all but become exhausted on
their planet. All of a sudden I was seized by a blind panic.
'That's none of your business, Squires!' I cried, lunging
forward in an unsuccessful attempt to snap his pencil in
two. I turned to the cyborgs, all of whose visors were now
concentrating on me and my unconsidered ululations,
continuing: 'Tell him nothing! Him and his gutter press
will destroy you!' Ed Squires looked at me and laughed
scornfully. 'Look at him,' he said to Trygon. 'He calls
himself the secretary of the L&H. He works in a library
and he objects to the sharing of information. What next,
McElhinney? Banning the internet? Don't make me
laugh! Secretary? You couldn't secrete an envelope to
save your life, you pathetic joker!'

To this day I cannot fathom what happened next.
Somehow, through a combination of guile and the
reporter's natural instincts, Squires succeeded in gaining
the cyborg's confidence, insisting that it was 'important'
that the more planets 'knew each other', the better. It
must have been a mere matter of minutes before information was pouring out of Trygon's mouth. 'No!' I cried,
'can't you see?' But it was useless. Being from another
culture, Trygon could not understand. How could he
have been expected to? What could he possibly have

made of my mindless rantings, those wild traffic controller-type gesticulations which accompanied my Cassandra-like strictures, the poorly-synchronised semaphore which endeavoured to embellish, for the purpose of mere comprehension, the admonitions which were now in my throat but mere squeaks? Throughout, Trygon's video data transmitter continued to operate, as was clear from the constantly changing colour patterns on the whirring, rotating visor, gathering details of socio-cultural behaviour for transmission back to his own planet. A huge melancholy overcame me as I considered what the elders might make of it all, gathered in some interplanetary projection booth to examine the behaviour of we humans. What could they possibly be expected to make of a species which threatened to 'tear the nuts off any scumbag cur' and 'Boot the skellies off asshole fisherman fucks!', in the course of the delivery of which, the entire pub was wrecked, Peter barely escaping with his life as the pool table was overturned by The Red Killeen in order to reveal the huddled, now not-quite-so-forthright Fair Isle bulk of Jimmy Skutch beneath.

Against Trygon and his fellow cyborgs, I bear no grudge. For them, it was and remains impossible to know our ways. What saddens me most is the fact that he allowed himself to be hoodwinked by the vulpine Squires, in the very same manner as the members of the L&H Society were only some months later, when they coolly ousted me, with a sang-froid many pith-helmeted tyrants would have baulked at, as chairman, installing the gutter press lackey in my place. Of course, out of all those involved that fateful day when interplanetary travellers from a solar system totally unknown to us came to our town, only he has done well. Only he has turned it to his advantage, with what might by most reasonably civilised human beings be described as most indecent haste, running it if you don't mind as his lead story the following day, complete with, in the coarse black type we have come to expect of *The Barntrosna Standard*, a huge – absurdly large, in fact – question mark above the words:

CYBORG WATER-STEALERS

followed by a 'report' on how local 'bookman' Pats McElhinney claimed to have not only encountered aliens somewhere in the vicinity of the Cloanaboghey Road, but to have been 'drinking with them' in The Bridge Bar.

I have no intention of dwelling on his elusive, would-be ironic decimations of my character and their tedious repetitiveness. Suffice to say that I may not yet venture out or receive books across the counter in my place of work without being subjected to clearly contrived queries as regards to 'aliens' and 'visitors'. There was a time when I would have taken the time to enlighten them with the truth of the story and derived great pleasure from their reactions, predictable as they might be, as the scales fell from their eyes and they stood there before me, humbled and aghast. But those days are long gone. If it is their wish to throw their lot in with a pencil-prodding nonentity, and thereby contribute to the advancing rot which will eventually consume the entire county as efficiently as an army of starving Colorado beetles a large kitchen table, then so be it.

But one day, they will find out the truth. I know. And that will be my crowning glory. For by then I will have completed my tome (currently standing at 200,000 words) and as I make my way to the lectern, I will clear my throat with dignity – not even giving a moment's thought to the L&H and its pathetically protracted debates over nothing – and, permitting a humiliated Squires a disinterested glance, I will cough ever so slightly and, in my practised dulcet tones, begin my tale, beside which men of flesh and wire are as nothing – *I was walking my dog Pongo one unspectacular autumn evening not long ago when I perceived directly before me the most unusual-shaped mushroom I had seen in some time. As I am well acquainted with the fungi to be found in that area, I could tell straightaway that this was clearly a discovery of some interest. But little did I realise the extent of this until, approaching it, it became quite clear that this was not an uncommon species of fungus but that indeed it was not one at all, but some kind of pod – which I now could plainly see was a living, breathing organism. Which was practically changing shape before my eyes! It was at that moment Pongo began to bark, and the creature burst forth with a heart-rending, blood-chilling shriek, sending bits of fleshy pod and wrinkly, polka-dotted skin all over Clonabooney Wood. . .*

kevin sampson

....

two star

It was a summer of almost incessant masturbation. He couldn't get girls off his mind. And when he wasn't thinking about them, he was out with the gang, looking for them. They looked everywhere, forlornly hoping that they'd stumble upon a lost colony of nymphets like in the Ayesha film – or at least a couple raping.

Liam's imagination was fuelled beyond combustion point by the stories that filtered down from the older lads. There had already been several rapings on the reservoir and a few goosings, too – and we weren't even in August, yet. But whenever Liam and the gang ambled up there, shitting themselves, there was nothing going on. No rapings, no blimps of any sort. No Jenny MacAdam.

Jenny MacAdam had let some of the older lads rape her. That was a fact. Alan's big brother told them that and he'd seen it with his own eyes. A few of them had gone up there with some ciggies and a Party Seven and Jenny had let Piggy Flynn goose her and then the others had taken turns. Alan's brother told them all about the Star System. One Star was Tit Outside. Wide-eyed, they couldn't imagine doing it anywhere else, but he explained that it meant feeling her tits through her clothes. Two Star was Tit Inside. The real thing. In the raw. No bra, nipples, the whole thing. Three Star was Fanny. Four Star was Hand On Dick and Five Star was All The Way. Piggy Flynn had been All The Way loads of times. He was an expert. But in spite of nightly pilgrimages to the rezzy, Liam never once saw Piggy or Al's brother, and never saw Jenny Mac, either.

The weather was getting hotter and that made it worse. Liam's mum kept making him wear shorts and telling him to play in the garden.

'Make the most of the weather, while it lasts!'

He was fourteen, for fuck's sake! And the garden? Barely a patio with a scrap of grass like all the other two hundred identical gardens on this new-built, nothing-happens, £100 deposit-move-in-today estate. What *could* you do in a garden the size of a Twister mat? Well – there was one thing. You could pretend to be weeding the feeble, foot-wide flower bed while you watched Mrs Crowe sunbathing next door. Rumours abounded when the Crowes first moved to Anglesey Close that Mrs Crowe was a former Miss Southport. She was tall and slim, had straight black shiny long hair and she smiled at Liam whenever she saw him. He just went red. But since the good weather broke she'd been out there every day, black bikini on, rubbing Ambre Solaire into those long brown limbs. And Liam hadn't missed a moment of it.

'I'm going up to the Kwiki, love. Is there anything special you want?'

Usually Liam's emotions jousted between intense

embarrassment at the notion that a fourteen-year-old, a near-man, should be considered wanting of Something Special. But then that would often give way to the concession that, actually, he did rather fancy a Heinz chicken and mushroom Toast Topper. But right now, the only emotion was glee. He knew exactly how this was going to go. The house would be empty. He'd lay out the two items he needed, in the place where he needed them, in the triangular recess behind the couch. The only problem was the curtains. You couldn't really close them on a hot summer's day. The neighbours'd think someone had popped it. So he'd limit potential exposure by opening the porch door, which would cut off all but about ten feet of any passerby's field of vision, should they so happen to be peering in just as a young lad with a hard-on was diving behind the couch, anxious to toss himself off.

He stole upstairs into Marie's room, which overlooked the garden. Prolonging the moment, he raked idly through her underwear drawer again, letting his fingertips stray over the purple satin cups of his sister's upholstery. She had terrific tits, his sister, but there was a problem with her too. She was his sister. Liam had never even been interested in blimping her, in spite of great pressure from the gang. He brought them a pair of her knickers once, and fished out a used jammy for Al. But that was as far as it went.

He went over to the window, already impatient to get on with it. Mrs Crowe was down there, only feet away, her tapering back glistening with the muggy coconut oil he could smell from where he now stood. Her bikini briefs had ridden up, exposing an inch of her perfect bottom. Liam could see the goose bumps when the sun went behind a cloud. He looked and gulped and perspired until he could look no more. The trick now was to get himself and his boner back behind the couch with as little fuss as possible. Climbing over into that confined space could be a bit tricky with an inflexible lob-on, but it was always worth it. The catalogue was ready and waiting at the lingerie page, and Marie's diary – which read like Catullus – was there as back up just in case his memory, his imagination and all those well-clad breasts failed to sustain him.

As ever, he was invaded by a black remorse the moment he'd wiped himself up. This was no good. There was the whole of the summer ahead. He'd have to get himself a girl. Any girl. Much more of this wanking and he'd have to start taking cold plunge baths and reading the Bible to take his mind off it. But then, even the Bible had its pervy moments and plenty of them.

It was the thought of cold baths that gave him the idea, though. Why had he not thought of this before? In a heatwave like this one, where would all the girls be? New Brighton Baths, of course. Obviously. There were other open air pools, but New Brighton had the highest diving board, with a Deep End of thirty-six feet. He'd heard all sorts of stories about goosings and rapings at New Brighton Baths. There'd been a few horror stories too, about lads off the Leasowe holding people up for their pocket money. One lad nearly drowned when the LEBB held him under in the Deep End for getting his tit off some girl from their estate. But Liam and the gang were hardly going to be a threat to the LEBB. They'd be looking for lads from Moreton or The Ford, big mobs trying to take over the place. Four lads from Thingwall wouldn't be much of a scalp to them.

'Even if we don't tap off, just think of the blimps!' choked a wild-eyed Paul Moran. Paul had only come to live in Axholme Drive last year, but everyone liked him. He was a bit of a daredevil and he talked about nothing but sex. He was obsessed.

'All those motts and groodies running around, and only a few scraps of material between us and them!'

Liam and Alan tittered, terrified. Stevie Bryan just gulped, as usual, and went white. He clutched the handrail of the seat in front as the bus trundled interminably towards Valhalla.

That's what it was, though. When they got there and found a place on the terracing, all they could do was stare. For a start, there was no chance – *no* chance – of Liam and the boys copping off. All the girls were like starlets in their pink and lime and miniscule gold lamé bikinis. But worse, the lads were all men. They had tattoos, muzzies, hairy chests and, where Liam's swimming trunks signified his gender with a modest popping at the crutch they had robust, vulgar bulges – great big ropey cocks that were already used to years of going all the way. They were men. But Liam could not have cared less. This was the world he'd been preparing himself for. This was real life.

He was happy to mind the clothes and try and look like he wasn't blimping while the others tooled around in the pool. It was just like the pool in *The Godfather*, when they go to Florida. Smooth white curving walls, all quite clinical yet throbbing with the muted bass notes of sex. Paul Moran went right up to the highest board. It was about a hundred foot high. Not even the most obdurate of muscle men had the front to go up there. The story was that the last person who made the leap from the highest board had overshot the pool by about thirty feet and got splatted against the bright white walls.

People started to point up at Paul. All around Liam, young men were calling him a tit and an arsehole, then betting that he wouldn't go through with it. Groups of girls were clustered together, holding on to each other. They'd obviously heard about the mess the last guy had made. Three girls stood right next to Liam, shielding their eyes from the glare of the sun as they followed Paul's progress. He was standing right on the lip of the wide diving board. At that height, it wasn't a springboard – just a sturdy shelf, matted with waxy canvas. You could see Paul's toes gripping the edge of the board, or Liam was sure that *he* could, anyway. The girls linked their spare arms together. Liam noticed that they, too, were exposing an inch or two of white bottom where their bikinis had risen, or been rearranged, just like Mrs Crowe's. He found himself getting a lob-on, and shifted position to accommodate it.

Paul stepped back away from the edge of the board. The girls in the crowd sighed their disappointment, while the man-boys smirked and puffed out their chests, their shows of affront ill-masking their relief. And then the blurred silhouette of Paul came plummeting from way up there, barely disturbed the surface of the water as he plunged into the chemical blue and, a moment later, emerged grinning. Liam ran over to the side and helped pull him out with Alan. They went straight back to the bottom rungs of the diving boards, Al clearly intent on emulating Paul's heroics. Liam ambled back to the towels. One of the three girls eyed him up. She started to walk over to him. Shit! She was coming over.

'That your mate, then?'

He could hear her voice, but he wasn't computing the words. He was focused absolutely on the beguiling wisp of hair that trailed from her belly button to the outskirts of her bikini briefs. There was a trace of hair at her groin too. Liam could not take his eyes off it.

'Cat got your tongue?'

If only, thought Liam. He looked up at her. This was going to have to be good. Whatever he said now was going to seal his fate. He was a sentence away from a Date here and, albeit belatedly, getting his goosing career on the road. Whatever he said, it was going to have to be gold. It would have to encapsulate what he was all about – his wit, his charm, his sense of fun. This throwaway reply was, quite simply, going to have to knock her out.

'You've got a fucking hairy fanny, haven't you!'

He very nearly said that. It was, really, the only thing on his mind. It was as much as he could do to tear his eyes away from that exotic feather of hair and concentrate on the girl. She was beautiful, slightly Spanish or Roman-looking. He'd never really thought he liked curly hair, but this girl had a wild tossing mane and a generous smile and pale brown eyes and it all seemed to work together. He was in love. He made a nervous remark, designed to show that he was clever and 'different'. He said something about the lads' macho performance on the diving boards being a cover-up for their insecurities with women. He immediately regretted the implication that he was a big mad shagger, but she didn't seem to take that meaning. She was quiet, but confident.

Julie. Julie Julie Julie. Stupid name, but he loved her. He found out all the essentials as she squeezed the moisture from her hair after a neat dive nearly took her bikini with it. Liam watched a droplet trickle down her flat tummy. She lived in the flats right behind the Arrowe Park Hotel. *Not* the Woody, she said about fifty times. She was no Virginia Woolf on the patter front, but they were going to meet at the kiosk by the golf course at half seven and that was all that mattered. They were going for a walk on the golf course. She'd agreed to a walk on Arrowe Park golf course. That was a basic yes. It was going to be Two Star. At least.

vicki hendricks

....

rebecca

As her Siamese twin joined at the skull, I know Becca
wants to fuck Remus as soon as she says she's going to
dye our hair. I don't say anything – yet. I'm not sure she's
even admitting it to herself. The idea doesn't sit well with
me, but I decide to wait and see just how she plans to go
about it.

It's a cool, clear night in Gainesville, not a bad walk to
Discount Drugs. Becca picks out a light magenta hair-
color that to me indicates heavy drug addiction. 'No,
siree,' I tell her. 'I know my complexion colors. I'm a fall,
and that's definitely a spring.' I might add, no spring that
ever existed in nature.

'Oh, stop it, Rebby. We'll do a middle part and you can
keep your flat black. I'll just liven up my side. I want to
get it shaped too – something that falls around my face.'

'It better not fall anywhere near *my* face. I'm going for
a center pigtail.'

'Poo,' she says.

I turn my head as if to look her in the eye, but of
course, I can't because her face turns away as I move. All

my life – at least the last ten of my twenty-four years – I've tried to stare that girl in the eye, but I can only do it with a mirror, and there's never one around when I need it. The time I almost had her, she closed her eyes.

When we get home from the drugstore, she reads the instructions aloud and there are about fifty steps to this process by the time you do the lightening and the toning. Then she starts telling me which hairs are hers and which are mine. We've gone around on this before. It's a tough problem because our faces aren't set exactly even. I look left and down while she faces straight ahead and up. We share a pair of ears. For walking we've managed a workable system where I watch for curbs and ground objects and she spots branches and lowflying aircraft. She claims to have saved our life numerous times.

'Oh, yeah? And for what?' I ask her. She always laughs. But now I know – so she can fuck Remus, the pale, scrawny clerk with the goatee who works at 'A Different Fish' down the corner. Now it's clear why Becca didn't laugh when I pointed out his resemblance to the sucker-mouth catfish. Ha! Also her sudden decision to raise crayfish. Those bastards are mean, ugly sons of bitches, but they suit Becca fine. They're always climbing out of the tank to dehydrate under the couch, so we have to go back to the store for new ones. Fuck – I'd rather die a virgin. We entertain ourself just fine.

Anyway, there's never been a solution to the hair-ownership problem. In high school when we had senior pictures taken, we each planned a side part for maximum volume. Of course, Becca went first and when it was my turn, the hair gel she globbed on had worked so well that I was stuck with the lower side of what looked like a bald man's comb-over unless I wanted a six-inch cowlick. Soon after that, I heard our aunt refer to Becca as the 'more attractive twin', when, as a matter of fact, we are identical.

So this time I decide to stick to my guns. I grab a handful of twist ties, and we spend hours counting out pinches of hair – fifty strands per pinch – and twisting them separately until we've measured out the distance between her left eye and my right. It comes out thirteen pinches, and we divide the middle one in half.

It's two a.m. when she finishes drying that magenta haystack and we finally get into bed. Then she stays awake mooning about Remus while I put a bean bag lizard over my eyes and try to turn off her side of the brain. I know where she's got her fingers. There's a tingle and that certain haziness in our head.

We barely make it to work on time in the morning. Then Becca talks one of our co-workers into giving her a haircut during lunch. The woman is a beautician, but she developed allergies to the chemicals, so now she works at the hospital lab with us.

They're snipping and flipping hair in the break-room to beat shit and I'm trying to eat my tuna fish. 'Yes!' Becca says, when she looks in the mirror. Her side is blunt cut into a sort of swinging page boy. She tweaks the wave over her eye, making sure we'll be clobbered by a branch in the near future.

She blows herself a kiss and giggles. 'If I smoked, I'd get a cigarette holder.'

'Don't even fucking consider it.' I straighten my pigtail. 'Imagine the second-hand smoke . . .'

We get home from work that evening and – surprise,

surprise – she counts up and reports another crayfish missing. I try to scramble down to look under the couch in case the thing hasn't dried out yet, but she braces her legs and I can't get the leverage.

'You know how much trouble it is for us to get back up,' she says. 'Anyway, it'd be covered with dust-bunnies and hair.'

At that moment I get a flash of guilt from her section of the brain – she's lying. There is no fucking arthropod under the couch. She wants badly to get back to that aquarium store.

Becca smiles sweetly. I forgive her.

She insists on changing into 'sleisure wear' – that's what I call it – to walk down the street. The frock's a short, fresh, pink number with cut-in shoulders that I have to say complements the new hair color. Nevertheless, I wouldn't be caught dead in it at Liz Taylor's umpteenth wedding.

I lean against the wall while Becca straightens and primps. I'm wearing my 'Dead Babies' tour T-shirt – the slit in the back cleverly velcroed – and cut-offs that I wore all last weekend. They're now comfortably loose for the evening. Becca has long given up trying to convince me to dress in tandem.

We see Remus through the glass door when we get there. He has his back to us dipping out feeders for a customer. His shaved white neck almost glows. The little bell rings as we step in. Becca tugs me toward the tank where the crayfish are, and I can tell she's nervous.

Remus turns. Straining my peripheral vision, I catch the smile he throws her. I can feel this mutual energy between them that I missed before. He's not too bad-looking with a smile. I start to imagine what it's going to be like. What kind of posture they'll get me into. Maybe I should buy earplugs and a blindfold. Hell, why not use a mirror?

Becca heads toward the crayfish, but I halt her in front of a salt-water tank of neon-bright fish and corals. 'We should start one of these,' I tell her. 'It's tricky enough that we'd have to come here almost every night.'

'Shh!' she says.

A goby pops its round pearly head out of a mounded hole in the sandy bottom and looks at us. 'He's like a little bald-headed man. Don't you just love him?'

Becca pulls me to the crayfish tank and pretends to be picking out a healthy specimen. Remus comes back with his dipper and a plastic bag.

'What can I do for you two lovely ladies tonight?'

Becca reddens and giggles. Remus reddens. I know he's thinking about his use of the number *two*. He's got it right, but he's self-conscious like everybody.

'How much are the gobies?' I ask.

Remus doesn't even hear. He's watching Becca.

She points to the largest, meanest-looking crawdad in sight. 'This guy,' she says. I figure she's after the upper-body strength, the easier he can knock off the plastic strip and boost himself out over the back side of our tank. 'Think you can snag him?' she asks Remus.

He takes it like a test. 'You bet. Anything for my best customer–s.' He stands on tiptoe so the metal edge of the tank is in his armpit, and some dark hair curls from his scrunched short-sleeve. He dunks the sleeve completely as he swoops and chases that devil around the corners of the tank.

Remus is no fool. He's noticed Becca's hair and the dress. I'm thinking, get your mind outta the gutter, buster – but I'm softening. I'm tuned to Becca's feelings, and I'm curious about this thing – although, it's frightening. Not so much the sex, but the idea of three. I'm used to an evenly divided opinion, positive and negative, side-by-side, give and take. We have strength in numbers on the rare occasions when we agree and perseverance that comes from a certain amount of opposition. Three could be a lonely number for me. We might be strange to the world, but we've evolved an effective system. Even his skinny bones on her side of the balance will throw it all off.

Remus catches the renegade and flips him into the plastic bag, filling it halfway with water. He pulls a twist-tie from his pocket and secures the bag. The crayfish is snapping around. 'You have plenty of food and everything?' Remus asks.

Becca nods slowly and pokes at the bag. I know she's trying to think of a way to start something without seeming too forward. Remus looks like he's fishing for a thought.

My portion of gray matter takes the lead. 'Hey,' I say. 'Becca and I were thinking we'd try a new brownie recipe and rent a video. Wanna stop by on your way home?'

Becca twitches. I feel the thrill run through her, then apprehension. She turns our head further to Remus. 'Want to?' she says.

'Sure. I don't get out of here till nine. Is that too late?'

'That's fine,' I say. I feel her excitement as she gives him the directions to the house and we head out.

When we get outside she shoots into instant panic. 'What brownie recipe? We don't even have flour!'

'Calm down,' I tell her. 'All he's thinking about is that brownie between your legs.'

'Geez, Reb, you're so crude.'

'Chances are he won't even remember what we invited him for.'

Suddenly, it hits me that he could be thinking of what's between my legs too – a natural *ménage à trois*. I rethink – no way, Remus wouldn't know what to do with it.

Becca insists that we make brownies. She pulls me double-time the four blocks to the Quickie Mart to pick up a box mix. I grab a pack of M & Ms and a bag of nuts. 'Look, we'll mix these in and it'll be a new recipe.'

She brightens and nods our head. I can feel her warmth rush into me because she knows I'm on her side now – in more ways than one for a change.

'Too bad we don't have some weed,' I whisper.

She clucks her tongue. I cluck mine.

We circle the block to hit the video store and Becca agrees to rent *What Ever Happened to Baby Jane?* She hates it, but it's my favorite – besides *Hard Day's Night* – and she's not in the mood to care.

I pick it off the shelf and do my best Southern Bette Davis, 'But, Blanche, you *are* in that wheelchair,' I tell her.

'I'll take *Baby Jane* over the Beatles again any day,' Becca says.

It's eight o'clock when we get home and the first thing Becca wants to do is hop in the shower. I'd rather start the brownies. We both make a move in opposite directions, like when we were little girls. She fastens onto the loveseat and I get a grip on the closet doorknob. Neither of us is going anywhere. 'Reb, please, let go!' she hollers.

'You want brownies or not?' I yell. Fuck. It's one of those times you'd just like to take a hatchet . . .

After a few seconds of growling, I realize we're having a case of nerves. I let go and race Becca into the bathroom. 'Thanks, Rebelle,' she says.

At nine-ten we slide the brownies into the oven and hear a knock. Remus has made good time. I notice Becca's quick intake of breath and a zinging in our brain.

'Take it easy,' I tell her. 'I won't leave you.'

She gives a pathetic chuckle and yanks me toward the door.

Remus has a smile that covers his whole face. I feel Becca's cheek pushing my scalp and I can figure a big grin on her too. I hold back my wise-ass grumbling. So this is love.

Becca asks Remus in and we get him a Bud. He's perched on the loveseat. Our only choice is the couch, which puts me between them, so I slump into my 'invisible' posture, chin on chest, and suck my beer. I know that way Becca is looking at him straight on.

'The brownies will be ready soon. Want to see the movie?' she asks.

'Sure.'

Becca starts to get up, but I'm slow to respond.

Remus jumps up and heads for the VCR. 'Let me,' he says.

I nod for us. 'Relax,' I whisper to Becca. I'm thinking, thank God we've got *Baby Jane* for amusement.

The movie comes on and we watch. Minutes go by and neither of them speaks. Maybe the video wasn't such a good idea. I start spouting dialogue just ahead of Bette whenever there's a pause. Becca shushes me.

The oven timer goes off. 'The brownies,' I say. 'We'll be right back.' We hustle into the kitchen and I get them out. Becca tests them with a knife in the middle. 'Okay,' I tell her. 'I'm going to get you laid.'

'Shh, Reb!'

'Look,' I whisper, 'you two have been dragging along with these extremely boring crayfish conversations for months now and that's fine – but I'm not going to endure this girlish sexual tension night-after-night while you work up to getting your clothes off.'

I feel her consternation, but she doesn't object.

The brownies are too hot to cut, so Becca picks up the pan with the hot pad and I grab dessert plates, napkins, and the knife. 'Just keep his balls out of my face,' I say.

That takes the wind out of her, but I charge for the living room.

Remus has moved to the right end of the couch. Hmm. My respect for him is growing.

We watch and eat. Remus comments on how good the brownies are. Becca giggles and fidgets. Remus offers to get us another beer from the fridge. Becca says no thanks. He brings me one.

'Ever had a beer milkshake?' I ask him.

'Nope.'

'How 'bout a Siamese twin?'

His mouth falls open and I'm thinking suckermouth catfish all the way, but his eyes have taken on a focus.

I tilt my face up. 'Becca would shoot me for saying this – if she could survive – but I know why you're here, and I know she finds you attractive, so I don't see a reason to waste any more time.'

The silence is heavy and all of a sudden the TV blares – 'You wouldn't talk to me like that if I wasn't in this chair –' 'But, Blanche, you are in that chair, you *are* in that chair.'

'Shut that off,' I tell Remus.

He breaks from his paralysis and does it.

I talk to Becca. 'Hey, we're free spirits. It's hereditary.'

I feel her face tightening into a knot, but there are sparks behind it.

'Let's get comfortable in the bedroom,' I state.

Remus gawks.

I'm named Rebelle so Mom could call both of us at once – she got a kick out of her cleverness – and I take pride in being rebellious. I drag Becca up.

She's got the posture of a houndog on a leash, but her secret thrill runs down my backbone. It seems our bodies work like the phantom-limb sensation of amputees. We get impulses from the brain, even when our own physical parts aren't directly stimulated. I'm determined to do what her body wants and not give her mind a chance to stop it. She follows along.

We get into the bedroom and I set us down. I crook a finger at Remus and scoot left. He sits next to Becca. Without a word, he bends forward and kisses her, puts his arms around her and between our bodies. I watch.

It's an intense feeling, waves of heat rushing over me, heading down to my crotch. We've been kissed before, but not like this. He works at her mouth and his tongue goes inside.

The kissing stops. Remus looks at me, then turns back

to Becca. He takes her face in his hands and puts his lips on her neck. I can smell him and hear soft kisses. The heat is pouring off all of us. My breathing speeds up. Becca starts to gasp.

He stops and I hear the zipper on the back of her dress. She stiffens, but he takes her face to his again and we slide back into warm fuzzies. This Remus has some style. He pulls the dress down to her waist and unhooks her bra. She shrugs it off.

'You're beautiful,' he tells her.

'Thanks,' I say. I get a jolt of Becca's annoyance.

My eyes are about a foot from her nipples, which are up like gobies, and he gets his face right down on them. His wet tongue flicks back and forth across her perfect creamy mounds and he takes the shining pink nubs into his mouth and suckles. I feel myself edging toward the warm moist touch of his lips, but the movement is mostly in my mind.

Remus pushes Becca onto the pillow and I fall along and lie there, my arms to my sides. He lifts her hips and slides the dress down and off, and exposes a pair of white lace panties that I never knew Becca owned, never even saw her put on.

He nuzzles the perfect vee between her legs and licks those thighs that are pale as cave fish. Becca reaches up and starts unbuttoning his shirt. He helps her, then speedily slips his jeans on down to the floor, taking his underwear with them. I stare. As skinny as he is, he's got a weapon, fully loaded. This is the first time we've seen one live. I feel a tinge of fear and I don't know if it's from Becca or me.

'Got a condom?' I ask him.

'Oh, yeah,' he says. He reaches for his pants and pulls a round gold package out of the pocket. Becca puts her hand on my arm while he's opening it, and I turn my chin to her side and kiss her shoulder. We both watch while he places the condom flat on the tip of his penis and slowly smooths it up.

He gets to his knees and strips down the lace panties and puts his mouth straight on her. His tongue works in and I can feel the juices seeping out of me in response. Becca starts cooing like those cockatiels we used to have, and I bite my lip not to make a noise. Remus moves up and guides himself in, and I swear I can feel the stretching and burning. I'm clutching my vaginal muscles rigid against nothing, but it's the fullest, most intense feeling I've ever had.

Becca starts with sound effects from *The Exorcist*, and I join right in because I know she can't hear me over her own voice, and Remus is puffing and grunting not to give a fuck about anything but the fucking. His hip bumps mine in fast rhythm, as the two of them locked together pound that bed. I clench and rock my pelvis skyward and groan with the need, and stretch tighter and harder, until I feel a letting-down as if an eternal dam has broken. I'm flooded with a current that lays me into the mattress and brings out a long, thready weep. It's like the eerie love song of a sperm whale. I sink into the blue and listen to my breathing and theirs settle down.

I wake up and look over at Becca. Remus has curled next to her side with one arm over her chest and a lock of the magenta hair spread across his forehead. His fingers are touching my ribs through my shirt, but I know he doesn't realize it. I have tears in my eyes. I want to be closer, held tight in the little world of his arms, protected, loved – but I know he is hers now, and she is his. I'm an invisible attachment of nerves, muscles, organs, and bone.

It's after one when we walk Remus to the door, and he tells Becca he'll call her at work the next day. He gives her a long, gentle kiss, and I feel her melting into sweet cream inside.

'Goodnight – I mean good morning – ' Remus says to me. He gives me a salute. Comrades, it means. It's not a feeling I can return, but I salute back. I know he sees the worry in my eyes. I try to take my mind out of the funk, before Becca gets a twinge.

Remus calls her twice that afternoon, and a pattern takes shape over the next three days – whispered calls at work, a walk down the street after dinner, a 9:10 Remus visitation. I act gruff, uninterested, and keep dressing for a coup in my cut-offs and black T-shirts.

When we go to bed I try not to get involved. You'd think once I'd seen it, I could block it out, catch up on some sleep. But the caresses are turning more sure and more tender, the sounds more varied – delicate but strong with passion, unearthly. I follow this course like nobody has probably ever done, ride along without subterfuge, without jealousy, stifling my desire. But my heart is cut in two – like Becca and I should be. I'm happy for her – I'm miserably lonely. I never had this need before.

On the third day, I can't hold back my feelings anymore. Of course, Becca knows already. It's time to compromise.

'I think we should limit Remus's visits to twice a week. I'm tired every day at work and I can't take this routine every night. Besides,' I tell her, 'you shouldn't get too serious. This can't last.'

Becca sighs with relief. 'I thought you would ask me to share.'

I don't say anything. It had crossed my mind.

'I know,' she says, 'Just give us a few more nights. He's bound to need sleep sometime too.'

I notice her use of the pronoun *us,* that it doesn't refer to Becca and me any more. Why are we leaving everything up to him?

I hold back my complaints for three more nights. I know how wrapped up Becca is. I'm tangled in this web myself, dangling off the edge.

Remus stays later and later. On the third night I don't fall asleep till after three and wake up at dawn to their whispering. They don't go back to sleep and neither can I. In the morning I grumble and throw out irritated looks while we serve Remus toast and coffee. Then it's time to go to work.

In the space of an hour I spill urine from a beaker twice before Becca brings up the dreaded subject.

'I love him,' she says.

'No shit.'

'He loves me too. He wants to move in. He's been living with his mother until the fish business picks up, but if we all split the rent, it will be easy. Better for you too.'

'We don't have money problems.'

'I know it seems fast, but I'm twenty-four. . . .'

'Me too. Remember me?'

She puts her arm around my shoulders and squeezes. 'I know it's hard, but . . .'

'Seems to me that's your only interest – how hard it is.'

I feel the heat of her anger spread into my scalp. I've hit a new nerve. She's like a stranger.

I let her pull me to the ladies' room. She closes the door. 'You can't undermine this on me, Reb. It's my dream. How many times is a man going to come along who's interested in me? How many guys won't be scared off by the staring and inconvenience, the lack of intimacy – much less put up with your obnoxiousness and cynical attitude.'

'Obnoxiousness? How far would you be if one of us didn't have the guts to speak up?' I stare at her in the mirror, but her eyes are downcast. 'We've been taking care of each other all our lives. Now you're treating me like a tumor. What am I supposed to do?'

Her body is shaking. 'What can *I* do? It's not fair!' she screams.

'It's not my fault, for Christ sakes.' I turn toward her, which makes her head turn away. 'Okay, we'll share.'

She completely breaks down. She starts to sob.

I take my hand to her far cheek. I wipe the tears. I can't cause her more pain. My heart is breaking along with hers. There's enough agony in life. 'I'm sorry,' I tell her. 'I know I'm cynical and obnoxious. If I don't have a right to be, who does?'

She reaches for a paper towel to wipe her eyes.

'I guess you have the same right,' I say. 'So how come you're not?'

'Nobody could stand us,' she says. She blows her nose.

I smooth her hair till she stops crying. 'I love you, Becca. I'll do anything to make you happy. Fuck. I'll get earplugs and a blindfold. I should have done it right off the bat.'

We take a taxi to Penney's after work and I get my rig. Becca picks out an aqua satin sleep mask and treats me to a matching pair of pajamas. I know the sensations won't be cut off completely, but maybe I can deal with them in a positive way.

That night we take our walk down the street. There's nobody in the store but Remus. He walks up and I feel Becca radiating pleasure just on sight. He gives her a peck on the cheek.

I smell his scent. I'm accustomed to it. I try to act cheerful. I've pledged to let this thing happen, but I can almost feel him inside of her already, and the over-whelming gloom that follows. I put a finger in my ear and start humming 'You can't always get what you want' to block them out. I can do it.

They stop talking. Remus looks at me.

Becca tilts our head. 'What's the matter, Reb? You okay?'

'I'm fine. A headphone – that's what I need. I can immerse myself in music.'

'What?' asks Remus.

I pause. Becca fills in. 'She's a little upset . . .'

'I'm not upset,' I say. 'I've found a good solution.' I give her a hug.

The little bell on the door rings. Remus turns to see behind us. 'Hey there, Rom,' he calls, 'how was the cichlid convention?' He looks back at us. 'Did I mention my brother? He's just back from Savannah.'

Becca and I turn and do a double-take. The door closes. In the last dusky rays of sunset stands a mirror image of Remus – identical, but a tad more attractive. A zing runs through my brain. I know Becca feels it.

christopher fowler

....

at home in the pubs of old london

The Museum Tavern, Museum Street, Bloomsbury
Despite its location diagonally opposite the British
Museum, its steady turnover of listless Australian bar
staff and its passing appraisal by tourists on quests for the
British pub experience (comprising two sips from half a
pint of bitter and one Salt 'n' Vinegar flavoured crisp,
nibbled and returned to its packet in horror), this
drinking establishment retains the authentically seedy
bookishness of Bloomsbury because its corners are
usually occupied by half-cut proofreaders from nearby
publishing houses. I love pubs like this one because so
much about them remains constant in a sliding world;
the smell of hops, the ebb of background conversation,
muted light through coloured glass, china tap handles,
mirrored walls, bars of oak and brass. Even the pieces of
fake Victoriana, modelled on increasingly obsolete pub
ornaments, become objects of curiosity in themselves.

At this time I was working in a comic shop, vending

tales of fantastic kingdoms to whey-faced netheads who were incapable of saving a sandwich in a serviette, let alone an alien planet, and it was in this pub that I met Lesley. She was sitting with a group of glum-looking gothic *Gormenghast* offcuts who were on their way to a book launch at the New Age smells 'n' bells shop around the corner, and she was clearly unenchanted with the idea of joining them for a session of warm Liebfraumilch and crystal-gazing, because as each member of the group drifted off she found an excuse to stay on, and we ended up sitting together by ourselves. As she refolded her jacket a rhinestone pin dropped from the lapel, and I picked it up for her. The badge formed her initials – L L – which made me think of Superman, because he had a history of falling for women with those initials, but I reminded myself that I was no superman, just a man who liked making friends in pubs. I asked her if she'd had a good Christmas, she said no, I said I hadn't either and we just chatted from there. I told Lesley that I was something of an artist and would love to sketch her, and she tentatively agreed to sit for me at some point in the future.

The World's End, High Street, Camden Town

It's a funny pub, this one, because the interior brickwork makes it look sort of inside out, and there's a steady through-traffic of punters wherever you stand, so you're always in the way. It's not my kind of place, more a network of bars and clubs than a proper boozer. It used to be called the Mother Red Cap, after a witch who lived in Camden. There are still a few of her pals inhabiting the place if black eyeliner, purple lipstick and pointed boots make you a likely candidate for cauldron-stirring. A white stone statue of Britannia protrudes from the first floor of the building opposite, above a shoe shop, but I don't think anyone notices it, just as they don't know about the witch. Yet if you step inside the foyer of the Black Cap, a few doors further down, you can see the witch herself, painted on a tiled wall. It's funny how people miss so much of what's going on around them. I was beginning to think Sophie wouldn't show up, then I became convinced she had, and I had missed her.

Anyway, she finally appeared and we hit it off beautifully. She had tied back her long auburn hair so that it was out of her eyes, and I couldn't stop looking at her. It's never difficult to find new models; women are flattered by the thought of someone admiring their features. She half-smiled all the time, which was disconcerting at first, but after a while I enjoyed it because she looked like she was in on a secret that no one else shared. I had met her two days earlier in the coffee shop in Bermondsey where she was working, and she had suggested going for a drink, describing our meeting place to me as 'that pub in Camden near the shoe shop'. The one thing Camden has more than any other place in London is shoe shops, hundreds of the bastards, so you can understand why I was worried.

It was quite crowded and we had to stand, but after a while Sophie felt tired and wanted to sit down, so we found a corner and wedged ourselves in behind a pile of coats. The relentless music was giving me a headache, so I was eventually forced to take my leave.

The King's Head, Upper Street, Islington

The back of this pub operates a tiny theatre, so the bar suddenly fills up with the gin-and-tonic brigade at seven each evening, but the front room is very nice in a battered, nicotine-scoured way. It continued to operate on the old monetary system of pounds, shillings and pence for years, long after they brought in decimal currency. I'm sure the management just did it to confuse non-regulars who weren't in the habit of being asked to stump up nineteen and elevenpence halfpenny for a libation. Emma was late, having been forced to stay behind at her office, a property company in Essex Road. The choice of territory was mine. Although it was within walking distance of her work she hadn't been here before, and loved hearing this mad trilling coming from a door at the back of the pub. I'd forgotten to explain about the theatre. They were staging a revival of a twenties musical, and there were a lot of songs about croquet and how ghastly foreigners were. I remember Emma as being very pale and thin, with cropped blonde hair; she could easily have passed for a jazz age flapper. I told her she should have auditioned for the show, but she explained that she was far too fond of a drink to ever remember anything as complicated as a dance step. At the intermission, a girl dressed as a giant sequinned jellyfish popped out to order a gin and French; apparently she had a big number in the second act. We taxed the barman's patience by getting him to make up strange cocktails, and spent most of the evening laughing so loudly that they probably heard us onstage. Emma agreed to sit for me at some point in the future, and although there was never a suggestion that our session would develop into anything more, I could tell that it probably would. I was about to kiss her when she suddenly thought something had bitten her, and I was forced to explain that my coat had picked up several fleas from my cat. She went off me after this, and grew silent, so I left.

The Pineapple, Leverton Street, Kentish Town
This tucked-away pub can't have changed much in a hundred years, apart from the removal of the wooden partitions that separated the snug from the saloon. A mild spring morning, the Sunday papers spread out before us, an ancient smelly labrador flatulating in front of the fire, a couple of pints of decent bitter and two packets of pork scratchings. Sarah kept reading out snippets from the *News Of The World*, and I did the same with the *Observer*, but mine were more worthy than hers, and therefore not as funny. There was a strange man with an enormous nose sitting near the gents' toilet who kept telling people that they looked Russian. Perhaps he was, too, and needed to find someone from his own country. It's that kind of pub; it makes you think of home.

I noticed that one of Sarah's little habits was rubbing her wrists together when she was thinking. Every woman has some kind of private signature like this. Such a gesture marks her out to a lover, or an old friend. I watched her closely scanning the pages – she had forgotten her glasses – and felt a great inner calm. Only once did she disturb the peace between us by asking if I had been out with many women. I lied, of course, as you do, but the question remained in the back of my head, picking and scratching at my brain, right up until I said goodbye to her. It was warm in the pub and she had grown sleepy; she actually fell asleep at one point, so I decided to quietly leave.

The Anchor, Park Street, Southwark

It's pleasant here on rainy days. In the summer, tourists visiting the nearby Globe fill up the bar and pack the riverside tables. Did you know that pub signs were originally provided so that the illiterate could locate them? The Anchor was built after the Southwark fire, which in 1676 razed the south bank just as the Great Fire had attacked the north side ten years earlier. As I entered the pub, I noticed that the tide was unusually high, and the Thames was so dense and pinguid that it looked like a setting jelly. It wasn't a good start to the evening.

I had several pints of strong bitter and grew more talkative as our session progressed. We ate Toad-in-the-Hole, smothered in elastic gravy. I was excited about the idea of Carol and I going out together. I think she was, too, although she warned me that she had some loose ends to tie up, a former boyfriend to get out of her system, and suggested that perhaps we shouldn't rush at things. Out of the blue, she told me to stop watching her so much, as if she was frightened that she couldn't take the scrutiny. But she can. I love seeing the familiar gestures of women, the half-smiles, the rubbing together of their hands, the sudden light in their eyes when they remember something they have to tell you. I can't remember what they say, only how they look. I would never take pictures of them, like some men I've read about. I never look back, you understand. It's too upsetting. Far more important to concentrate on who you're with, and making them happy. I'd like to think I made Carol feel special. She told me she'd never had much luck with men, and I believe it's true that some women just attract the wrong sort. We sat side by side watching the rain on the water, and I felt her head lower gently onto my shoulder, where it remained until I moved – a special moment, and one that I shall always remember.

The Lamb & Flag, Rose Street, Covent Garden

You could tell summer was coming because people were drinking on the street, searching for spaces on the windowsills of the pub to balance their beer glasses. This building looks like an old coaching inn, and stands beside an arch over an alleyway, like the Pillars Of Hercules in Greek Street. It's very old, with lots of knotted wood, and I don't suppose there's a straight angle in the place. The smoky bar is awkward to negotiate when you're carrying a drink in either hand, as I so often am.

This evening Kathy asked why I had not invited her to meet any of my friends. I could tell by the look on her face that she was wondering if I thought she wasn't good enough, and so I was forced to admit that I didn't really have any friends to whom I could introduce her. She was more reticent than most of the girls I had met until then, more private. She acted as though there was something on her mind that she didn't want to share with me. When I asked her to specify the problem, she either wouldn't or couldn't. To be honest, I think the problem was me, and that was why it didn't work out between us. Something about my behaviour made her uneasy right from the start. There was no trust between us, which in itself was unusual, because most women are quick to confide in me. They sense my innate decency, my underlying respect for them. I look at the other drinkers standing around me, and witness the contempt they hold for women. My God, a blind man could feel their disdain. That's probably why I have no mates – I don't like my own sex. I'm ashamed of the whole alpha male syndrome. It only leads to trouble.

I made the effort of asking Kathy if she would sit for me, but knew in advance what the answer would be. She said she would prefer it if we didn't meet again, and yelped in alarm when I brushed against her hip, so I had to beat a hasty retreat.

The King William IV, High Street, Hampstead

Paula chose this rather paradoxical pub. It's in the middle of Hampstead, therefore traditional and oaky, with a beer garden that was packed on a hot summer night, yet the place caters to a 'raucous gay clientele. Apparently, Paula's sister brought her here once before, an attractive girl judging from the photograph Paula showed me and such a waste, I feel, when she could be making a man happy. I wondered if, after finishing with Paula, I should give her sister a call, but decided that it would be playing a little too close to home.

We sat in the garden on plastic chairs, beside sickly flowerbeds of nursery-forced plants, but it was pleasant, and the pub had given me an idea. I resolved to try someone of the same gender next time, just to see what a difference it made. I picked up one of the gay newspapers lying in stacks at the back of the pub, and made a note of other venues in central London. I explained my interest in the newspaper by saying that I wanted to learn more about the lifestyles of others. Paula squeezed my hand

and said how much she enjoyed being with someone who had a liberal outlook. I told her that my policy was live and let live, which is a laugh for a start. I am often shocked by the wide-eyed belief I inspire in women, and wonder what they see in me that makes them so trusting. When I pressed myself close against her she didn't flinch once under my gaze and remained staring into my eyes while I drained my beer glass. A special girl, a special evening, for both of us.

The Admiral Duncan, Old Compton Street, Soho

Formerly decorated as a cabin aboard an old naval vessel, with lead-light bay windows and a curved wood ceiling, this venue was revamped to suit the street's new status as a home to the city's homosexuals, and painted a garish purple. It was restored again following the nail bomb blast that killed and maimed so many of its customers. Owing to the tunnel-like shape of the bar, the explosive force had nowhere to escape but through the glass front, and caused horrific injuries. A monument to the tragedy is inset in the ceiling of the pub, but no atmosphere of tragedy lingers, for the patrons, it seems, have bravely moved on in their lives.

In here I met Graham, a small-boned young man with a gentle West Country burr that seemed at odds with his spiky haircut. We became instant drinking pals, buying each other rounds in order to escape the evening heat of the mobbed street beyond. After what had occurred in the pub I found it astonishing that someone could be so incautious as to befriend a total stranger such as myself, but that is the beauty of the English boozer; once you cross the threshold, barriers of race, class and gender can be dropped. Oh, it doesn't happen everywhere, I know, but you're more likely to make a friend in this city than in most others. That's why I find it so useful in fulfilling my needs. However, the experiment with Graham was not a success. Boys don't work for me, no matter how youthful or attractive they appear to be. We were standing in a corner, raising our voices over the incessant thump of the jukebox, when I realised it wasn't working. Graham had drunk so much that he was starting to slide down the wall, but there were several others in the vicinity who were one step away from being paralytic, so he didn't stick out, and I could leave unnoticed.

The Black Friar, Queen Victoria Street, Blackfriars
This strange little pub, stranded alone by the roundabout on the north side of the river at Blackfriars, has an Arts and Crafts style interior, complete with friezes, bas-reliefs and mottoes running over its arches. Polished black monks traipse about the room, punctuating the place with moral messages. It stands as a memorial to a vanished London, a world of brown trilbys and woollen overcoats, of rooms suffused with pipe smoke and the tang of brilliantine. In the snug bar at the rear I met Danielle, a solidly-built Belgian au pair who looked so lonely, lumpen and forlorn that I could not help but offer her a drink, and she was soon pouring out her troubles in broken English. Her employers wanted her to leave because she was pregnant, and she couldn't afford to go back to Antwerp.

To be honest I wasn't listening to everything she was saying, because someone else had caught my eye. Seated a few stools away was a ginger-haired man who appeared to be following our conversation intently. He was uncomfortably overweight, and undergoing some kind of perspiration crisis. The pub was virtually deserted. Most of the customers drinking outside on the pavement, and Danielle was talking loudly, so it was possible that she might have been overheard. I began to wonder if she was lying to me about her problems; if, perhaps they were more serious than she made them sound, serious enough for someone to be following her. I know it was selfish, but I didn't want to spend any more time with a girl who was in that kind of trouble, so I told her I needed to use the toilet, then slipped out across the back of the bar.

The Angel, Rotherhithe

Another old riverside inn – I seem to be drawn to them, anxious to trace the city's sluggish artery, site by site, as though marking a pathway to the heart. The interesting thing about places like The Angel is how little they change across the decades, because they retain the same bleary swell of customers through all economic climates. Workmen and stockbrokers, estate agents, secretaries, van-drivers and tarts, they just rub along together with flirtatious smiles, laughs, belches and the odd sour word. The best feature of this pub is reached by the side entrance, an old wooden balcony built out over the shoreline, where mudlarks once rooted in the filth for treasure trove, and where you can sit and watch the sun settling between the pillars of Tower Bridge.

As the light faded we become aware of the sky brushing the water, making chilly ripples. Further along the terrace I thought I saw the red-haired man watching, but when I looked again, he had gone. Growing cold, we pulled our coats tighter, then moved inside. Stella was Greek, delicate and attractive, rather too young for me, but I found her so easy to be with that we remained together for the whole evening. Shortly before closing time she told me she should be going home soon because her brother was expecting her. I was just massaging some warmth back into her arms – we were seated by an open window and it had suddenly turned nippy – when she said she felt sick and went off to the Ladies. After she failed to reappear I went to check on her, just to make sure she was all right. I found her in one of the cubicles, passed out.

The Ship, Greenwich
The dingy interior of this pub is unremarkable, with bare-board floors and tables cut from blackened barrels, but the exterior is another matter entirely. I can imagine the building, or one very like it, existing on the same site for centuries, at a reach of the river where it is possible to see for miles in either direction. I am moving out toward the mouth of the Thames, being taken by the tide to ever-widening spaces in my search for absolution. There was something grotesquely Victorian about the weeds thrusting out of ancient brickwork, tumbledown fences and the stink of the mud. It was unusually mild for the time of year, and we sat on the wall with our legs dangling over the water, beers propped at our crotches.

Melanie was loud and common, coarse-featured and thick-legged. She took up room in the world and didn't mind who knew it. She wore a lot of make-up, and had frothed her hair into a mad dry nest, but I was intrigued by the shape of her mouth, the crimson wetness of her lips, her cynical laugh, her seen-it-all-before eyes. She touched me as though expecting me to walk out on her at any moment, digging nails on my arm, nudging an elbow in my ribs, running fingers up my thigh. Still, I wondered if she would present a challenge, because I felt sure that my offer to sketch her would be rebuffed. She clearly had no interest in art, so I appealed to her earthier side and suggested something of a less salubrious nature.

To my surprise she quoted me a price list, which ruined everything. I swore at her and pushed her away, disgusted. She, in turn, began calling me every filthy name under the sun, which attracted unwanted attention to both of us. It was then that I saw the ginger-headed man again, standing to the left of me, speaking into his chubby fist.

The Trafalgar Tavern, Greenwich

I ran. Tore myself free of her and ran off along the towpath, through the corrugated iron alley beside the scrapyard and past the defunct factory smokestacks, keeping the river to my right. On past The Yacht, too low-ceilinged and cosy to lose myself inside, to the doors of The Trafalgar, a huge gloomy building of polished brown interiors, as depressing as a church. Within, the windows of the connecting rooms were dominated by the gleaming grey waters beyond. Nobody moved. Even the bar staff were still. It felt like a funeral parlour. I pushed between elderly drinkers whose movements were as slow as the shifting of tectonic plates, and slipped behind a table where I could turn my seat to face the river. I thought that if I didn't move, I could remain unnoticed. In the left pocket of my jacket I still had my sketchbook. I knew it would be best to get rid of it, but didn't have the heart to throw it away, not after all the work I had done. When I heard the muttered command behind me, I knew that my sanctuary had been invaded and that it was the beginning of the end. I sat very still as I watched the red-headed man approaching from the corner of my eye, and caught the crackle of radio headsets echoing each other around the room. I slowly raised my head, and for the first time saw how different it all was now. A bare saloon bar filled with tourists, no warmth, no familiarity, no comfort.

When I was young I sat on the step – every pub seemed to have a step – with a bag of crisps and a lemonade, and sometimes I was allowed to sit inside with my dad, sipping his bitter and listening to his beery laughter, the demands for fresh drinks, the dirty jokes, the outraged giggles of the girls at his table. They would tousle my hair, pinch my skinny arms and tell me that I was adorable. Different pubs, different women, night after night, that was my real home, the home I remember. Different pubs but always the same warmth, the same smells, the same songs, the same women. Everything about them was filled with smoky mysteries and hidden pleasures, even their names. The World Turned Upside Down. The Queen's Head and Artichoke, The Rose And Crown, The Greyhound, The White Hart, all of them had secret meanings.

People go to clubs for a night out now, chrome and steel, neon lights, bottled beers, drum and bass, bouncers with headsets. The bars sport names like The Lounge and The Living Room, hoping to evoke a sense of belonging, but they cater to an alienated world, squandering noise and light on people so blinded by work that their leisure time must be spent in aggression, screaming at each other, shovelling drugs, pushing for fights. As the red-haired man moved closer, I told myself that all I wanted to do was make people feel at home. Is that so very wrong? My real home was nothing, the memory of a damp council flat with a stinking disconnected fridge and dogshit on the floor. It's the old pubs of London that hold my childhood; the smells, the sounds, the company. There is a moment before the last bell is called when it seems it could all go on forever. It is that moment I try to capture and hold in my palm. I suppose you could call it the land before time.

The Load Of Hay, Haverstock Hill, Belsize Park

The red-haired officer wiped at his pink brow with a Kleenex until the tissue started to come apart. Another winter was approaching, and the night air was bitter. His wife used to make him wear a scarf when he was working late, and it always started him sweating. She had eventually divorced him. He dressed alone now and ate takeaway food in a tiny flat. But he wore the scarf out of habit. He looked in through the window of the pub at the laughing drinkers at the bar, and the girl sitting alone beside the slot-machine. Several of his men were in there celebrating a colleague's birthday, but he didn't feel like facing them tonight.

How the hell had they let him get away? He had drifted from them like bonfire smoke in changing wind. The Trafalgar had too many places where you could hide, he saw that now. His men had been overconfident and undertrained. They hadn't been taught how to handle anyone so devious, or if they had, they had forgotten what they had learned.

He kept one of the clear plastic ampoules in his pocket, just to remind himself of what he had faced that night. New technology had created new hospital injection techniques. You could scratch yourself with the micro-needle and barely feel a thing, if the person wielding it knew how to avoid any major nerve-endings. Then it was simply a matter of squeezing the little bulb, and any liquid contained in the ampoule was delivered through a coat, a dress, a shirt, into the flesh. Most of his victims were drunk at the time, so he had been able to connect into their bloodstreams without them noticing more than a pinprick. A deadly mixture of RoHypnol, Zimovane and some kind of coca-derivative. It numbed and relaxed them, then sent them to sleep. But the sleep deepened and stilled their hearts, as a dreamless caul slipped over their brains, shutting the senses one by one until there was nothing left alive inside.

No motives, no links, just dead strangers in the most public places in the city, watched by roving cameras, filled with witnesses. That was the trouble; you expected to see people getting legless in pubs.

His attention was drawn back to the girl sitting alone. What was she doing there? Didn't she realise the danger? No one heeded the warnings they issued. There were too many other things to worry about.

He had been on the loose for a year now, and had probably moved on to another city, where he could continue his work without harassment. He would stop as suddenly as he had begun. The only people who would ever really know him were the victims – and perhaps even they couldn't see behind their killer's eyes. As the urban landscape grew crazier, people's motives were harder to discern. An uprooted population, on the make and on the move. Fast, faster, fastest.

And for the briefest of moments he held the answer in his hand. He saw a glimmer of the truth – constancy shining like a shaft through all the change, the woman alone in the smoky saloon smiling and interested, her attention caught by just one man, this intimacy unfolding against background warmth, the pulling of pints, the blanket of conversation, the huddle of friendship, but then it was gone, all gone, and the terrible sense of unbelonging filled his heart once more.

irvine welsh

....

elspeth's boyfriend

Thir's some cunts thit ye hit it oaf wi, n some cunts thit ye dinnae. Take Elspeth's boyfriend fir example; a right fuckin case-in-point, that yin. Ah mean, ah'd nivir even met the cunt until Christmas day, but aw wi'd goat fi the auld lady leadin up tae it wis 'Greg this' n 'Greg that' n 'eh's an awfay nice laddie'.

So that gits ye thinkin tae yirself, right away; aw aye?

Christmas, eh. Some cunts lap it but tae me it's a load ay shite. Too commercialized. It's usually just the faimlay for us. But ah've fuckin moved in wi ma burd Kate, oor first festive season the gither. We hud a big row aboot it n aw; mind you, ye eywis dae at Christmas. Wouldnae be a fuckin Christmas withoot every cunt gittin oan each others nerves.

As ye kin fuckin guess, she's moanin thit wir gaun tae muh Ma's instead ay hers. The thing is thit ma brar Joe n eh's wife Sandra n thir two wee bairns n ma sister Elspeth wid be thair. Tradition n that. That's what ah telt Kate, ah eywis go tae ma auld girl's at Christmas. That cow ah used tae be wi, that June, she's takin the bairns tae *her* auld lady's. No thit it bothers me, but it means thit muh Ma'll no see thum at Christmas. That's June but: fill ay fuckin spite.

Ye cannae fuckin win wi burds at Christmas. Aye, Kate wis aw humpty n aw. She goes, well you go tae your Ma's n ah'll go tae ma faimly's. Ah sais tae her, dinnae start gittin fuckin wide, wir gaun tae muh Ma's n that's that. Dinnae try n snub ma auld girl.

So that wis that settled. Nearer the time ah git's oantae the auld lady, askin her when she wants us roond. She gies ays aw this, 'oh lit me see, when did Elspeth say thit her n Greg wir gaunnae come roond again . . .'

Well, ye git the fuckin picture. By the time it's Christmas day, me n Joe've hud wir fuckin fill ay Elspeth's boyfriend, this fuckin Greg cunt or whatever they call um. Ah'd been oot oan the pish aw Christmas Eve wi some ay the boys, n Joe wis in the same boat, ye could see it fae the cunt's eyes, he wis fucked n aw. Aye, it goat fuckin well messy that night. Lines ay charlie racked up every five minutes; boatils n boatils ah champagne bein guzzled. That tae me's what Christmas is aw aboot, jist littin yirsel go. Specially the champagne; ah love that stuff, could quaff it till the cows come hame. Must be the aristocrat n ays. Blue fuckin blood.

Ye suffer the next day but, no half ye fuckin dinnae.

So that Christmas mornin, me n hur huv this big arguemint again. Ma heid is fuckin nippin, n ma sinuses feel like some cunt's went poured a load ay concrete intae them. Tryin tae git ready tae go roond tae muh Ma's hoose, n feelin like that, she asks ays, – What dae ye think ah should wear the day Frank?

Ah jist looks at her n goes: – Clathes.

That shuts ur fuckin mooth fir a bit.

Then ah sais, – How the fuck should ah ken?

She looks at ays n goes, – Well, should ah git aw dressed up?

– Wear whit ye fuckin like, ah telt ur, – ah'm no gittin aw trussed up like a fuckin turkey jist tae sit peevin n watchin the telly roond at muh Ma's. Levis, Ben Sherman n Stone Island cardy, that'll dae fir me.

So that seems tae satisfy hur, n she pits oan this sports gear. Casual but quite smart, ken.

Aye, ah could tell a mile away thit she'd taken the fuckin strop, but. Ah jist thoat, well, if she wants tae be aw anti-social this Christmas, that's fuckin well up tae her.

Wi heads doon the road n gits tae the auld girl's. Joe n that wis awready thair.

– Aye, aye Franco, that Sandra goes tae me.

– Aye, ah goes. Nivir saw eye-tae-eye wi her. Too much ay a mooth oan it. Dinnae ken how oor Joe kin be daein wi that. His choice but. Widnae fuckin well be mine anywey. At least her n Kate git oan, n that's a good thing, cause it keeps the bairns oaf Joe's back n lits us git a peeve in peace. Ah git a can ay Rid Stripe open. Ah'm gaunny git fuckin well hammered; it's what Christmas is aw aboot.

Wi firin intae the lagers awright. Wir jist sittin thaire, thinkin through oor hangovers, 'if this cunt Greg or whatever ye call the boy, if eh starts gittin wide, eh's gaunnae git a fuckin bat in mooth, Christmas or nae fuckin Christmas.'

Eftir a bit the door goes, n it's Elspeth. This tall, dark-heided cunt wi a side-partin comes in behind her. Eh's aw done up tae the nines in a smart coat n suit, ye kin tell that this cunt really fanices ehsel. What goat me wis the side partin. Ken how some things jist git oan yir fuckin nerves fir nae reason? Bit then what *really* wound ays up wis thit eh wis cairryin a bunch flooirs. Flooirs, oan fuckin Christmas Day! – For you Val, eh goes tae the auld girl, giein her a wee peck oan the cheek. Then the cunt comes up tae me n goes, – You must be Frank, n eh pits ehs hand oot.

Ah'm thinkin, aye, who the fuck wants tae ken likes, but ah lit it go, cause ah didnae want tae cause a scene. Jist didnae take tae this smary poof at aw but, ye ken how it is wi some people? Try as ye might, ye jist cannae fuckin well take tae thum.

But ah bites the bullet n shakes the cunt's hand, thinkin, Christmas n that, the season ay goodwill.

– Good tae meet ye finally, eh sais. – Elspeth talks about ye a lot. In very glowing terms, I should add, the cunt goes.

Ah feel like asking the cunt what the fuck eh's oan aboot, is eh tryin tae git wide or what, but eh's turned away n eh's ower tae Joe. – And you must be Joe, eh goes.

– Aye, sais Joe, shakin ehs hand, but no gittin up oot the chair. – So you're oor Elspeth's felly then, aye?

– I certainly am, eh smiles, at her, n ah catch um giein her hand a squeeze. She's lookin aw that daft wey at um, like she's nivir been oot wi a gadge before.

– Love's young dream, that Sandra goes, cooin away, like one ay they big fat fuckin pidgeons thit the auld man used tae keep. Ah mind ay wringin a couple ay the cunts necks eftir eh'd battered ays once. The best thing tae dae wi they cunts though, is tae set thum oan fire. It's barry watchin thum tryin tae take oaf, whin thir blazin away n screamin in agony. Ah'll gie yis fuckin cooin, ya cunts.

Sometimes ah used tae jist go doon tae the loft oan ehs allotment and burn a couple ay the bastards thair, or git yin n nail it tae the hut. Jist tae see the expression oan the auld fucker's face when eh came hame, aw pished n upset. Blamed every cunt n aw; vandals, gypos, neighbours, publicans. Wanted tae kill half ay fuckin Leith. Ah'd be sittin thair in the chair opposite, lookin aw innocent, jist gaun, – Ohhh . . . which one wis it they goat this time dad? N he'd be fuckin well jist aboot in tears. The cunt wid smash up the hoose in a fit ay rage, before hittin the boozer again. Come tae think ay it, it wis probably me that drove the cunt tae drink! Him n eh's fuckin daft pidgeons.

That fuckin Sandra. Nivir mind the fuckin turkey, stick that fat cunt in the oven n wi'll be feedin half ay fuckin Leith through until next Christmas. Ah dinnae ken aboot stuffin it but, ah'll no be volunteerin fir they fuckin duties anywey. Nae fuckin chance!

So this big, bloated rooster's right up tae Elspeth's boy. – Ah'm Sandra, Joe's wife, she sais tae this Greg, aw that flirty, slutty wey.

This cunt goes up and kisses her twice, once oan each cheek, like some fuckin weirdo. Ah dinnae hud wi that, kissin a woman ye dinnae ken, in somebody's hoose. At Christmas, at a fuckin faimlay gatherin. Aye, ah'm watchin Kate, thinkin thit if eh does that tae her, eh's fuckin well gittin the nut rammed oan um. Fuckin smarmy poof.

But she sees me lookin at her, n she kens how tae behave. Goat her well fuckin trained. Aye, *she* kens no tae show ays up. Must huv a word wi Joe aboot that Sandra, embarrassin um like that. Ah ken that big cow; a leopard nivir fuckin well changes its spoats, right enough. Used tae call her the thirty-two bus, back in the day. That wis cause every cunt rode her roond the schemes. Still, it's no fir me tae say. So Kate pits her hand oot for him tae shake, n keeps her eyes doon, away fae his. – Ah'm Kate, she mumbles.

Handled that yin well. Aye, mibbee the message aboot eggin boys oan is startin tae git through. Jist as fuckin well, fir her sake. The wey ah see is thit whin a lassie's wi somebody, she's no meant tae be giein other boys the come-on aw the time. Ye cannae trust a fuckin cow like that, n yuv goat tae huv trust in a relationship.

This Greg looks aw surprised, n gies a wee smile. Somethin creepy aboot that bastard. Ken how some cunt's jist set yir fuckin teeth oan edge? The fucker reminds ehs ay that cunt ay an insurance man thit used tae come roond oor bit whin wi wir bairns. Eh'd eywis gie us these sweeties; really crap yins like dolly mixtures, aw that cheap shite. Aye, ye could tell he wis a fuckin right oily cunt underneath it aw. Ah ey took the sweeties oaf the cunt, but. Too fuckin right ah did. Nivir liked that fucker though.

The auld girl's been in the kitchen aw mornin, workin oan the meal. Her face is aw rid. She likes tae make a big effort fir Christmis. Widnae be me anywey. Fuck slavin ower a hoat stove oan Christmas day. Ye cannae work oot what's gaun oan in some cunt's heid's but. Now she's tryin tae organise every cunt: makin a big fuss aboot us aw openin oor presents under the tree. Ah'm no bothered wi aw that shite. Whae cares aboot fuckin presents? As far as clothes n aw that goes, ah've goat the money tae git what the fuck ah want. Ye like tae git what you want tae wear, no what some other cunt wants tae gie ye. Ay gied the burd two hundred quid fir clathes, n muh Ma the same. Then ah gied Joe a hundred tae git somethin fir the bairns, n fifty bar tae oor Elspeth for whatever she wanted. The only presents ah goat wis fir ma ain bairns. That wis only because ah kent thit if ah gied June the money tae git thum somethin, like a fuckin Play Station or a bike, they'd end up wi some plastic shite fae Ali's Cave. Aye, the rest wid go oan fuckin snout fir her. So that wis aw. The rest ay thum, it wis jist; here's yir fuckin Christmis offay me, jist git what the fuck ye want.

It's the best fuckin wey. Aw that fuss aboot wrappin fuckin presents up? Ah couldnae be daein wi that. Fuck wrappin presents.

Rap some cunt's fuckin jaw.

Ah'm lookin ower at that Kate. Two hundred fuckin bar fir clathes ah gied her, n she comes intae muh Ma's dressed like a fuckin frump, showin ays up. Oor Elspeth's made an effort, she's goat a nice black perty dress oan, aw fir that smarmy Greg cunt n aw. Even that fuckin cow Sandra hus. Scrawny auld fuckin hen done up as spring chicken, mind, but at least shi's fuckin well tried. Kate but: a fuckin jaikey on Christmis Day! In muh Ma's hoose n aw!

Thir aw makin a big fuckin fuss aboot presents. It's 'ooh, this is lovely' n 'oooh, it's jist what ah eywis wanted'. Then thir aw at me tae open mine, so ah jist thinks, might as well, keep the cunts happy. If it fuckin well means that much tae thum. Ah gits a blue pastel-coloured Ben Sherman oaffay Kate, n a yellaw Ben

Sherman offay Joe n Sandra. In ma auld girl's parcel thir's another Ben Sherman; a black, broon n light-blue striped yin. Ah think ah must've asked fir Ben Sherman's offay every cunt; mind you, ye cannae go wrong wi shirts. Thir's one left, marked oan the gift tag: To Francis, from Elspeth and Greg. Merry Christmas.

It feels like another fuckin Ben Sherman, but whin ah rips it open it's a sweater wi the new club crest oan it.

– That's nice, muh mother sais. Elspeth goes, – Aye, it's the new yin. It's goat the original Harp crest, wi the ship for Leith, n the castle fir Edinburgh. Thaire smilin at ays, n it gits right oan ma fuckin tits. Tryin tae take the fuckin pish here. Tae me, whin ye buy some cunt official club merchandise, it's like yir sayin tae thum thit ye think thir a fuckin wanker. Ah widnae be seen deid wearin that shite. That's fir fuckin wee bairn n fuckin dippit cunts, that. – Ta, ah goes, but through gritted teeth, ken?

Ah'm thinkin; that's gaun right in the bucket whin ay git hame, tell ye that fir nowt.

Ye kin understand it if it wis Elspeth thit made the mistake. Ah mean, that's birds fir ye. But if that Greg cunt wis in oan buyin it, it meant thit eh wis tryin tae take the pish. Ah'm fuckin well fumin at that disrespect, so tae stoap masel fae sayin somethin ah shouldnae, ah go ben the scullery tae git another can fae the fridge. Then ah'm thinkin thit that Greg's such a big fuckin lassie ehsel, he probably disnae huv fuckin a clue either.

Ma heid's still nippin n ah swallay a couple ay extra-strength Annadin wi a moothfae ay beer. Whin ah gits back ah sees this fuckin Greg cunt's playin away wi Joe's bairns, oan the fuckin flair wi aw thir toys. Meant tae be the fuckin bairn's new toys, no fir some big pansy tae

ponce aroond wi. Ah pills Joe aside n back intae the
kitchen, n goes: – Ye want tae watch that cunt aroond
the bairns. Touch ay the fuckin Gary Glitters thaire, ah'll
tell ye that fir nowt.

– Ye reckon? Joe sais, pittin ehs heid roond the door tae
check it oot.

– Defo. Ye ken how fuckin plausible they cunts kin be.
That's the thing. Ah'd lay ye even money thit that cunt's
oan the stoats register. Ye kin spot the type a mile away.

Muh Ma sees us n comes ben. – What are you two oan
aboot, standin here in the kitchen drinkin like fishes! Git
oot thaire n try n be social, it's meant tae be Christmas!

– Right Ma, ah goes, lookin at Joe. That Greg cunt
might huv brainwashed her; that's wimmin fir ye, no goat
much brains tae fuckin wash in the first place, bit Joe n
me huv been aroond long enough tae see right through a
cunt like that.

Best keepin the auld lady fuckin sweet but, or shi'll huv
a coupon oan her aw day. So wi gits back through wi the
rest ay thum n ah sits doon n picks up the *Radio Times*.
Ah starts tae circle aw the programmes wir gaunny
watch. The wey ah see it is thit some cunt's goat tae
decide, tae stoap every fucker fae squabblin, so it might
as well be me. That's what ah like best aboot Christmas,
jist sittin back wi a few cans n watchin a good film.

Ya beauty! James Bond's oan. Doctor No, n it's jist
aboot tae fuckin well start.

Sean Connery, the best fuckin Bond. Ye dinnae want
some fuckin poncey English cunt, no fir James Bond.

Mind you, no thit ah really agree wi huvin some cunt
fae Tolcross as Bond. Thir's cunt's fae Leith thit could've
done that joab jist as well as Connery. Auld Davie Robb,

drinks in the Marksman, he must be aboot ages wi Connery. A fuckin hard cunt n ehs day, everybody'll tell ye that. Intae everythin, he wis. Cunts like that could've been good Bonds, if they'd goat the fuckin trainin likes.

– Wir no watchin Doctor No, muh Ma sais, – come on Francis!

– Ah'd awready picked it but Ma, ah tells her.

She's standin thair, wi her airms aw folded, the fuckin billy ay the wash-hoose, like she wants ays tae gie her the remote. Nae chance ay that. Sometimes ah think thit muh Ma forgets thit this is as much ma hoose as it is hers. Ah might no huv steyed here fir years, bit this wis the hoose thit ah grew up in, so ye still eywis think ay it as your hoose. Ah think she sometimes firgets that. – Yuv seen it loads ay times! She moans. – The wee yins might want tae watch the cartoon video's they goat fir Christmas!

– Toy Story Two . . . one ay the bairns goes. That wee Philip, a sneaky wee bastard, that yin. Takes eftir ehs ma.

Some cunts are that fuckin clueless thit ye huv tae explain everything. – Naw, cause that's the whole point ay gittin a fuckin video, ah goes tae thum, – thit ye kin watch it anytime ye like. Ye cannae watch the Bond film anytime ye like. Ye either watch it or ye dinnae, n yuv goat tae watch a Bond film at Christmas. Joe? Ah turns tae ma brar.

– Ah'm no bothered, Joe goes.

Sandra looks acroas at him, then at me, then at Kate. Ye jist ken that big cow's gaunny say somethin cause she goes aw that huffy, puffed-up wey. – So wi huv tae watch what Frank wants again, ah take it. Fine, she goes, aw sarcastic.

– Dinnae fuckin start, Joe goes, pointin at her.

– Ah'm jist sayin what yir Ma's sayin, thit the bairns . . .

Joe cuts her oaf. – Ah sais dinnae fuckin start, eh lowers ehs voice. – Ah've telt ye.

She sits bristlin away on the fuckin couch, bit she's no lookin at anybody n she's no sayin nowt.

Joe looks at me, n shakes ehs heid.

It wis aboot time eh wis gittin her telt.

Muh Ma looks ower at Greg n Elspeth. They've been sittin oan thir ain; jist whisperin away, n laughin tae thumselves in the corner, aw anti-social. Meant tae be a fuckin faimlay Christmas wir huvin here. If the cunts wanted tae dae that, they could fuckin well dae it ootside. – What dae youse two want tae watch? Muh Ma asks thum.

They look at each other like thir no bothered, and this smarmy cunt, this Greg poof goes, – Well, ah'm with Frank. Ah think it would be a good laugh tae watch the Bond movie. Then the cunt goes in this posh voice, – Ah Mr Bond, I've been expecting you . . . n muh Ma laughs n ah even sees a wee smile oan the corner ay Joe's lips.

Of course, the bairns are aw laughin now, n every cunt suddenly thinks it's aw a fuckin great idea tae watch the Bond movie, now thit this fuckin Greg wanker's intae it.

Ruined ma fuckin enjoyment ay the film.

These cunts; that two, that Greg n Elspeth: thuv been whisperin tae each other aw the wey through the fuckin picture anyway. Eftir makin aw that fuss aboot it, that cunt wisnae even watchin the film right. At the end ay it, the pair ay thum git up n stand in front ay the telly. Ah'm jist aboot tae tell thum tae sit the fuck doon cause ah want tae change channels tae see that fuckin *Snowman* cartoon, fir the sake ay the bairns ken, n thaire blockin the signal fae the remote.

– We've got a little announcement to make, this Greg cunt goes, and Elspeth moves close tae um and they hud hands. Muh Ma's lookin aw excited. It's like she's waitin fir the last fuckin number oan her caird doon at the Mecca. The Greg cunt coughs, – It's difficult tae know how to say this, but, well, yesterday, I asked Elspeth if she would do me the great honour of becoming my wife, and I'm delighted tae say that she said yes.

Ma auld girl stands up, aw delirious, n stretches her airms oot like that Al Jolson cunt, aw ready tae burst intae song. But it's tears she bursts intae, n she's sayin how beautiful it is; her wee lassie n she cannae believe it, n aw that crap. What a fuckin fuss tae make ower nowt. It's like some cunt hud slipped an ecky intae her sherry. Ah widnae pit it past yon Greg. Sly-lookin gadge, ken? Aye, Sandra n Kate are aw excited n Joe's wee yin says, kin she be a bridesmaid, and they say, aye, of course ye kin, n aw that shite. Ah couldnae fuckin believe ma ears. Gittin mairried! Oor Elspeth n this fuckin nonce cunt in the suit!

Her heid's in the clouds. That's Elspeth but, eywis thinkin thit she's better thin any cunt else. Spoiled rotten by bein the youngest, n the only lassie, that's what it wis. Nivir hud it rough, no like me n Joe. Thinks thit she kin jist suit ehrsel. Some cunt should tell her; it disnae fuckin well work that wey, no in the real world.

So ah'm fuckin well sittin thair, ma nut poundin, n thair aw shriekin away as she pills oot a ring n sticks it oan her finger, showin it oaf. – It's beautiful, muh Ma goes.

– Very nice, that Sandra sais, – Did eh git doon oan the bended? Bet eh did, she goes, lookin at that Greg, then glancin doon at ma brar like eh's nowt.

Fuckin Elspeth but. Ah dinnae ken what she's playin at. Ah mind ay that last boy she wis gaun oot wi, he wis a good cunt. Keith, the boy's name wis. He hud a big motor n aw, and a no bad flat. The pit the perr fucker away though, jist fir dealin a wee bit ay bugle. It's fuckin well oot ay order, cause jist aboot every cunt's at that game these days. Ye cannae really class charlie as drugs, no in ma book. Ah mean, it's no like it's schemies fuckin killin thirsels wi smack. What it is, is a designer accessory fir the modern fuckin age. That's the problem wi this fuckin country though; too many cunt's livin in the dark ages, no prepared tae move wi the times.

This Greg cunt vanishes for a bit, then eh comes back wi a huge boatil ay champagne n some glesses. The wey that Sandra's lookin at the boatil, ye'd think it wis a fuckin vibrator thit she wis gaunny stick up her fanny. So fuckin pretty-boy pops the cork n it flies acroas the room, hittin the ceilin. Ah'm ower n checkin tae see if it's left a mark whaire it hit the paintwork, n if it hus, that cunt kin pey fir muh Ma tae git her fuckin ceilin redone. Lucky fir him it husnae. Eh pours the drink intae the glesses. Joe takes a gless fae the cunt, but ah wave um away. – Dinnae like that stuff. That's crap, ah tell the boy.

– Stickin tae the beer, aye, eh goes.

– Aye, ah sais.

– Come on son, it's a special occasion, yir sister's engagement, muh Ma goes.

– Disnae bother me, ah dinnae like they fizzy bubbles. They git up ma nose, ah tell her, lookin ower at the Greg poof, wi ehs fuckin side-partin n ehs suit n crew-neck shirt withoot a tie. Ah wanted tae tell her that *he* gits up ma fuckin nose, but ah kept quiet, Christmas n that.

Aye, it's no fir me tae say nowt, but ah'll run a check oan this cunt. Somethin fuckin right iffy aboot that radge. Eh looks the type ay cunt that's no too sure aboot whether tae catch the one or the six, if ye ken what ah mean. Probably one ay they fuckin bent-shots that shag the young poofs up the Calton Hill. In the fuckin closet, n usin oor Elspeth as cover.

See if that cunt gie's her AIDS; eh's fuckin well deid.

– Well, that fuckin loudmoothed hoor Sandra goes, raisin her gless in a toast, – Tae Elspeth n Greg!

– Elspeth n Greg, every cunt sais.

Ah'm sayin nowt, but ah never take ma eyes oaf that cunt. Aye, pal, ah'm fuckin well wide fir you. Every cunt else's makin a big fuss, n even Joe shakes the boy's hand. Ah'm shakin nae cunt's hand, that's a fuckin cert.

– Well, ah'd best git the dinner served up, the auld lady sais, – this hus been the happiest Christmas I've hud in years. See if yir faither wis here . . . she bubbles at Elspeth.

If oor faither wis here eh'd huv fuckin well done what eh eywis did; drunk us oot ay hoose n hame n made a fuckin exhibition ay ehsel.

This cunt Greg puts ehs hand oan muh Ma's wrist n slides ehs other airm around oor Elspeth's waist. – Ah was just sayin tae Els last night Val, it's my one big regret that I was never able tae meet John.

What's that cunt sayin aboot ma fuckin auld man? He didnae ken ma fuckin auld man! This fuckin cunt thinks eh jist come in here n take ower everything, jist cause eh caught oor Elspeth at a vulnerable time. Jist cause she wis oan the rebound so tae speak, wi that fuckin perr Keith boy gittin sent doon. Ah've seen smarmy cunt's like this Greg before, seen thum in action. Eywis oan the look-oot fir some lassie tae take a len ay.

Naw, she's makin a big mistake n she hus tae be telt.

So wir sittin doon at the table tae oor dinner, n the auld lady's only went n arranged it soas thit ah'm sittin next tae this fuckin smarmy, side-partin, child-molester. Ah'm gled now thit that fuckin June took oor bairns tae her hoor ay a Ma's hoose.

– So what line ay work are ye in mate, Joe asks the Greg boy.

Elspeth buts in before the cunt kin speak. – Greg works fir the council.

– Huv a word wi the cunts aboot that council tax, fuckin well oot ay order, ah goes. Muh Ma n Joe n Sandra nod away, agreein wi that, n ah've fuckin well goat the cunt thair. The council's a fuckin waste ay money as far as ah kin see. They could shut the whole fuckin loat doon the morn n nae cunt wid notice any fuckin difference.

Elspeth gits aw snooty, – That's no Greg's department. He's in Planning. A Principal Officer, she says, aw fill ay it.

So it's planning were gittin now, is it? Aye, n ye ken what that cunt's fuckin well plannin awright; plannin tae git ehs fuckin feet under the table. Well, no in this hoose eh's no.

Sittin thaire, drinkin ehs wine, chompin intae that dinner like eh's tae the fuckin manor born. The crawlin cunt goes, – You've really pulled oot aw the stops here, Val. Delicious. Cooked tae a treat.

Ah'm sittin next tae um, ragin, n ah swallays a moothfae ay grub. Thir's somethin, a wee bone or the likes, stickin a bit in ma throat. Ah takes a sip ay wine.

– Ah'd like tae propose a wee toast, the Greg cunt goes, raisin ehs gless. – Tae family.

Ah tries tae cough up, but it's stuck fast. Ah cannae git any air, ma fuckin nostrils are aw blocked up wi that charlie fae last night . . . ma sinuses are packed solid wi crap . . .

Fuckin hell

– Uncle Frank's no well, the wee boy says.

– Ye awright Francis son? Somethin no gaun doon? Muh ma goes. – Eh's gaun red . . .

Ah waves the cunts away, n ah stands up. That daft cow Sandra's tryin tae gie me a bit ay breed, – Force this doon, force it doon . . . she goes . . . but ah'm fuckin well chokin anywey, she's fuckin tryin tae kill me . . .

Ah pushes her aside, n ah'm gaspin n chokin, n ma heid's spinnin n ah see the horror in thaire faces roond the table. Ah cough, n this sick comes up n catches in ma fuckin throat n flies back doon, aw hoat n burnin, right back intae ma fuckin lungs . . .

YA CUNT

AH'M FUCKIN CHOKIN

Ah'm grabbin the table, n bangin oan it, then grabbin at ma throat . . .

AW YA FUCKER . . .

Ah feels this bang oan the toap ay ma back; one dunt, then another, n ah feels somethin loosen n it aw comes up, that fuckin blockage is away n ah kin breathe . . .

Sweet fuckin air . . . ah kin breathe . . .

– Awright Franco, Joe asks.

Ah nods.

– Well done Greg, ye saved the day thaire, eh goes.

– Ye certainly did, that Sandra says.

Ah'm gittin ma puff back, tryin tae work oot what happened. Ah turns tae this Greg. – Some cunt battered ays oan the back thaire. Wis that you?

– Aye, ah think ye swallowed the wishbone, eh goes.

Ah smacks the nut oantae the cunt, n eh faws back, hudin ehs face. Thir's screams fae the women n the bairns n Joe's ower n eh's goat a grip ay ma airm. – What ur ye fuckin daein Franco, the boy helped ye! Eh saved yir fuckin life!

Fuckin baws tae aw that: ah brushes ehs hand oaf. – Eh battered ays oan the back in muh Ma's hoose! Nae cunt lays thir hands oan me! In muh Ma's hoose, oan Christmas Day? That'll be fuckin right!

Muh Ma's screamin, callin ays an animal, n oor Elspeth's daein her nut. – That's it, that's us finished, she goes, lookin at me, shakin her heid. – We're gaun, she sais tae muh Ma.

– Aw dinnae, please, hen, no the day! Muh Ma pleads.

– Sorry mum, we are off. She points at me, – He's ruined everything. Eh'll be happy now. Good. We'll leave yis to it. Merry fucking Christmas.

This Greg cunt's goat ehs heid up, wi a servette oan ehs nose, tryin tae stem the blood. A bit ay it's goat oantae ehs shirt though. – It's awright, it's awright, eh laughs, tryin tae calm thum aw doon. – It wis nothing! Frank's hud a bad fright, eh's in shock, eh didnae ken what eh wis daein . . . it's nae bother, ah'm fine . . . it looks worse than it is . . .

Ah mind ay thinkin, ah'll gie ye a loat worse thin that,

ya cunt. Ah sits doon, n ah'm still gittin ma breath back. Thaire aw arguin like fuck. Elspeth's greetin n he's tryin tae calm her.

– It's awright, eh didnae mean it darlin, let's just stay for a bit. For Val's sake, eh's gaun.

– You dinnae ken um! Eh hus tae spoil everything, she sobs.

It's aw a big excuse fir her tae go aw greetin-faced n spoiled, as usual.

Joe n Sandra ur sortin oot muh Ma n the bairns. She's moanin aw that usual shite aboot whaire did she go wrong n aw that. It's me thit fuckin well went wrong, comin here oan Christmas day.

Ah jist heaps some mair sprouts oantae ma plate, n fills up ma gless. Ah feel like sayin tae thum, if yis are gaunny eat yir Christmas dinner, fuckin well sit doon n eat it. If yis urnae, git the fuck away n gie me peace tae finish mine.

Aye, mibbee ah should've cooled it, n goat a hud ay the cunt ootside, instead ay littin fly like that in muh Ma's hoose. That cunt wis too wide fir ehs ain good, but. Far too wide. Awright, eh did try n help, but eh gie'd ma back a fuckin right dunt. Nae need fir that. N ah suppose thit what it aw boils doon tae is thit thir's jist some cunts ye cannae take tae. Ye fuckin try, but ye ken deep doon thit yir nivir gaunny see eye-tae-eye, n that's that.

Aye, oor Elspeth's makin a big mistake gittin mairried tae that.

salena saliva godden

flies that whore in kitchens

Tap, tap, tap and mowing lawns as the world opens its windows, breathing for the first day of spring, for the first time. So, the day begins and life starts afresh and shiny and flowers rear and open their delicate heads in blankets and pillows of onion and chive greens.

Knotted woollen tights are left at the back, with errands and tasks to be done another day, perhaps when it rains.

Hair shines and swishes in red and yellow over-under sunglasses, wine glasses drain and sparkle clean wanting filling.

Summer dresses shift over soft swaying arses, smoking the very finest green grasses.

Butterflies flutter fly, flutter sexily by, bisexual, any sexual, but very sexual and butter melts on café tables and in kitchens flies whore.

Deciding not to die today in that wretched wretching welling of poisoned bodily organs and human eternal fear of mortality, blank stark, staring, brick-hard reality, she slowly opened one eye. Then the other.

The daylight screamed through the crack in the curtains.

It was when she was naked, alone in bed, working out what she had done the day before, where she had been and how she had got home when the phone rang, chilling, loud and shrill.

A shaft of light is filled with dust which sparkles. She lights a half-stubbed joint as she husked out a Good Mornin' and the smoke swirls in the light shaft grey and silver. Instant head dizzy rush. Her head is deep, heavy in the pillows and her soft leg slips out of the side of the sheet and bends at the knee.

'Hello, it's me, what are you up to? You are not still in bed are you?'

'Well . . . yes, why, what time is it?' then inhale more for the tobacco than the hash.

'It's two in the afternoon, wake up!' he cheerily barks down the phone.

She thinks about the barking sunlight, the barking voice, the whole damn dog of the day.

'Well, I'm taking you to lunch, its a lovely day, if you fancy it?'

'OK, thanks.'

'I'll come and pick you up in about five minutes, I'm around the corner.' The phone cuts out.

'Fuck!' she hollers at the air, placing the joint in the ashtray. She pulls back the duvet and walks over to the window, scratching her arse. It is a glorious day, she reluctantly admits, opening the curtains and the window, setting the room alight, on fire with sunshine and the shaft becomes the room. Someone somewhere is cutting grass, lawnmower music. She walks into the kitchen, opens the fridge and glugs at a carton of orange juice; it's been opened wrong, it leaks and splashes onto her right tit and to the floor. She leaves that puddle for the ants.

Her bedroom is a tip of clothes, books, records and papers strewn across the floor. Three-day-old coffee stands firm in a mug on the floor asking to be kicked over.

She finds the dress with the daisies, cannot find any clean knickers, drags the dress on, pulls her dark hair into some kind of bunch at the back, goes into the bathroom and splashes a bit of water in the direction of her face, puts in her brown-coloured contact lenses and then there is a tap bang at the door because the doorbell needs batteries and she is suddenly very hungry. She grabs her keys and sunglasses and is glad to leave the house.

'Have you read *Communion*?' he said, unravelling a fresh pack of cigarettes.

'No, why?' she said as a short-haired waitress with no bra walks over.

'Can I take your order?'

'I'll take a mineral water, a bottle of house red and I'll start with the rocket salad,' he said certainly.

'And you?'

'Umm . . . I'll take the salad and start with a Bloody Mary.'

The waitress leaves them.

'Top tits.'

'What was I saying? Oh yeah, *Communion*, it's by Whitney Striber, they made a movie about it and stuff, did you ever see it?'

'No.' She watches him, twitching slightly.

'It really plays with people's paranoia. It's a heavy book about aliens. This guy, yeah, really believes it happened to him, that he has been taken away by aliens. He reckons that they take people all the time and do weird shit like anal probes to take samples of the intestine, rip out unborn babies. They even programmed him so he wouldn't know they were in the room with him! Weird shit, man, one seriously heavy book, it really gets you thinking . . .'

The waitress bounds over bringing the drinks.

She takes a gulp of water, it is tangy and fizzy and warm against the smooth ice, she then stirs the Bloody Mary after removing the second ice cube.

'I am an alien.'

'Yeah right!' He guffaws into laughter. 'That's what I love about you, you just come out with comments like that all the time.' He smiles warmly. She shrugs her shoulders and there is a crick, click in her neck. He stops grinning and pours two glasses of wine as the salads arrive.

'Anyway, if you were an alien, you wouldn't admit it just like that, would you?' he says.

'That's what everyone thinks! Everyone thinks that aliens would be so secretive and surreptitious, creeping around planet Earth in remote areas, in Midwest America or Wales, in the middle of the night, like burglars. Doing secret sadistic tests on human specimen victims, experimenting on household pets, and farm animals which we kidnapped in the middle of the night, that it's a government conspiracy and they know all about us and keep it so fucking secret, bullshit . . .' Her neck aches and cramps, she pummels the muscles with her forefingers as she speaks, hurriedly, 'If there is a superior alien race, which there is, assuming, of course all alien beings would be advanced and therefore superior, we wouldn't pussy around doing kidnaps and secret tests, would we? Fuck it, we'd just steam in, take what we wanted and fuck off home or stay and take over, whatever we wanted, right?' Her neck is wearing thin.

He blinks and then says, 'I suppose so,' and eats a huge lettuce leaf like a hungry tortoise, munching and folding the leaf with his teeth and fingers; salad dressing glistens on his lips.

She tilts her head forward and it cracks further until it fractures and eventually snaps. The salad bowl globs in balsamic vinegar, olive oil and shavings of parmesan, as a ladybird flits down and lands on the baby pink table cloth. It flutters nervously, until it eventually closes its wings to reveal that crisp red shell with six perfect black dots.

She licks her lips and picks out a piece of lettuce, teases the ladybird to walk onto the leaf, then she slowly wraps it in the raddichio.

There is a subtle ripping sound as her fleshy skin splits, bloodily sheds and falls away into her lap, blood staining the daisies.

A toad-green reptilian face, slimy, blinks as her snaky chameleon tongue flicks, licks out at the speed of light to

240 *flies that whore in kitchens*

claim the ladybird and lettuce aperitif. He looks up from the menu to say he fancies the tagliatelle with . . .

Accidently, during the struggle, as she climbs onto the table, sinew legs bent crouching, she knocks over the last smeared glob of tomato Bloody Mary which mixes with the blood, she notices the two shades of scarlet red.

'That makes three, three shades of red,' she smiles, pouring the remainder of the wine over the half-eaten face of her spasm-jolting and now silent dining partner.

The restaurant would have been utter pandemonium, scream-filled with chaotic, terrorised and horror-struck patrons and staff who instead, nibble at flies that whore in kitchens as butter melts at the tables.

ben richards

....

penalty fare

When Tammy phoned, I was sprawled on the sofa doing what I had been doing for the last three weeks: nothing. I hadn't had a drink for three weeks but my feelings of virtue had passed their sell-by date. My restlessness had led me to keep switching the radio dial and I had settled temporarily on Melody FM. The DJ was playing 'Love on the Rocks'. When I realised it was Tammy on the phone, I turned the volume up to make an ironic point. I hoped he might play 'Stand by your man' next so that I could wisecrack about her name but it was 'Hello' by Lionel Richie so I turned it right down. Anyway, the great surprise was that Tammy wanted to meet me that day at 3.30 in town.

'And don't be late, Paul. No messing me about. I'll wait fifteen minutes and then, if you're not there, I'm off and you'll never see me again. Understood?'

I put the phone down and the radio back up. The DJ was playing 'Daniel' but I couldn't read too much into that. The song always made me sad when I was younger because I wanted a brother to compensate for my three sisters, and 'Daniel' was a reminder that I didn't have one, not even to say goodbye to. I decided to stop listening to Melody FM because I was beginning to feel as if my flat was turning into a barber's shop or the back of a minicab. Just as I was about to change the station, the travel news told me that there were northbound tailbacks due to a burst watermain on the Finchley Road but that *there were no major delays on the buses or tubes.* I switched the radio off.

Tammy's ultimatum was fair enough. I don't know why I'm always late, it pisses me off almost as much as it does the person waiting for me. And my lateness preceded my drinking so there was no excuse. Today, though, I was sober and I was going to be early. I was going to leave a full hour to get from Whitechapel to Tottenham Court Road. I would be there first and then Tammy would come home again and I would stop sprawling on the sofa feeling sick and ill with inactivity and missing her. There was no grace or charm in my decline, no elegant loneliness, just unwashed dishes in the sink, half-watched day-time television, and messy sleep.

I took the tube to Liverpool Street where I changed onto the Central Line. In between Liverpool Street and Bank the train shuddered and then came to an abrupt, jolting stop. It was not the kind of slowing down stop owing to congestion on the line ahead, it was a dramatic something's happened kind of stop. I stared at the soot-furred purple cables on the walls that curved around the carriage. Then the lights went out.

For a few minutes, there was almost-silence punctuated only by the tut-tutters. But the first whimpers of the claustrophobes indicated that this was no routine and it was then that I knew with absolute certainty that I would not meet Tammy, that she would be cursing her moment of weakness and stalking away into the crowds while I was trapped hundreds of feet underground on a tube line towards which I have always felt a strong antipathy. The injustice of it brought a lump of desperation to my throat. Along the carriage, I could hear others moaning about job interviews, childminders and needing the toilet. The voices in the darkness were edging into neurosis as imaginations became fear-fevered. One man began to cry that he could smell smoke. Another told him to shut up. Somebody asked to borrow a mobile and there was a titter from the less cowardly when another impatient voice shouted 'mobiles don't work hundreds of feet underground, you silly cunt'. I felt a sneaky sympathy for silly cunt because I have never had a mobile and it is the kind of mistake that I am capable of making.

The lights came back on after thirty minutes but the train did not move for a further hour. Some people had actually begun to cry, one woman began hammering on the windows and had to be calmed down by a qualified nurse, the man next to me took big puffs on an asthma inhaler. Tammy's fifteen minutes extra had long expired but I carried on to Tottenham Court Road because there was nothing else to do. My mind was dangerously cold, I had anaesthetised my anger and fear and despair, I was staring in front of me like a young conscript waiting in the trench for the whistle.

Tammy was not at Tottenham Court Road, of course, but I began to walk down Oxford Street hoping that I might bump into her. The night had begun to darken, rain spat onto the pavement and the shops were overloaded for Christmas. I wandered into HMV and stared blankly at all the CDs, there were millions of them, just too many, far too many – it brought a mixture of nausea and panic to my throat. I went into Marks & Spencers and found myself in the food department looking at salads that had been chopped and washed, potatoes that had been peeled and impregnated with oil for roasting, sliced pineapples, diced carrots, topped and tailed beans, podded peas. I padded down the aisles looking at all the bright packaging – the tubs of different patés, the Italian, Indian and Chinese ready-made meals, the Christmas biscuit selections. I hadn't eaten all day but I felt no hunger.

It was then that the foetus of anger that was inside me began to stir, clenching its tiny fists just a bit tighter. There was so much stuff it was almost unbearable, it was as suffocating as the stalled tube train on the Central Line, it was as enervating as my empty flat. I went out into the cold air and was nearly crushed by teenage boys and girls carrying souvenirs of some boy band that had just turned on the Oxford Street Christmas lights. The puffy little thirteen-year-old faces of the kids glowed with cold and excitement. Just for a second, as I watched them heading home, misery held me by the throat and shook me with gentle menace.

I didn't want to get the tube again so I went to wait for a 25 bus. There was already a big crowd at the bus stop and suddenly my desire to get away from the West End became so strong that I went back to the tube station. It was unlikely that the same thing would happen twice in one day.

I was right. There were no problems with the eastbound service, a train came quickly and I even managed to get a seat. I rested my head against the window and tried to imagine Tammy's face. As I contemplated her anger and disappointment, I was filled with melancholy but I knew that it was pointless trying to get a message to her to explain my non-appearance. None of her friends would speak to me, her feral brothers had always been waiting for the time when they would have an excuse to give me a kicking, and her mum was a Seventh Day Adventist who believed that I had been sent personally by Satan to corrupt her beloved daughter.

'Ticket, please.'

I jumped, because I had had my eyes closed and not noticed the gold-capped inspectors boarding the train. The inspector stared at me impatiently as I began searching in my pockets for my ticket. What the fuck had I done with it?

'I can't find it,' I said. 'I did buy one but I can't find it.' I tried another pocket and then gave up because I was too tired to carry on looking. The inspector sighed contemptuously.

'I'm going to have to charge you a ten-pound penalty fare,' he said. People started to look at me. Most of them did not have the judgemental faces from the adverts but showed a resigned sympathy. I gazed into the face of the inspector. He was heavy-jowled, his moustache bristled impatiently.

'I can't pay,' I said.

'Then I'll need to take your address, and see some proof of . . .'

'No, you don't understand. I don't care if the fine is ten pounds or a million pounds. It's not the money. I've got ten pounds in my pocket but you're not having it. I've got rights as well as responsibilities. You fuck up people's lives and then you fine them. Today I got stuck for an hour and a half on the tube because of you bastards. I saw people nearly dropping dead with fear, I let someone down again. It wasn't my fault but there's nothing I can do about it.'

There was desperation as well as anger in my voice. It was as if all the impotent fury I had ever endured had been condensed down into this one moment. Another inspector came up and they both stood over me. I felt the suffocating sensation that I had experienced staring at all the CDs and the food packaging and the prepubescent pop fans. I tried to get up, I just wanted to walk away from them, but I felt so heavy and so tired, it was as if something was holding me back and I started to shout and to flail about, pushing at the inspector. Suddenly, there were arms holding me, grabbing at me, one civic-minded passenger bidding for a Community Action Trust award had hurled himself on top of me, somebody was shouting about scaring the kiddies and I could hear crying. I thought about Tammy and how it hadn't been my fault and Melody FM and Daniel my brother and all the CDs and pre-prepared salads and mobiles not working hundreds of feet underground and the Christmas fucking lights after some grinning clones had flicked the switch and how sometimes you couldn't do anything about anything. But, after everything that had happened, I couldn't give these inspectors ten pounds, I couldn't even give them the wrong address.

I was hauled from the train and handed over to the British Transport Police by the Inspector and Mr Crime-watch UK – both of whom were acting like they had just caught Lord Lucan on the Central Line. They were brothers separated at birth. To their enormous disappointment, however, the search carried out by the police did not unearth drugs, or knives but it did produce the missing ticket which had hidden itself under my keys. Even in my distressed state, I allowed myself a quick smirk at the Inspector as the ticket emerged. He began to plead for me to be done for assault instead of fare-dodging but we had been followed onto the platform by an irate woman who said that she was a lawyer and she would be advising me to pursue a counter-claim of assault and even kidnapping in which she would gladly act as my witness. She waved her copy of the *Guardian* about and generally made a total nuisance of herself demanding names, ranks and numbers – using the kind of voice that coppers both hate and fear – until finally they became so pissed off that they let me go.

Back at home that night, I found a message from Tammy on the answerphone. She had wanted to see me because she was probably going away but since I hadn't cared enough to make the effort to keep our appointment she was phoning to say goodbye. I numbed out the message and decided that I had better eat something, so I started to make some mashed potato. I stood at the sink peeling potatoes while I listened to Roy Orbison singing 'In dreams' on the radio. When the potatoes were done, I took the masher and attacked them as if there were a face staring up at me from the pot. The self twins – Pity and Loathing – were beginning their familiar jitterbug, sniggering at the very concept of a soothing candy-coloured clown. So I abandoned the potatoes, took out the ten-pound note that I had so fiercely protected from the ticket inspector and went to the off-licence to buy myself a bottle of vodka.

jim dodge

....

bathing joe

An elegy for Bob, 1946–1994

The summer of '94 at French Flat, on a scorching afternoon in mid-July, my brother Bob suggested we bathe
his dog Joe, a sixteen-year-old Kelpie. Since Bob held
intractably to the notion that bathing dogs more than
once a year destroys their essential skin oils, I hustled to
gather the leash, towels, and doggie shampoo before he
changed his mind.

Joe – 112 in human years – truly needed a bath. He
suffered every affliction of elderly canines: deaf as dirt;
a few glimmers short of blind; lumpy with warts and
subcutaneous cysts; a penis pointing straight down; a
scrotum so saggy his testicles banged against his hocks;
prone to drool; given to a seemingly constant flatulence
that would be banned under the Geneva Accords; and
possessed of what the genteel call 'doggie odor,' which in
Joe's unfortunate case ranged between gaggingly rank
and living putrefaction. When Joe dozed by the
woodheater on a winter's eve, enjoying dinner was diffi-

cult – considering one's watering eyes and the instinct to cover the food.

So I had the leash on Joe before Bob, whose right leg had been amputated near the hip years earlier, could get up on his crutches. With Bob herding from behind, I led Joe around back of the cabin, where we'd set up an old bathtub for starlit soaks. We hadn't used the bathtub lately, so I scooped out the accumulated litter of madrone leaves and pine needles before I lifted in Joe. As I slipped off his collar, Joe grunted and sat down, settling into what we called the ODZ, or Old Dog Zone, where Joe seemed to be watching methane sunsets on Jupiter, or flights of birds invisible to human eyes. I turned on the water, hot and cold mixing in a single hose, while Bob opened the shampoo.

I asked him, 'Want me to put in the plug?'

'Jesus, no,' Bob said. 'Rising water freaks Joe out bad. In fact, better make sure that drain ain't clogged.'

'How could it be?' I reminded him. 'Remember when you couldn't find the rubber plug one night and hammered in that chunk of redwood for a stopper? Knocked out all those little cross-pieces?'

'Aw,' Bob dismissed the memory, 'they were rusted all to shit anyway. Besides, the tub drains on the ground – not like there's a pipe to clog.' He squirted some shampoo on his palm. 'You gonna stand there yakking or are we gonna get on it – it's broiling out here.'

Joe returned from Jupiter when the stream of water hit him. He bolted for safety but couldn't get traction on the tub's slick bottom. Bob grabbed him around the neck and Joe slid to the front of the tub. He held still, warbling softly as I soaked him down.

'It's ok, Joe, you're ok,' Bob comforted his pooch, working the shampoo into a grey lather. Joe struggled again, scrambling to get his back legs under him, then suddenly stopped. His yellowish dingo eyes began to widen.

'Brain-lock,' I opined.

Bob ignored me to encourage Joe: 'Good dog, good dog. Just keep still and we'll be done in a few minutes. You can't help being old, can you?'

Joe answered with a low, trembling yowl.

'What's he yodeling about?' I wondered aloud.

'Hell if I know.' Bob rubbed Joe's neck. 'What's the matter, buddy?'

I noticed the greyish-yellow scum building in the bathtub and gratuitously advised Bob, 'I wouldn't bathe that dog without some industrial-strength, eight-ply latex gloves. You wake up tomorrow, you might not have fingernails.'

Bob glanced at the rising scum. '*That's* the problem. Joe's sitting on the drain, got it blocked, and the water's rising – thinks he's gonna drown. Let me scoot him back down, off the drain.'

But when Bob tried to slide him toward the middle of the tub, Joe's yowl leaped an octave and he twisted his head free of Bob's grasp. He huddled against the front curve of the tub, a strong shiver passing through him from flank to nose.

I turned off the water. 'Now what?'

'Beats me,' Bob declared, then cooed at Joe, 'What's your problem, buddy? You're not gonna drown.' Bob slipped his hand underwater and felt beneath Joe. When he withdrew his hand he gave me a funny look. 'You're not gonna believe this,' he said solemnly, 'but Joe's got his nuts caught in the drain.'

'Impossible,' I assured him. 'The drain's too small for his nuts to fit through.'

Bob shook his head. 'Maybe not if they were soapy and slid through one at a time. Better take a look under there. I'll hold Joe.'

The tub was set about eight inches off the ground on a wooden frame, so I had to brace both legs and lift with a shoulder to rock the tub back far enough to see. Sure enough, Joe's testicles were dangling from the drain, side by side in his flaccid, mottled scrotum.

Bob took a break from consoling his dog to ask, 'See anything?'

I eased the tub back down. 'Yeh, I see your dog's nuts caught in the drain. I trust you appreciate my reluctance to believe it.'

'Well,' Bob said impatiently, 'try to poke them back through. Ol' Joe's about to go into shock.'

Joe whimpered piteously in confirmation.

'You're kidding,' I said. 'Try to *poke them back through*. Hey bro, he's *your* dog and those are *his* nuts – *you* do it. Poking Joe's stuck nuts is not even *on* my list of 25,000 things I'd do for fun or money.'

'Sweet Jesus,' Bob sighed with pained exasperation, 'show class or show ass.'

I'd forgotten that Bob, with only one leg, probably couldn't leverage the tub, so I gracefully offered, '*I'll* lift the tub; *you* handle his nuts.'

'Ah, come on,' Bob objected, 'someone's got to hold Joe. If he panics, he'll either tear them off or stretch his sack so bad his balls will be bouncing along behind him the rest of his life.' He scratched Joe's head, murmuring, 'Hang on, old pal, we'll get you loose.'

I had an idea. 'Maybe we could take a sledgehammer to the tub – sort of break it out around him.'

'Right, good thinking,' Bob mocked me. 'Take a twelve-pound sledge to a metal bathtub. We'd have him loose by next month easy.' He shook his head. 'How would you like *your* nuts caught in the drain and some utter dimwit pounding away on the tub with a sledge-hammer?'

'All right,' I said, 'but it'll cost you.'

'Why doesn't that surprise us?' Bob asked his dog. Then to me, 'What?'

'Dishes for a week plus that little Shimano reel you hardly ever use anyway.'

Bob explained to Joe, 'You're gonna be here a long time, buddy, because my brother is a no-class, show-ass jerk.'

Swabbing sweat off my brow, too hot for prolonged negotiations, I surrendered. 'Hand me that damn bottle of shampoo.'

I lifted the tub again, sweat-blind in the heat, and awkwardly squirted some shampoo on Joe's scrotum for lubrication. Taking a deep breath, I began working Joe's testicles around in his sack, trying to arrange them verti-cally for a push upward, all the while providing a running commentary on my feelings for Bob's amusement and to deflect all but essential attention from the task at hand: 'Forty-nine years I've been alive. Representing the present culmination of millennia of species evolution. Of exacting natural selection. Years of formal education. Diligent study. Developing skills. The long, excruciating refinement of sensibility. And now I understand my whole life has been a preparation for this moment: trying to get your dog's nuts unstuck from a bathtub drain. And I don't know if that's perfect or pathetic or both or none of the above.'

'Well,' Bob offered with a dry sweetness, 'for sure it's better than something worse.' Then to Joe, 'Listen to him snivel.'

I saved my breath and, working by touch, manipulated Joe's nuts around till they were stacked, then, using sort of a reverse milking move, squeezed his scrotum from the bottom. The top testicle popped through, then the other. Joe was free. With an agility he hadn't shown in years, he leaped from the tub and started rolling in the dirt, moaning.

Bob smiled. 'There you go, buddy! Happy dog!'

When I dropped the tub off my numb shoulder, the dirty water sluiced forward and slopped over the rim, drenching me.

I sniveled some more: 'Oh great, I free his worthless old nuts and what do I get – soaked with mutagenic Joe scuzz.'

Bob laughed. 'Plus you get our eternal gratitude – don't forget that.'

I won't.

tania glyde

....

baby heaven

It's a Saturday night and I'm queuing to get into Heaven.

You on the list?

Well, I suppose so . . .

What do you mean, you suppose so?

I'm not in the mood, really I'm not.

The man at the door runs his finger up and down the list. The queue heaves.

Let's have a look . . . no, your name's not down.

But my friend Nick's gonna be in there, you must know him, tall dark guy, he'd've got a plus one—

No, no plus one's here, love.

What, so I'm not wearing the right gear, am I? Sorry I don't have no leopardskin diving suit on tonight!

Nothing to do with that, love. You're just not one of us.

Oh please, haven't we moved on from there?

I run up and down the queue.

Can I borrow your mobile? Can you get me guested? Oh go on, oh go on! My mate Nick's in there. I've got to see him!

A sad-eyed girl with a weird skimpy dress of suction

caps and wires that does nothing to hide her terrible scar touches my arm with a pitying look.

Sweetheart, you're not going to get in tonight.

Why not? What the fuck's going on? I've come a long way, you know!

Didn't you read your T-shirt when you put it on this morning?

Huh?

Well, you topped yourself, didn't you? Didn't you realise you'd done it?

Oh God, yeah! They don't let suicides into Heaven, do they! Ah, fuck it!

The day it happened, I remember someone called me and told me Nick'd had a fatal accident. Something about a dispatch cyclist in Tottenham Court Road. It wasn't my fault, I know, but I felt so powerless that I just threw myself into my work. Turning my love and my grief into something better, I suppose. And I survived that way, for a while.

But then I started to miss him, so I killed myself. Paracetamol with a temazy chaser and a glass of wine, and here I am at the door of Heaven to find him, and I can't even fucking get in.

Hey, love, don't cry, says the girl in the queue, *there's an all-nighter round the corner for people like you. They'll let you in.*

I walk round there, wiping my eyes. At least there's no queue at this place. Not surprisingly perhaps, given the two dusty cheese-plants and dribbling fish-fountain inside. Well, that too is a style!

A nun stands inside, holding a tray. Things are looking up.

Complimentary drink, dear?

Oh, it's a woman.

The choice is Baileys with a squirt of UHT, or a horrible-looking concoction I can't really see properly in the bad light.

Ooh lovely, a blue cocktail! If you can't get into Heaven, you get to go to a Tory bop! Oooh! You're funny, aintcha!

The nun raises her eyebrow in a strange way, as if I have caught onto something.

No, no, dear, it's methadone with homemade lemonade and a splash of gin. The extra colouring we've put in is entirely additive-free, I assure you.

No, no! I'll get my own thanks!

I go to the bar and order a *boy-type* drink, you know, a pint of Extra with a double Macallan chaser. Since it looks as though I'm gonna be here for a long time, *well, forever,* I'll start as I mean to go on because, of course, things probably aren't gonna be all that different here, are they? Which means I must continue to embrace the postfeminist culture of masculinity: gambling, football and types of beer; academic philosophy, fighting and *really understanding animals.*

And of course, it's not ok now for a woman to admit her failings, it's not ok to lose armwrestling matches and it's definitely not ok to admit someone treated you really badly, because all your friends start being really condescending, *Don't call him! Oh, are you all right? . . .*

. . . but FUCK, what am I on about? I'm *dead,* for God's sake. It's time to live a little. Though, oddly enough, there are a hell of a lot of women here. Quite arty women, actually.

I look around at the other guests. For a while, it's fun. You know, I actually know a few people here.

Oh look, there's that bloke from the DSS I met in the pub and fucked later on. He, er, lent me some money afterwards – and then reported me for not declaring earnings! I never got him back for that. He looks really unhappy!

Oh and look, interesting! There's the the blind beggar whose hat I accidentally kicked one day as I was walking down Glasshouse Street. Oh sorry, mate, sorry. I bent down to put the money back and add some more of my own when I looked more closely at him and whaddyer-know! He turned out to be a man I shagged ages ago who gave me crabs and then went round telling everyone I'd given them to him! This was a man so stupid that he used to let off fireworks *during the day*. Then, one afternoon, without telling me, he went off to Germany with some mates to visit Hitler's grave and came back with a dwarf hippy chick wearing *wooden earrings!* And he's not even fucking blind either!

Oh sorry, mate, sorry, I continued to say as I bent over him, Hey, mate, hold on for a minute, I'll get you a beer. I spiked him with acid and he ended up in the middle of Piccadilly Circus thinking he was a photocopier and sobbing over his little guinea pig he had when he was five. He doesn't look very happy now, does he?

Schadenfreude! It's better than sex!

Then up comes a personable but slightly pratty-looking young man in a suit with gold-rimmed glasses, just like one of those restaurant greeters who you think's a friend of yours and you spend ten seconds wondering who the hell it is. He speaks.

Hello there, lovey! Who would you most like to have a One-to-One with?

He's really put me on the spot.

H G Wells? Nah. St Augustine? No, definitely not. Got it! [snap fingers] Ted Moult! He topped himself, didn't he? No wonder after all that double glazing and gardening. Ted'll be here, won't he, flogging poppy heads by the ounce. This isn't purgatory at all, it's really quite nice! Music's not bad either!

The man holds up his glass of white wine and says to me,

You know, I've been thinking. Do you think Chardonnay's become a meme?

What?

Well, I was just wondering if society's really caught on to the social and commercial implications of a type of grape that's demographically egalitarian, you know, spread all over the world. It won't be long before it's a fully-fledged unit of cultural inheritance!

Nice to find a few thinkers here, I yawn. He goes on talking.

Well, speaking of myself, I've always been a cultural relativist, you know.

Cultural relativist? I know what you mean, I say, like how the Mwug-Mwug tribe of the upper Congo slit young virgin girls' throats on the occasion of the chief's birthday and leave them on the hillside for the vultures to finish off – but who are we in the West to judge? We have to PAY for water, we have to QUEUE for buses, we have to actually RENT a space, just for somewhere to live!

He doesn't laugh.

Oh, for God's sake, I shout over the music, d'you just wanna go for a shag?

I can't believe I said that, I love Nick! The man's eyes light up – maybe he's been here for a while, his clothes are a bit strange. But anyway, now he's dragging me towards the toilet. But I love Nick.

Hey mate, why the toilet? We're dead, aren't we? Can't we just go behind the bar?

(But I love Nick, I was faithful to him, mostly.)

We're in the toilet for two hours. He has still not come and nor have I.

What's wrong, I ask.

Didn't you know? No orgasms here. We can't.

So we could just be stuck in this toilet forever?

Of course.

I start to cry. I want Nick. The man pulls out of me rapidly and goes away. I go back to the bar and get another Macallan, but my way is blocked by a large geezer who is talking far too loudly.

I was off my fuckin' 'ead last night! I 'ad fifteen pints and four grammes of sulphate, and then me mate turned up with an ounce of the devil's dandruff and then I necked, oooooh, ten Es, at least, and I got so fucking paranoid about this fucking bitch in a phone box with her shoppin' that I fucking raped her, didn' I?!

An' then we dropped a couple a trips an' then me other mate came round with some kickin' rocks and when we was on our way to the pub, this old biddy comes along in 'er Merc to

*ask for directions like – so we took 'er for a little ride, didn't
we? With 'er stuffed in the boot!*

*I was so fuckin' monged I ran over a coupla schoolkids,
didn' I? Stupid little cunts.*

*So we legged it back to me mate's house and then I bit 'is
ear off! And then I 'ad about an 'undred vallies and fell asleep
wiv me 'ead on the gas ring! An' while I was out of it, me
mate turned it on and burnt all me 'air – 'an I didn' even
notice! Wot a night, WOT a night!*

I smile, generously. And he bends, turning his face to
mine and whispers, his piggy eyes glittering like a cobra's.

*You look 'ungry darlin'! Did you hear all that, love? Me
an' me mate, we can get you anyfing you like, darlin',
anyfing you like!*

Oooh, good, can you get me some smack, then?

His face changes completely.

*Wot? Wot did you just say? Oofff, smack is for really sad
people, real fuckin' losers who just wanna get off their 'eads an
destroy other people's lives! Whhhooooo-o, no, sorry, love, you
won't catch me doing that!*

He turns his back.

Oh, for God's sake, I don't want any fucking drugs
anyway, I want to find Nick! I walk round and round. I'm
really missing him now.

Why are you here? says a nice-looking girl.

I killed myself, I say, thinking I might have found a new
friend. But she gasps.

That's really disgusting, that's really immoral. [superior] *I
got run over by a bus.*

Oooh, get the little victim! I spit, forgetting myself.
What right've you got to talk about morality?

I catch myself going off on one. Not like usually.

Morality's the most overrated concept in the universe! Remember those politicians going on about teaching morality to children in schools? If you do that, you're gonna have to ban history, because as we all know, brute force and selfishness win every time; you'll have to ban politics too – lies and deceit win without exception; and you'll definitely have to ban biography: the lives of the eminent bear very little scrutiny. Most artists are cunts to their nearest and dearest. *And* your make-up's horrible!

That's just the politics of envy. You don't want anyone to do well at anything because you're a failure yourself, and that's why you committed suicide.

Envy is just another form of dissent, I reply. So why are you here anyway, if you died accidentally?

But she's gone. But the failure thing stings. I drink more.

You know, I'm starting to see a pattern here. A dancer rubs up against me and giggles before disappearing.

A woman in curiously smart, very good quality, if dated, clothing, appears beside me.

So what are *you* doing here then? I ask. Top yourself as well, did you?

No.

Well, what then? Drug addict? Cultural relativist?

No, no.

Well, what then? You don't have to worry about showing your vulnerability to a stranger here, I mean, we're all dead, aren't we? I mean, I'm not going to use it against you.

I wrote a book, actually.

Christ, what was it, *How I murdered my baby?*

No, no, you might have heard of it, actually.

Oh yeah? What was it called then?

The Story of O.

The story of fucking O. Oh yes, I see what you mean now.

I grab her lapel.

Yeah! I know your bloody book – source of every justification of abuse you've ever heard! So many women I know cling desperately to the idea of the ritual, ideas that you helped to spread! *He abused me, but it was a ritual: we just had to work it out;* or *I'm abusing you, aren't I? But it's just a power thing between you and me, isn't it?*

The *beginning's* good, I'll give you that, yeah, I could get off on that, but frankly, all you're doing is promote . . . promote self-abnegation for women, the annihilation of the self! And no wonder she's naked at the end, labial rings that size would *ruin* the line of your clothes!

You're getting awful worked up about a book that came out forty years ago! It obviously had some effect on you, didn't it?

No!

Well, you just told me you killed yourself, I mean, that's, er, pretty self-annihilating, isn't it?

You're just trying to fuck with my head, aren't you, Miss Pauline Reage! Fuck you! I bet you used to collect cuddly toys, didn't you? Sure sign of a hard bitch!

And I am about to shout some more when I think I've caught sight of Nick across the room, at the cigarette machine. (You have to pay for fags, even here!)

I leave her and push my way towards him, but then I trip on something and stumble. I put my hand out and find myself grabbing hold of something small and slimy.

People look at me with pity but go on talking.

Oh, WHAT? Errrrrrrrgh!

No, no, this isn't funny any more, someone must have slipped me something.

There's no nice way of putting this.

It's an aborted foetus.

Several of them, in fact. Alive and well, though not exactly kicking. Some of them are in bits, crawling round in formation on the patchy, sweaty carpet.

I pick myself up and shout at the nun who's passing by with an enormous tray of Ferrero Rochers.

What the hell are they doing here, and what are they doing on the floor?

They're people just like you and me, she admonishes, sneerily, *have you got a problem with that?*

Whadayamean? What? Even here, where we're been denied entry to Paradise, there's free drinks but no crèche?! Nowhere for all these poor little fuckers to go? All right, all right, out with it! Are we actually in hell here? I mean, I did start to wonder . . . Is this the joke? It's not a halfway house, is it? It's not Purgatory, is it?

No dear, this isn't Hell. You weren't nearly bad enough for that. Suicide is a very regulation abuse of the Good Lord's gift of life.

The foetuses crawl about. The nun smiles even more patronisingly.

Well, dear, now you're experiencing one of those agonising moments in the life of the liberal intellectual when political beliefs don't quite match up to personal experience. Have a nice day now, won't you!

I bang the tray from underneath and the Ferrero Rochers fly up like sparks from a Roman candle. The nun merely kneels down on the floor and starts picking them up, one by one!

No, no no no no no no no no no no NO!

I push her away, tip the Ferrero Rochers off the tray and begin putting the foetuses on it. One of them's trying to speak, for fuck's sake! I grip the tray and talk to them.

Right, you lot, you're with me now. Let's find you a nice place to hang out, huh?

No one seems to take any notice as I carry the tray of foetuses through the room, and over the dance floor. The chill-out room is packed with people listening to drum 'n' bass remixes of Bartók and Motorhead.

Then I see a door with a sign on it. Maybe that'd do. I get nearer and read it.

Mother and Baby Room, it says. Gritting my teeth, I push through the door, put the tray down and arrange some towels on the changing table.

Ok, there you go.

I pick up each one, little and raw and all different sizes, and arrange them on the towel, praying they are too underdeveloped to understand group power relations.

Ok, ok, there you go, my voice is getting all sing-songy for some reason. I go looking for milk. All there is is more of that Baileys and cream stuff. I figure, here at least, it's ok to give alcohol to an unborn child. The music thuds outside. There's a mirror, but I don't want to see myself in it. I smear it with body lotion.

We sit for a while. Occasionally I look outside for Nick. Maybe he wasn't christened, maybe he is here. I snooze as the foetuses play silently on the towel. The party, of course, does not end.

I open the door. The music's changed. Some cunting

freak has sampled that vile song, you know, the one where she does all sorts of things 'like a woman', but she 'breaks like a little girl'. The person who wrote that is the pits of piss. This girl's not for breaking, I'll tell you that for nothing.

And then, a skinny bloke with a beard and piercings which frankly do not look as if they've healed too well, walks in.

Whoo-hoo, you should get your money back on those, I say sympathetically, looking at his hands. Why didn't you just go for the belly button? Mind you, they say you've got to wear hipsters for three months and not go in the bath, nor the sea. Don't go anywhere near the sea, will you? Have you seen your feet? Oh, you poor lamb!

He looks at me.

I've been here for hours, something is strobing behind my eyes. Of course, I can't be tired, can I? The bloke looks so sad that I suddenly feel really horny.

I'd ask you to go down on me but I really can't handle facial hair. No, you can't kiss me either.

His eyes are expressionless.

Tell you what, I'll do it to you! If you can't get off yourself, well, you can always do it to someone else!

I nod an apology to the foetuses.

He stands perfectly still. I give myself a time limit, as I guess he's going to be just like the rest of us down here. But in fact he does come. It's weird, like sort of cough mixture. I decide to spit it out. It's sort of greenish and linctusy-looking.

He looks down at me and says something incomprehensible, at which a woman comes in the door behind him, shouting,

Come on, don't be silly darling, nobody speaks Aramaic any more, except for somewhere in Syria and we're not in Syria now, darling, are we?

The woman is tall, blonde and elegant, and is smoking a slim panatella.

All right, all right, you're his mum, aren't you! I get it! Sorry sorry sorry. I should have realised . . .

Oh, no problem, we thought we'd just check in for a bit. I must admit I don't really like coming down here, but we do own it.

I didn't think you two'd be spending much time down here, frankly.

Well, my son was going to come anyway to try out his trendy new way of doling out the scripts – honestly, he's a saint, my son – but of course, you're a suicide, aren't you, not an addict. It was lucky you spat it out really . . . Is there anything you'd like to ask?

I have ceased to be surprised by anything by now. So I'm not gonna muck about.

Well, yes, there is, actually. Um, let's get straight down to brass tacks. How did you feel when you got pregnant?

Well, it just happened really. A lovely man came down to see me, and then nine months later, there was Jesus!

What do you mean it just happened? What, after all those sex education classes, *Cosmo* quizzes and Black Lace books – it just happened? I've heard that one before.

We didn't have Cosmo *back then, darling.*

You're just like every other woman, aren't you. Or is it that all women think they're the fucking virgin Mary . . .

You've never been pregnant, have you?

Well, at least if I had I would have got a fuck out of it, I say.

I'm about to reply when the door opens wider.

Ah yes! Wait a minute! I think you know Nick, don't you?

He's here! Nick Nick! It's you! But how did you get down here?

I throw my arms around him and bury my head in his neck. But he lets his arms hang limp, and sighs, viciously.

I don't believe it. I just don't fucking believe it. That poor fucking cyclist got *three years*! I should never have done it. I thought it was the one foolproof way of getting you off my back! And now I'm stuck here forever! Fuck!

And he storms out. I fall back against the table.

The bearded man puts his arm round me.

Don't worry about it, love. My dad's a fascist cunt! That's life, innit!

notes on contributors

Nicholas Blincoe was born in Rochdale and now lives in London. He was a founder member of Britain's first white rap group, signed to Factory Records and has a Ph.D in contemporary philosophy. He has published four novels, including *Manchester Slingback* which won the 1998 CWA Silver Dagger Award, and several short stories. Along with Matt Thorne he co-edited the collection *All Hail the New Puritans*.

Paul Charles, originally from County Derry, now lives in London. He is one of Europe's leading music promoters and agents representing artists such as Tom Waits, Jackson Browne, Warren Zevon, Ray Davies, Christy Moore and Nick Lowe. He has published four books featuring the adventures of Camden based detective Christy Kennedy, the latest of which is *The Ballad of Sean and Wilko*.

Lana Citron was born in Dublin in 1969. A history graduate of Trinity College, Dublin, she now lives in London. Her short stories have appeared in *Shenanigans* and *New Writing 8* and her debut novel *Sucker* is also available.

Jim Dodge is the author of three novels, *Stone Junction*, *Fup* and *Not Fade Away*. He lives on an isolated ranch in western Sonoma County, USA.

Stella Duffy was born in London and brought up in New Zealand. She has written four thrillers featuring Saz Martin: *Calendar Girl*, *Wavewalker*, *Beneath the Blonde*, *Fresh Flesh* and three other novels, *Singling out the Couples*, *Eating Cake* and *Immaculate*

Conceit. She is also an actor, improvisor, comedian and occasional radio presenter.

Christopher Fowler is a director of The Creative Partnership, a film promotion company based in Soho, and is the author of nine novels, including *Roofworld*, *Spanky*, *Soho Black*, *Psychoville*, *Disturbia* and *Calabash*, and of the short story collections *City Jitters*, *Sharper Knives*, *Flesh Wounds*, *Personal Demons* and *Uncut: 21 Short Stories*.

Tania Glyde lives in London and has had two novels published, *Clever Girl* and *Junk DNA*. She also appears in the *Disco 2000* Anthology. She has performed her poetry all over the UK and in Europe.

Salena Saliva Godden, part poet, part twisted songstress, is known for taking poetry into clubs with her band, the PC Collective. She is also the editor and producer of *Salpetre*, CDs, and radio. *www.salpetre.com*.

Sparkle Hayter is a Canadian stand-up comedian and an Afghan War TV reporter. She has published five novels featuring newswoman and reluctant sleuth Robin Hudson. She lives in the Chelsea Hotel, New York.

Vicki Hendricks lives in Pembroke Pines, Florida, where she teaches at Broward Community College. She has written several short stories and three novels, *Miami Purity*, *Iguana Love*, and *Voluntary Madness*.

Patrick McCabe was born in Clones, County Monaghan, Ireland in 1955. He has twice been short-listed for the Booker Prize with his novels, *The Butcher Boy* and *Breakfast on Pluto*. He co-wrote the screenplay for Neil Jordan's highly acclaimed film of *The Butcher Boy*. He lives in Sligo with his wife and two daughters.

Ben Richards was born in 1964 and lives in East London. He has worked as a housing officer for Newham and Islington councils and lectured at the University of Birmingham. He has had four novels published, *Throwing the House out of the Window*, *Don't Step on the Lines*, *The Silver River* and *A Sweetheart Deal*.

Kevin Sampson lives and works on Merseyside. He has published three novels, *Awaydays*, *Powder*, *Leisure* and a football memoir, *Extra Time*.

Matt Thorne was born in Weston Super Mare in 1975 and currently lives in London. His journalism has appeared in the *Guardian*, *Independent on Sunday* and *The Times*. He has published three novels, *Tourist*, *Eight Minutes Idle* and *Dreaming of Strangers*.

Lynne Tillman is the author of *Haunted Houses*, *Absence Makes the Heart*, *Motion Sickness*, *Cast in Doubt*, *The Madame Realism Complex*, *The Velvet Years: Warhol's Factory 1965–7*, *The Broad Picture*, *No Lease on Life*, and *Bookstore: The Life and Times of Jeannette Watson and Books & Co.* She lives in New York City.

Will Self is the author of *The Quantity Theory of Insanity*, *Cock & Bull*, *My Idea of Fun*, *Grey Area*, *Junk Mail*, *The Sweet Smell of Psychosis*, *Great Apes*, *Tough, Tough Toys for Tough, Tough Boys* and *How the Dead Live*. He was born and lives in London.

Irvine Welsh's first novel, *Trainspotting* came out in 1993 and has been turned into a play and film. He has also published *The Acid House*, *Marabou Stork Nightmares*, *Ecstasy*, and *Filth*.

John Williams was born and lives in Cardiff although he has also lived in Paris and London. He is the author of four books, *Into the Badlands*, *Bloody Valentine*, *Faithless* and his latest, *Five Pubs, Two Bars and a Nightclub*, a collection of short stories based in Cardiff.